How Ocean Merlani Stole their Navigator

✦ **A Strange Space Novel** ✦

KATIE SILVERWINGS

Memphis, TN

PEPTALK PRODUCTIONS, LLC

Publisher's Cataloging-in-Publication Data
provided by Five Rainbows Cataloging Services

Names: Silverwings, Katie, 1991-

Title: How Ocean Merlani stole their navigator : a strange space novel / Katie Silverwings.

Description: Second edition. | Memphis, TN : PepTalk Productions, 2025. | Series: Strange Space Adventures, bk. 3.

Identifiers: LCCN 2024923973 (print) | ISBN 978-1-959922-34-6 (paperback) | ISBN 978-1-959922-35-3 (hardcover) | ISBN 978-1-959922-36-0 (ebook) | ISBN 978-1-959922-37-7 (audiobook)

Subjects: LCSH: Extraterrestrial beings--Fiction. | Families--Fiction. | Friendship--Fiction. | Houston (Tex.)--Fiction. | Science fiction. | Illustrated works. | BISAC: FICTION / Science Fiction / General. | FICTION / Coming of Age. | FICTION / Family Life / General. | FICTION / Friendship. | GSAFD: Science fiction.

Classification: LCC PS3619.I58 H69 2025 (print) | LCC PS3619.I58 (ebook) | DDC 813/.6--dc23.

Published by PepTalk Productions, LLC 2024
Memphis, Tennessee, USA
www.PepTalkProductionsLLC.com

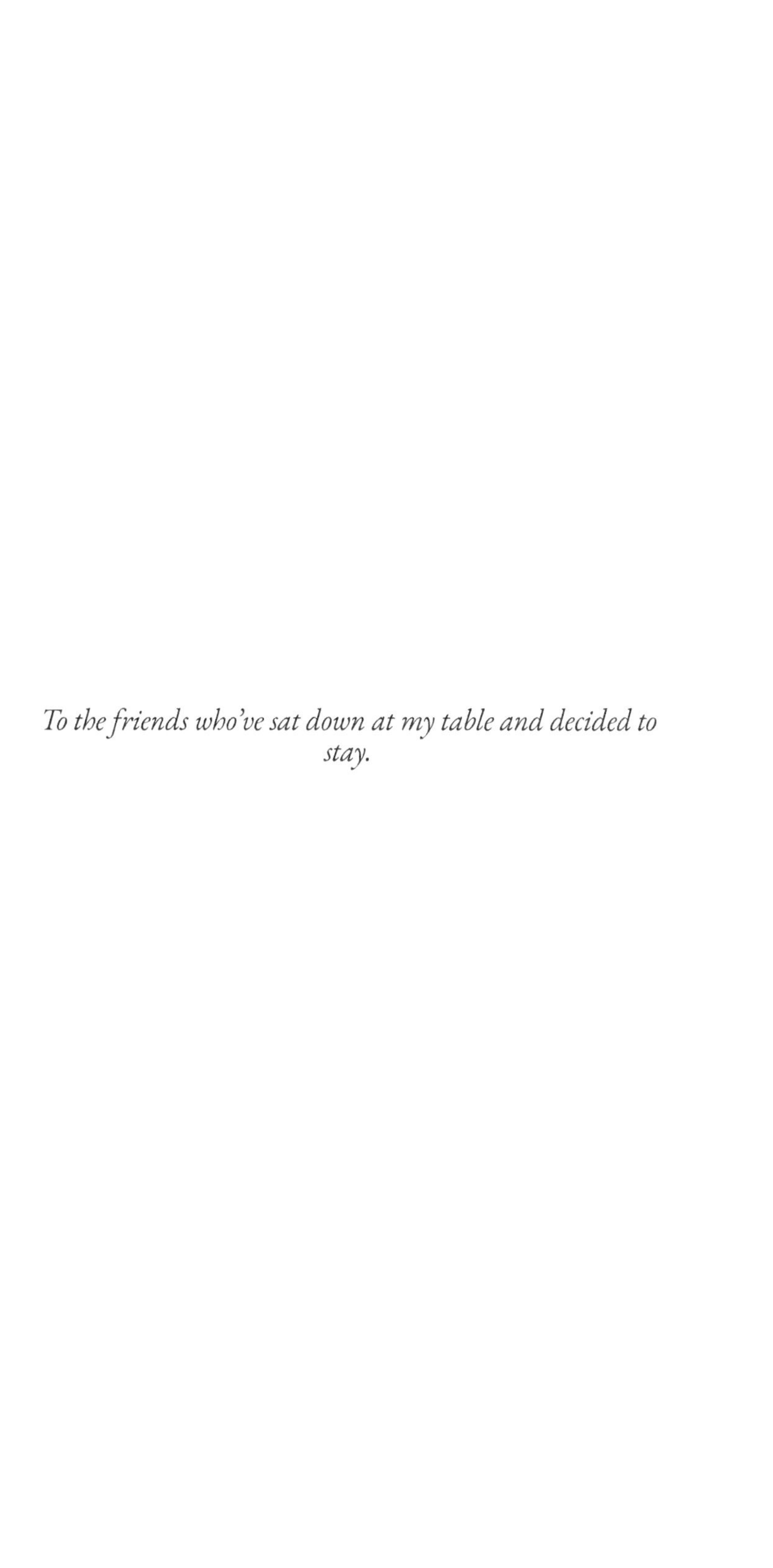

To the friends who've sat down at my table and decided to stay.

Books by Katie Silverwings

FEATHERED FRIENDSHIP
✦ A Strange Space™ Novella ✦

CELADON
✦ A Strange Space™ Novel ✦

HOW OCEAN MERLANI STOLE THEIR NAVIGATOR
✦ A Strange Space™ Novel ✦

WARMTH AND DARKNESS
✦ A Strange Space™ Novella ✦

THE GARDEN IN THE DARKNESS
✦ A Strange Space™ Novel ✦

TALES OF THE NAVIGATORS: VOLUME 1
✦ Strange Space™ Short Stories ✦

ON THE SUBJECT OF KITTENS AND MITTENS
✦ A Strange Space™ Novella ✦

The printing of this edition of *How Ocean Merlani Stole their Navigator* was made possible through the generous support of the members of the Strange Space Fan Club, including:

Astral Navigator

Sharon T. Hinton

Space Adventurer (1 Year)

Tabitha

Thank you so much to all of my Fan Club members and supporters! I couldn't do this without you.

To find out more about the Strange Space Fan Club and join for free, visit:

www.KatieSilverwings.com/Fan-Club

Characters Appearing in this Story

The following list of characters is divided by species and arranged in order of their appearance in the narrative. Only characters with significant "speaking roles" have been detailed here. All others present are listed as a group for the reader's reference; characters who are mentioned but do not appear are not included. Listed family connections are not exhaustive.

Florivans

Ocean Merlani Barker Hämäläinen

They/them. Also known as "Cinny". A second-year cadet at the Sol Central Space Service Academy (Advanced Geosciences, Quantum Space Drive Engineering, and Exoplanetary Mineralogy). Former survivor-smallest kitten. Child of **Ocean Marbree** and littermate of **Sky Miradyn** and **Storm Melbryl**. Adoptive child of **George Barker** and **Taimri Hämäläinen**. Nibling of **River Myrval** and adoptive nibling of **Jade Ilmi**, **Cerulean Mirawynd**, and **Elias Rudolph.** Adoptive grandchild of **Elder Celadon**.

Cerulean Mirawynd

They/them. Also known as "Wyndi". A former survivor-smallest kitten. Lead Quantum Space Drive Engineering instructor, Sol Central Space Service Academy. Former 2nd Darter Squadron mascot. Counterpart to **Julian Potts**. Member of the household of **Elder Celadon**. Adoptive entile of **Ocean Merlani** and their siblings.

JADE ILMI

They/them. Also known as "The Fleet's Phantom". A former survivor-smallest kitten. Star-Keeper and Agent of the Florivan Council of Elders. Child of **Elder Celadon.** Adoptive entile of **Ocean Merlani** and their littermates.

ELDER CELADON TOREVAL

They/them. Also known as "Dons". Primary Quantum Space Drive Engineer, LSS *Starbright*. Member of the Florivan Council of Elders; 'Defense Fleet Elder'. Parent of **Jade Ilmi**. Counterpart to **Elias Rudolph**. Adoptive grandparent of **Ocean Merlani** and their littermates.

OTHER FLORIVANS APPEARING

QDE Cadets Kingfisher, Bunting, and Jay. Sky Miradyn Barker and Storm Melbryl Barker. QDE Cadet Mist. Lt. Cyan Rillni

Humans

COMMANDER JULIAN POTTS

He/him. Also known as "Sarge". Lead Astral Navigation instructor, Sol Central Space Service Academy. Defense Fleet veteran and former 2nd Darter Squadron pilot. Counterpart to **Cerulean Mirawynd**. Member of the household of **Elder Celadon**.

TERESA VASQUEZ

She/her. Also known as "Reese". A final-year Command and Tactical Piloting dual-focus cadet at the Sol Central Space Service Academy. Co-captain of the Martial Arts Competition and Demonstration team. Niece of **Esteban Vasquez**.

BENNINGTON LEWIS

He/him. A new Astral Navigation cadet at the Sol Central Space Service Academy, recently transferred from the Command department.

COLONEL PENNY ALBRIGHT

She/her. Lead Tactical Piloting instructor and assistant Security/Tactical instructor for Judo, Sol Central Space Service Academy. Head of the Academy's Martial Arts Competition and Demonstration team. Defense Fleet veteran and former 2nd Darter Squadron pilot. Adoptive aunt of **Ocean Merlani**. Member of the household of **Elder Celadon**.

TOBIAS DA SILVA

He/him. Also known as "Toby." A final-year Security and Tactical Piloting dual-focus cadet at the Sol Central Space Service Academy. Co-captain of the Martial Arts Competition and Demonstration team.

PAUL KOUASSI

He/him. A final year Command and Tactical Piloting dual-focus cadet at the Sol Central Space Service Academy. Member of the Martial Arts Competition and Demonstration team.

ANTOINETTE MARTINS

She/her. A second-year Security focus cadet at the Sol Central Space Service Academy. Member of the Martial Arts Competition and Demonstration team.

BECK LAVINE

They/them. A second-year Command focus cadet at the Sol Central Space Service Academy. Member of the

Martial Arts Competition and Demonstration team.

SIMON KATZ

He/him. A second-year Engineering and Command dual-focus cadet at the Sol Central Space Service Academy. Member of the Martial Arts Competition and Demonstration team.

ANTON CONDREY

He/him. A new Astral Navigation cadet at the Sol Central Space Service Academy, recently transferred from the Engineering department.

RICHARD MALTBY

He/him. A new Astral Navigation cadet at the Sol Central Space Service Academy, recently transferred from the Astral Cartography department. Twin brother of **Robin Maltby**.

ROBIN MALTBY

They/them. A new Astral Navigation cadet at the Sol Central Space Service Academy, recently transferred from the Navigation Technology department. Twin sibling of **Richard Maltby**.

ELIAS RUDOLPH

He/him. Also known as "Rudy". Primary Astral Navigator, LSS *Starbright*. Counterpart to **Celadon Toreval**. Line-adopted uncle to **Ocean Marbree** and their littermates. Veteran of the Defense Fleet, former mechanic of the 2nd Darter Squadron.

DR. REBA KIELY

She/her. A physician and instructor at the Sol Central Space Service Academy's Medical Center. Wife of

Julian Potts. Adoptive aunt of **Ocean Marbree** and their siblings. A member of the household of **Elder Celadon**.

LT. COMMANDER GEORGE BARKER

He/him. Assistant Tactical Piloting and Astral Navigation instructor, Alpha Centauri-New West Space Service Academy. Defense Fleet veteran and former 6th Darter Squadron pilot. Former Astral Navigator counterpart of **Ocean Marbree**. Adoptive father of **Ocean Merlani** and their littermates. Husband of **Taimri Hämäläinen**. A member of the household of **Elder Celadon**.

COLONEL ESTEBAN VASQUEZ

He/him. Retired career Defense Fleet officer and former head pilot of the 6th Darter Squadron. Great-uncle of **Teresa Vasquez**.

RANGER CAPTAIN TAIMRI HÄMÄLÄINEN

She/her. Also known as "Tam" or "Äiti". Co-Captain of the Lone Star Ranger Corps' starship LSRV *Atascosa*. Astral Navigator counterpart to Ranger Captain **River Myrval**. Wife of **George Barker** and adoptive mother of **Ocean Merlani** and their siblings. A member of the household of **Elder Celadon**.

LIEUTENANT SEAN MARSHAL

He/him. Also known as "Marsh". Secondary Astral Navigator, LSS *Starbright*. Counterpart to **Cyan Rillni**.

OTHER HUMANS APPEARING

Astral Navigation Cadet "Dix" Perkins. Commander Saleh. Jacob Vasquez-Montoya.

CONTENTS

CONTENTS

Part 3: The Meddling of Navigators in the Course of Fate

Appendix

How Ocean Merlani Stole their Navigator

✦ A Strange Space novel ✦

KATIE SILVERWINGS

Part 1: The People We Call Home

Prologue

Two Florivans stand in a small office in the Nav/Quan wing of the Sol Central Academy's Houston Primary Campus.

It's a cozy sort of office, filled with warm-colored decorations which compliment the standard wood-paneled interior. The two-seat couch on the far wall is upholstered in grey, but draped with no fewer than five bright-colored blankets on one side to match the two geometric-pattern-embroidered pillows nestled on the other. A simple wood and steel desk takes up the center of the room, its surface neatly arranged with framed photographs around the outer edge. The computer interface built into the center of desk's surface is currently disengaged, as is its usual set of large holoscreen projections. Behind the desk, a sheer ivory curtain obscures the scene of the campus green space and other buildings which could otherwise be seen out of the large windows.

The younger of the two Florivans stands at attention in front of the desk beside the matching high-backed wooden guest chair. They're wearing the pale grey uniform of an Academy cadet and have all four of their hands clasped together behind their back. Two narrow departmental stripes run around the cuff of each of their four jacket sleeves: one in rusty orange and the other in bright blue. The upper half of their chin-length silver hair is pulled back with two narrow braids into a grey barrette at the top of their head, just behind their catlike ears. The cadet's skin is a deep greenish-blue tone underneath the signature silver stripes of the species. The fluffy silver tuft at the end of their long prehensile tail twitches erratically, betraying a nervousness which the cadet is otherwise doing their best to conceal.

The older Florivan is roughly the same height as the cadet, although both of them are nearly a head shorter than average for their species. Their skin is a brighter true-blue color than the cadet's, while their long silver hair is arranged into an ornate braid which coils all the way around their head. They're dressed in a charcoal-grey Academy Instructor's uniform, complete with ivory collar and a Commander's insignia pin on their lapel. A second pin marks them as a reserve officer of the Sol Coalition Defense Fleet.

The cadet has been standing in the Commander's office for at least ten minutes now, waiting to either be disciplined for something they don't remember doing or be told whatever it is that made the Commander call them in after training hours in the first place.

At the moment, the Commander is over by their office door, occupied with a hushed conversation with their human counterpart. Said counterpart is leaning on the door frame: a tall, bald human man of the paler variety with a salt-and-sand beard, also dressed in an Academy Instructor's uniform. An additional silver insignia pin over his breast pocket of a winged star marks him as a fully qualified pilot. Whatever it is the two of them are talking about, their voices are both pitched softly enough that even the cadet's keen ears can only make out a few words here and there. If the posture of the Florivan instructor's ears and long silver-tufted prehensile tail are any indication, it's nothing too terribly serious.

After a few more minutes, the human instructor half-chuckles at something the older Florivan has said. He gives his counterpart an affectionate pat on the head, nods to the cadet, and leaves.

The Commander turns back from the doorway and strides gracefully over towards the desk. "Thank you for your patience, dear." They smile at the cadet. "I didn't expect we'd be interrupted like that—usually Sarge can handle the antics of his Nav cadets without my advice."

"Of course, Commander Cerulean." One of the cadet's ears twitches curiously. "May I ask why you wanted to see me?"

The Commander sets a hand lightly on the cadet's shoulder for a moment as they pass by in a gentle, affectionate way. "I'm just a bit concerned for you, dear, that's all—and since we just finished compiling next year's roster, I thought it might be good for the two of us to talk about a few things."

"Commander," the cadet says, hesitantly and still with a somewhat forced formality to their tone, "I assure you, I'm *fine*. I just... didn't click with anyone this time around. I'm hardly the first jumper to go into their second year without a counterpart."

"True. Your cousin Mereday took almost six years before we finally found a human who suited them..." There's a flicker of sadness that crosses the Commander's trio of golden eyes for a moment or two. They pause at the corner of the desk to blink it away and then look back to the cadet. "That isn't what I wanted to talk to you about, though. I *know* you'll find a Navigator for yourself eventually. Most of us do, sooner or later."

"Then why *am* I here, Commander?" The cadet seems genuinely confused.

The Commander remains silent for a moment as they sit down behind the desk, leaning on their lower set of elbows with their hands folded together. They fix their three golden eyes on the cadet with a pointed expression and gesture vaguely with one of their upper hands. "I had a chance to look over your class schedule for next term."

"Oh." The cadet's ears droop slightly.

"I know you're enthusiastic about your secondary course, dear," says the Commander, gesturing abstractly with one of their upper hands, "and I've spoken to a number of your instructors about the potential workload conflicts, considering that you're attempting to complete the full Advanced Geosciences and Exoplanetary Mineralogy tracks instead of choosing one or the other like most of the other undergraduate students do—but I was hardly expecting to have to do the same with *Colonel Albright* of all people."

The cadet hesitates. "I *did* talk with her about the scheduling before I turned in my registration forms—"

"—I'm sure you did." The Commander shakes their head. "It's just... Well. *Highly* unusual, you realize?"

The cadet's tail swishes disappointedly. "You don't want me in her classes at all, then, Commander?"

"I'm not sure I understand why you want to be in them in the first place, to be frank." The Commander lets out a concernedly exasperated sigh. "Or, for that matter, why you seem to think that it's physically possible for you to keep up a course overload in *three* different departments at the same time. *Two* is pushing it to begin with."

"I'm only taking four physical skill units across in Sec/Tac, Commander," the cadet protests. "That's *hardly* an overload—"

"—It *is* when one of those units represents participation in an intra-system ranked competition team." The Commander pauses and gestures for the cadet to sit down in the chair they've been standing beside all this time.

The cadet complies, although with an awkward hesitation.

"I was aware of your extracurricular pursuits when we signed you, dear." The Commander folds their hands back together. "*Unusual*, for sure, but considering your background I suppose it wasn't too surprising. I have a quirk or two of my *own* from being raised by humans—but we both know who and *what* we are, when it comes down to it."

"...Yes, Commander." The cadet's ears slip into a less confident position. They have all four hands folded together in their lap now, holding their sets of four long fingers tightly interlaced as if forcing themself not to fidget.

"Not that I was planning on stopping you from pursuing them in your free time, of course..." The Commander tilts their head curiously. "But I'll admit I didn't realize you intended to actually *compete* with the humans."

"I'm..." The cadet hesitates. "I'm not in it for the competing, really."

"Then what is it?"

The cadet looks away now from the Commander's eyes, all three of their own turning down to stare at their hands instead. "...I don't know how to explain."

"Try, if you would, please."

The cadet forces back a sigh while trying to find the right words. "The Colonel's been letting me sit in on her recreational classes all year. When she asked if I'd like to sign up for the full-credit ones and join her team next term, I... I couldn't turn down the invitation, Commander Cerulean. I just... *couldn't*. That's all it is."

"Hmm. I see." The Commander is silent for a few moments, the same way they are when one of the Nav cadets has done something wrong and they're waiting for their counterpart to point it out first.

"I..." The cadet sighs again, their ears drooping further even as their third eye glances back up at the older Florivan. "It means a lot to me, that she thinks I'm skilled enough to ask."

After another long silence, the Commander nods slightly. "Well, I'm not going to try to stop you if you're set on it, dear. Colonel Albright is one of my oldest friends, and I trust her judgment... but if this starts impacting your performance in the Strange or your other studies, I *will* have to intervene. Do you understand that?"

"Yes, Commander."

The Commander looks at the cadet for another long moment and then shakes their head with a small sigh and makes a shooing motion towards the door. "That's all I wanted to say, dear, I know you have places to be."

The cadet stands and turns to go, and has just waved the door open when the Commander speaks again. "And Merlani?"

The cadet turns back to look at the Commander. Their ears perk back up at the use of their private name and the unspoken signal that they're now talking as family members rather than instructor and student.

"You *know* I'm here if you need to talk, don't you? You don't have to face everything alone."

"I know, Entile Wyndi. But I'm fine. Really. You don't have to worry about me." The cadet dips their head with a reassuring smile before they leave the office.

The Commander lets out a long sigh now as their eyes fall on two of the many framed pictures arranged on the corner of their desk. In the first, a young Florivan who shares their bright, clear blue coloring stands beside a young pinkish-pale human woman with curly red hair who's posing in her Academy-Medical graduation outfit. In the second, a young human man of the mildly tan variety with mousy-brown martian curls sits on a garden bench beside the same young Florivan. A little girl who matches the human and seems to have borrowed his uniform jacket is perched on the young Florivan's lap, smiling shyly at the camera.

"It's in my nature, though, kitten," the Commander says, even though the cadet is no longer there to hear them. They absently run their fingers over the beads woven into the knotted-thread bracelet they wear hidden under the cuff of their lower-left sleeve. "I never stop worrying about *any* of you…"

Threw days into the first term of their second year at the Academy, the young Florivan known as Ocean Merlani sits alone at a booth in the far corner of the campus mess hall. They've set up their pocket-com to display a trio of holoscreens in front of them above the table, each one showing one set of their homework assignments. The keyboard projection takes up the space directly below the center holoscreen, aligned so they can type on it with their lower set of hands while their upper pair are busy with moving things around on the holoscreens themselves. A pot of tea, a mug, and a plate with a half-nibbled blueberry muffin sit beside them.

Outside in the walled courtyard between the mess hall and the campus library, very little is going on aside from the nightly show of the local bats hunting moths in the glow of the lights which illuminate the courtyard and paths between buildings. Merlani isn't watching the bats tonight, but their keen catlike ears can still pick up the sound of them. It's a pleasing sound, in their opinion, if one they'd never expected to encounter when they first moved here.

As much as Merlani does enjoy watching the aerial dances of the bats, their focus at the moment is solely on their homework. Their self-imposed task for the evening: trying to sort out their notes for one of the six different assignments they've already been given. Merlani knew from the beginning they were going to have a lot to juggle between all of their classes this term, but a day one research paper on hydrodynamics and geomorphology was *not* something they'd taken into account. The way they see it, though, anything is manageable as long as they start on it well before the deadline.

It's past midnight now—by several hours, even. The mess is practically empty, save for a few human cadets at one of the tables on the other end of the room who are playing cards, another pair closer to the automat service line who seem to have come in for a late night snack, and what sounds like a group of four or five up on the mezzanine level holding some form of extracurricular club meeting. The window-encircled space of the campus mess hall holds hundreds during its busiest hours, but outside of standard diurnal mealtimes, it tends to be a bit of a ghost town. That's somewhat Merlani's point of studying here this time of night, though; no one ever bothers them, but they don't have to feel completely *alone.*

Or rather, until *now*, no one has ever bothered them.

"Hello! Mind if I sit with you?"

The unexpected brightly accented voice interrupts Merlani's train of thought. They turn their third eye up from the notes they were arranging on their right-hands holoscreen.

The young human standing over them is tall and deeply tan, with dark brown eyes and a long wavy mess of black hair pulled up into a high ponytail. She has to be a cadet of some kind, but she's out of uniform, so there's no way of telling what department she belongs to. She looks like she's just come from the athletic center, though: loose red tank top with wide armholes, grey sports bra underneath, grey cropped leggings. A set of delicate black line-work tattoos traces halfway up her right arm from her wrist, all in a pattern of stars and Earth-based constellations.

Before Merlani can say anything, the human is already in the process of scooting herself into the red-upholstered bench seat across the table from them and settling in with her back in the corner between the wall and the bench.

"You *do* know there are other tables, right?" Merlani is more confused by the human's insistent manifestation than they are annoyed, although both emotions make their way into their tone. They flick an ear in the direction of those many empty tables, just for good measure.

"Oh, I know—but *you* looked like you could use bit of company!" The human has now started to remove her plates and mug from the tray she's set down directly behind Merlani's main holoscreen. Once the tray is clear, she stashes it somewhere underneath the table and then stretches out her long legs across the rest of the bench, crossing them at the ankles.

"You aren't going to leave, are you?" Merlani asks, fixing the rest of their eyes on her pointedly.

The human picks up her mug in both hands. She lets out a contented sigh before blowing away some of the steam rising from it and taking a long sip.

Merlani catches a whiff of strong coffee smells from the steam wafting across the table—it's a familiar smell, one that stirs up a lot of old memories in the back of their mind. Coffee is the smell of *family*, even though for Florivans like them it's poisonous to ingest. Merlani's always thought it a pleasant smell, ever since they were a small kitten snuggling in the pockets of their coffee-loving human parents.

"You sit in here practically every night," says the human between sips. "I've seen you, you know? Ever since the beginning of last year: same table, pot of tea, holoscreens— never any company—it's *interesting*."

"So why bother me now?" Merlani turns their eyes back to their homework and tries to keep the majority of their attention on the document in front of them instead of the perplexing human sitting behind it. It isn't easy. "If I'm so 'interesting', why wait a whole year?"

The human grins at Merlani through the translucence of their holoscreen. "Well! *Now* I know who you *are*, and it's not nearly as weird to sit down and say hello to a classmate as to a total stranger, is it?"

"I don't think we've been introduced?" They turn all three of their eyes back to her curiously. Merlani is *certain* they would have remembered this human if they'd met her before. Her voice is too distinctive for them to have forgotten. It has a bright, warm citrus-and-spice sort of quality to it that would be quite pleasant, really, if only she wasn't using it to pester them in the middle of their studies.

"We haven't—well, not *formally*, at least," the human says, letting out a small laugh. "I can't remember your name, but I *know* you're the same Florivan that managed to pull an ippon gachi out of their opponent inside of two minutes during the practice spars in Colonel Albright's advanced judo class yesterday. I don't think I've ever seen anyone manage that so quickly before, you know? *Especially* not anyone who just switched in from the recreational class. Made a bit of an impression on all of us—but since you scurried off so fast after we were dismissed, no one had a chance to properly welcome you."

"Ah!" Merlani slides their pocket-com and holoscreens over towards the window enough to give their classmate a bit more room at the table. "You're one of the Sec/Tac folks! I should have recognized you sooner. Nice to meet you, then."

"I'm Teresa Vasquez. Reese, if you like." She extends a hand across the table to them through the space between the holoscreens, still holding her coffee in the other.

"Ocean." Merlani takes the hand just long enough to shake it. Somewhere in the back of their mind, it registers that Reese's hand is warm—probably because of the coffee in the mug she's been holding.

"Nice to meet you, Ocean!" Reese takes another sip from her coffee, then tilts her head curiously towards their holoscreens. "So, what *is* all this nonsense, anyway?"

"Homework." Merlani gestures at the holoscreens in turn. "Geophysics, crystallography, and gravimetry on that one, Nav/Quan methodology and jump protocols in the middle... and *this* is environmental geology, for which I'm supposed to have a research paper outline ready to turn in *next week*."

"Already?" Her eyes widen. "And I thought *my* professors were intense."

"As I was warned last year, Dr. Olsen takes no prisoners." Merlani shakes their head ruefully, then glances back to their notes and list of references. "That's why I'm trying to get a head start on it tonight—I have *two* more classes with her that start tomorrow, and I have no doubt she'll be assigning things like this during both of them."

"Oof. That's what, two-thirds of a planet you're working on tonight, then?" Reese smiles teasingly at them over the edge of her coffee mug.

"Something like that, yes." Merlani stifles a laugh.

"So, why study here, then, if you have all of that to get done?"

Merlani shrugs. "They have tea and muffins here, mainly. Plus the library closes at ten, and it's annoying to have to stop in the middle of what I'm doing and set everything back up somewhere else... and it's too quiet in my quarters."

'Too quiet' is something of an understatement. Merlani had *thought* it was quiet last year, when they'd first started coming to the mess hall to study. Now that their housemates have all graduated, even the common area of the flat they once shared is empty all the time. Theoretically they'll be receiving new housemates by the end of the week, but the folks from the Campus Accommodation lottery haven't told them yet who or how many to expect.

"It's pretty quiet in here this time of night, though, isn't it?"

"Oh, there's enough activity going on to make it interesting." Merlani is the one to smirk teasingly now. "Although *usually* the activity is polite enough not to come over and interrupt me."

"Hey, you've been here since what… dinner service? You *looked* like you could use a good interruption!" Reese nudges the smaller of her plates over to them under the holoscreen display. "Concha?"

"What sort?"

"Vanilla and cinnamon."

Merlani looks between their new acquaintance and the plate of sweet bread buns decorated with white crackled sugar shells. They smile at her. "All right, Reese, you can stay."

"Excellent!" Reese takes another long sip from her coffee. "I had a feeling you'd like pan dulce. It's a good middle-of-the-night-going-into-morning sort of thing, I think—and don't worry, I checked that they had the little 'won't poison your new Florivan friend' symbol on the tag."

"Thank you." Merlani stifles a giggle. "I *do* appreciate not being poisoned in the middle of my homework."

They disengage the keyboard projection and nudge the pocket-com and holoscreen displays over a bit further out of the way, then take a concha from the plate. The mess always features a variety of traditional regional foods as part of the standard menu, but somehow they missed seeing these when they went through the line earlier. It *is* a good time to stop for a break, anyway. Merlani takes the opportunity to pour more tea into their cup to go with it.

They'll have to get up and refill the pot soon; what little remains in it has gone cold.

"Speaking of the middle of the night…" Merlani begins, looking to Reese with a curious twitch of their ears. "Why are *you* here, anyway? I thought most humans were diurnal when they're planetside and did the whole seven-or-eight-hours-sleeping thing?"

Reese tears off a portion of her own concha and gestures back and forth with it as she talks. "Oh, you know, couldn't sleep; needed to get some workouts in anyway; first class tomorrow—well, this morning, now—is an early one… that sort of thing."

"Ah. So now you're topping up on caffeine and sugar instead of actually trying to sleep tonight?"

"Got it in one." She pops the bit of sweet bread into her mouth and washes it down with more of her coffee.

"Ah. Okay, then." Merlani twitches an ear. Reese has succeeded in piquing their curiosity now. "What's the morning class?"

"The ever-delightful 'Senior Seminar in Personnel Management and Effective Communication' with Professor Bloom." Reese rolls her eyes dramatically.

"That's one of those 'boring and redundant but required to graduate' sort of things, I take it?"

"Yeah." Reese chuckles brightly. "I'd probably like it better if it *weren't* at eight in the morning, but at least I have 'Ship-based Combat Tactics and Maneuvers' right afterwards to wake me back up. I'm doubling between Tactical Piloting and Command—makes for some odd mixes of subjects."

"Fellow sleepless overachiever, then?" Merlani chuckles lightly, wondering what Entile Wyndi would think of this human's schedule compared to theirs.

Reese raises her coffee mug to them in a mock toast. "Seems like it."

Merlani raises their teacup silently to match the gesture.

Grinning, Reese tears another piece off her concha and dips the end of it in her coffee before taking a bite. "Granted, I should *probably* be reading up some more on the first battle of the Teegarden Expanse right now, since we're running through simulations based on it after the lecture on Friday... but I can do that later, you know?"

Merlani nods, although they're not sure that in her place they'd put off the reading themself. "Which class is that for?"

"Mm..." Reese pauses to take another sip of her coffee. "'Advanced Interstellar Combat Theory and Historical Parallels'. It mostly boils down to the play-by-plays of the battles in the Novan war, you know? The idea is to look at those against all the *other* significant conflicts in human history and see what could've been done differently. Commander Saleh said we'll be running a lot of sims and they'll be bringing in people who were *there* and making decisions to talk during some of the lecture sessions."

"That sounds..." Merlani can't find the word that would fully describe what they're thinking, so they settle on one that at least comes close. "*Intense.*"

"It can be. That's kind of the point? The Commander served under Admiral Setiawan back when she was Captain of SCV *Strix*. They were there at the Expanse and at Procyon *both*—their whole goal with the class is to make sure we all know the reality behind the stats." Reese gestures vaguely with another torn-off bit of concha. "Make us better leaders if the Defense Fleet ever has to get called out of mothballs again and all that."

Merlani takes a slow sip of their lukewarm tea.

It's an odd collection of mixed emotions that her description of the class draws up for them. The Defense Fleet is far smaller now than it was at the height of the Novan War, but there's still a good number of ships patrolling around the eight star systems that make up the little slice of the galaxy Merlani's people share with humanity—particularly in the deep space border regions near the old Novan claims. Their own parent had volunteered as one of the Fleet's Quantum Space Drive Engineers towards the end of the War, too, and had stayed with the Fleet for a long time after it was over.

Merlani themself is decades removed from the War, of course, but they were *raised* by people who lived through it. More than that, they're Florivan. Their people are instinctive pacifists and were officially neutral and theoretically protected during the War, but that didn't mean anything to the Novans in the end. Their entire *species* was almost wiped out of existence when Procyon fell and the Florivan Sanctuary planet was destroyed. Even now, there are barely enough Florivans left scattered across humanity's seven systems to stand a chance of ever recovering their numbers. If it weren't for their role jumping starships across space with their human friends, *none* of Merlani's people would have survived at all.

"Hopefully," Merlani says, quietly, pushing all those thoughts away, "the Fleet will never be needed again."

Reese looks at them for a moment, then seems to realize something and nods slowly. "Hopefully. But we'll be ready if it ever is."

Merlani raises an eyebrow as they attempt to subtly redirect the conversation. "You're aiming to be a Fleet Captain someday, then?"

"Someday!" Reese brightens, gesturing with a bit of her concha again. "That's my whole family, really. More of us in the Fleet than out, even before the War. Sort of a legacy to build on, you know?"

Merlani nods. "I know what you mean."

Reese grins at them now, a conspiratorial glint shining in her dark eyes. "Who knows, Ocean? When I *do* make Captain, maybe you'll end up being my jumper. Wouldn't that be *stellar*?"

"It might at that..." Merlani agrees, hesitantly. "Although I'm not sure the Fleet has much need for QSD engineers with geology degrees. My two littermates are doing engineering and medical secondaries, though. One of them might suit your needs better."

Reese is the one to raise an eyebrow this time. "Either of *them* go in for Judo?"

"Oh, no. It's just me, I'm afraid—they don't exactly get any of my 'hobbies' to begin with." Merlani shakes their head, stifling a laugh at the memory of Mir and Mel trying to help them practice their fall breaks. Neither of their littermates have ever shown an interest in joining them, even when they were kittens. Now, both regularly ask if they've grown out of playing 'human warrior' yet when they have a chance to talk—half of it's teasing, of course, but Merlani gave up on trying to explain the appeal of martial arts to other Florivans years ago.

"Well, then." Reese sets her mug down on the table with a dramatic clink. "That settles it! I'm keeping *you*."

"Oh?"

"Naturally! Who needs an extra engineer or medic when I can have a second-Dan geologist around to kick butts with me?"

It could be because it's late and they're more tired than they'd be willing to admit, and it could be because of the tone of her voice, but for one reason or another, that statement is enough to send Merlani into a fit of giggles like nothing has in *years*.

Reese cracks up in return. If any of the handful of other people in the mess happen to be watching the two of them, it must be quite the odd sight: a Florivan and a human, laughing like idiots on either side of a table covered in holoscreens.

"All right, *Captain* Reese," Merlani says at last, wiping a laughter-tear out of one of their lower eyes, "you find yourself a ship, I'll find myself a Navigator... and we can go kick all the butts in the galaxy if that's what you want. They'll never see us coming."

"I'm going to hold you to that, Ocean!" Reese says as her own giggles finally die down.

Merlani shakes their head again and takes a sip of their tea. A stray thought flits through their mind that they wouldn't be upset at all if this particular human *does* turn out to be their Captain someday. She's the first person they've met since LSS *Starbright* dropped them off at

Earth last year who's been so easy to talk to. It's refreshing, somehow.

Reese finishes off the last of her coffee and then stretches and starts putting her empty dishes back onto the tray.

Merlani finds themself inexplicably disappointed to see their new friend gathering her things. "Leaving so soon?"

"Well, you do have a paper to work on, don't you? Wouldn't want to overstay my welcome." Reese stands and stifles a small yawn before stretching some stiffness or other out of her arms again. "Besides, I need to shower before I get ready for class. Professor Bloom expects us to be *presentable* regardless of how early it is."

"It's not that late already, is it?" Merlani looks back to their holoscreens to check the time. It's close to four in the morning.

"Mm..." Reese giggles. "Well, late or early or whatever, if you're still here at breakfast service, I might come back and pester you some more."

"I'll probably be off to catch an hour or two of sleep by then, I think. My first class isn't until ten."

"*Hasta luego*, then—good luck on your homework."

"Thank you."

Reese turns to go, then pauses and turns back to them with a grin that makes her dark eyes sparkle. "Just you wait, though, Ocean. I'll have you for my jumper someday. That's a *promise*."

All Merlani can do is chuckle. "Okay, Captain Reese. I won't forget."

As Reese leaves, Merlani turns their full attention back to their main holoscreen to try and find the paragraph they'd been reading when she first appeared. The thought occurs to them, albeit briefly, that they might actually be looking forward to the next time this particular human decides to interrupt them.

ON THE FINAL DAY OF THEIR FIRST WEEK OF classes, Merlani finds themself holding back an awkward sort of frustration as they attempt to get to their locker in the Nav/Quan department's central room.

The frustration isn't due to the round of jump simulations they just got out of—that went well enough, particularly because it was just the "test all the new Nav Cadets over the Quantum Space intercom channels to check who can actually hear them before we assign training partner rotations" exercise that their instructors run at the beginning of each school year. There's no point having one of the Florivan cadets paired with a human whose voice can't reach them in the Strange, after all.

Just like last year, Merlani was able to hear all four of the humans who've been brought into the program as potential Navigators. They'd even been able to pick up one cadet's voice when none of the other three un-partnered Florivans could. Granted, Kingfisher and their littermates Jay and Bunting are new arrivals to the program, younger by almost six years, and don't have nearly as much practical experience working with different Navigators as Merlani themself does.

The fact that Merlani had been the *only* Florivan in the entire department aside from their Entile Wyndi who could hear Cadet Lewis is, ultimately, the source of their current frustration. The young man in question is a tall, blond-ish variety of pale human with a somewhat scraggly goatee who happens to be standing *between* Merlani and their locker, attempting to carry on a conversation with them that they aren't particularly interested in having in the first place. It's not that they *dislike* him, really, just that they have places to be and he's been talking at them ever since they came out of the simulation chamber.

"So, anyway, Ocean," he says, coming to the end of a long ramble about how happy he is not to have washed out of the program on his first day and how surprising it is that even the already-partnered Florivan cadets couldn't hear him, since he's *so* highly qualified for Nav. "It does look like we'll get to work together, doesn't it?" The eager grin on his face strikes Merlani as *particularly* grating, for some reason.

"That's up to the Commanders," Merlani replies. Their tail swishes with some of the frustration, although they do their best to keep their expression neutral. "They won't post the first rotation roster for a week or two, though."

"Still!" Cadet Lewis laughs, leaning against the lockers—and annoyingly, although they're sure he doesn't realize it, directly on the door of Merlani's. "You seem neat, and you *could* hear me—so I like to think we'd be a great pair."

There are a lot of things Merlani considers saying in response to this, not least of which is that it takes far more than simply being able to *hear* a human through the veil to make the sort of a connection a Florivan has with their counterpart work. They settle for a neutral statement paired with a flick of their ears. "Well... We'll see how things turn out."

Cadet Lewis seems to take this as encouragement rather than the polite dismissal they intend it as. "Great! Say, you're coming to the welcome dinner at the Commanders' house tonight, right? Maybe we can sit together..."

Merlani is only half-listening now; a familiar set of clicking-boot footsteps from down the hallway has caught their attention. They turn their third eye in that direction and are incredibly relieved to see that it is, in fact, someone capable of extracting them from the awkward situation they've found themself in. The tall, highly muscular older woman approaching from the direction of Commander Potts' office has her tightly wound white curls pulled back into two poofy ponytails at the base of her neck. Her complexion is even paler than that of the annoying young man standing in front of Merlani—the result of the same albinism which has her wearing specially modified wraparound glasses with tinted lenses to shield her eyes from bright lights and help them see correctly. She's dressed in a Tactical Piloting instructor's uniform, although paired with a vintage Defense Fleet Darter pilot's jacket rather than an Academy-issue one. As with all such jackets, the short ivory garment features her surname embroidered both over the breast pocket under her pilot's wings pin and over her squadron's signature crossed swords and fleur-de-lis design on the back.

Merlani waves subtly to her with one of their lower hands. They couldn't ask for someone better to show up.

"Ah! There you are, Little Ocean!" their rescuer's crisp martian-accented voice calls to them, "Sarge told me you'd probably still be back here. You ready to go?"

"Yes, Ma'am!" Merlani turns and salutes her. "I'll be ready as soon as I get my things out of my locker, Colonel Albright." They make a point of sounding as formal and respectful as possible, even though this woman is, in truth, a member of their extended family. Merlani knows she likes it better when they call her 'Aunt Penny,' but they don't particularly want Cadet Lewis to know who their family members are.

"Good! Go on and get it, then, we don't want to be late. And who's this young man?" Aunt Penny tilts her head curiously.

"Ah! Astral Navigation Cadet Bennington Lewis, Ma'am." He nearly comes out of his skin as he scrambles to come to attention and salute as well.

Conveniently, this means he's no longer leaning against Merlani's locker. They take the opportunity to slide the door open and retrieve their gym bag.

"Nice to meet you, cadet." Aunt Penny smiles cheerfully. "You're a first-year?"

"Second-year, Ma'am." Out of the corner of one of their lower eyes, Merlani spots a timid blush spreading across Cadet Lewis' face. "But I just transferred into Nav from Command—I read about you and the other darter development test pilots for a group project last year, actually! It's an honor to really get to meet one of Admiral Marvin's Musketeers in *person*..."

"Well, young man, you must not have paid attention since you transferred." Aunt Penny shakes her head with a chuckle, still using her brightest and most charming teasing tone. "Try asking that Commander of yours what unit he got his wings with sometime."

"Ma'am?" Cadet Lewis sounds utterly confused.

"Oh, trust me, cadet, Sarge has *stories*... and if you ever get him started telling them, you may not be able to get him to stop." She laughs again. "Well, at any rate, I'm sorry to interrupt your conversation, but we have somewhere to be. Ocean?"

Merlani latches their locker door and scampers to catch up with their aunt, who's already striding towards the exit. "Coming, Colonel!"

Once the two of them are well away from Cadet Lewis' line of sight, Aunt Penny chuckles and sets an arm around Merlani's shoulders. "Well, now, *he's* a high-strung one, isn't he?"

"Thanks for the rescue, Aunt Penny." Merlani smiles up at her, then lets out the sigh of frustration they've been holding in. "We just met this morning and I've already known him too long."

"Oof, I know the type." She gives them a little pat on the shoulder. "Let's hope he mellows out sooner rather than later, then."

Merlani nods, although they're not sure from their first impression that Cadet Lewis is *capable* of mellowing out.

"Anyway!" Aunt Penny grins down to them. "Your teammates are waiting for us. I think you'll like them."

"I hope they like *me*," Merlani says softly. Their tail swishes behind them with a mild apprehension.

"I know they will, kiddo. Half of them are from my department, and they're pretty decent pilots, too—and we both know how well you get on with pilots!" She chuckles again, then shakes her head. "I still wish I could get your Dad to come out on an instructor exchange and show some of my seniors a thing or two, though. They're getting too used to flying with me."

Merlani stifles a giggle themself. "Well, maybe after Sky and Storm graduate? I think he's pretty set on staying at AC-NW as long as they're both there."

"I don't blame him one bit." Aunt Penny gives Merlani's shoulder another affectionate pat. "Glad you're here with us, though, Little Ocean—*especially* because you're just what I needed to shake my team up."

"Well..." Merlani hesitates, then grins up at their aunt. "It'll *surprise* them, at least."

"That's the fun part!"

When Merlani and their aunt reach the campus Athletic Center, she guides them into a small locker room just off of her Martial Arts Competition and Demonstration team's designated training space. She pops open one of the lockers to retrieve her own workout clothes and then gestures to the handful of empty, open lockers nearby. "Go ahead and claim whichever one you like, Little Ocean." She pauses, her darter pilot's jacket now slung loosely over her shoulder, and looks between Merlani and the selection of unclaimed lockers, all of which are a foot or more above their head. "Ah. Stepladder's in the corner there. Remind me and I'll see if one of our folks on the lower row will switch with you."

"It's fine, Aunt Penny." Merlani sets their bag down and goes to retrieve the stepladder. "I don't mind. I'm just glad there *is* one of these here. It must be the only one in the building." They aren't particularly in the mood to have to scale a wall of lockers just to put their bag away this evening—it's bad enough that they have to do that when they use the rest of the athletic center's facilities because the only locker available to claim when they enrolled was on the very top row.

"Well, perks of being one of my kiddos, Little Ocean," she calls, slipping into one of the curtained changing alcoves, "you have access to this room now. It may be small, but it's *ours*. Just don't let my stepladder wander off, okay?"

"I won't." Merlani smiles, sitting down on the bench in front of the lockers to remove their shoes. "Thanks, Aunt Penny. For letting me do this, I mean."

"Hey, now, I know how hard you've worked to get here." She pops her head out from behind her curtain to fix them with an affectionate but pointed look. "Don't go thinking this is me making good on one of the favors I owed your

Nida or anything—I'd have asked you to join the team even if we weren't family."

"I know."

"Good." Aunt Penny nods and disappears back behind her curtain.

While Merlani is sorting out their own clothes, their keen catlike ears pick up the conversation that's going on in the training area. They hear two voices, not quite *arguing* but somewhat teasingly exasperated. To Merlani's surprise, one of the voices is unmistakably that of their recently-acquired friend, Teresa.

"All right, that's everyone accounted for?" asks a masculine voice Merlani doesn't know.

"I think so," says Reese, "except for the Colonel."

"Wait, no, someone's missing... let me see... Barker? Is Cadet Barker here yet?"

"Do we even *have* a Barker?"

"We should, there's one here on the roster. Must be the new cadet the Colonel said she was bringing in as Josie's replacement."

"Let me see that... huh. Barker, O. M.; 'they'—Freshman, you think? I don't recognize their name..."

"Vasquez, you'd forget your *own* name if it wasn't attached to you."

"Don't start that with me again, Toby." Reese laughs, but with a promise in her tone. "I can and *will* make you regret it, mister."

Merlani shakes their head, giggling softly at the ongoing joke the Academy rosters have been making at their expense all week. Somehow, it's actually *funny* this time. "Aunt Penny, from the sound of it, I think your team might start sparring without you…"

Aunt Penny emerges from her changing alcove wearing her loose-fitting green workout gear and stuffs her uniform into her own locker, keeping her signature jacket slung loosely over her shoulder. "Oh, they do that sometimes. Don't worry about it, I promise they don't ever actually *try* to hurt each other." She chuckles. "Take your time getting changed, Little Ocean, I'll introduce you properly once I'm done straightening the others out."

"Yes, Ma'am."

As they hear her footsteps and the swinging of the door to the other room, Merlani catches the continued conversation between Reese and the teammate with whom she's been debating the roster.

"Fine, fine," says the voice Reese had addressed as 'Toby'. "Either way, the Colonel is going to have a *fit* when she gets here if our new cadet is still missing."

"She won't have the fit at *us*," Reese points out. "She'll have it at this Baker person when they show up late to the first practice of the term."

"There you go again. It's *Barker*, Vasquez, we're missing *Barker*."

Aunt Penny's brightly martian-accented voice cuts into the conversation. "Are the two of you done with your little argument so we can get down to business?"

"Colonel Albright, Ma'am! We were just taking the roll call—"

"—Heard all of it. Don't worry, da Silva, I brought our new recruit with me."

"…*Where*, ma'am?" Reese asks.

"I left them in the other room so they could finish changing. Now, is everyone *else* here?"

"Yes, ma'am," says da Silva. He sounds embarrassed, somehow.

"Stellar! That means I don't have to hunt anyone down this evening." The distinctive sound of Aunt Penny cracking her knuckles punctuates her words. "Good to see some of you finally learned how to get here on *time*."

In the locker room, Merlani is almost done tying their narrow black cloth belt on over the modified white judogi top that matches the loose trousers they're wearing. The belt sits comfortably just below their lower set of arms. They stretch their limbs out experimentally for a few moments to make sure they have everything fastened correctly.

Somehow, despite their aunt's reassuring words, Merlani just *knows* this is going to keep being one of those days where things don't go quite right for them. They should be excited, of course, and to a certain extent they are—and honored that Aunt Penny wants them on her team, too—but at the moment they're mostly just nervous.

They're aware, though, that their nerves are probably less to do with the prospect of meeting the team and more to do with the fact that so far today, every interaction they've had with a new human has been nothing but *awkward*. Especially with that Cadet Lewis—he was just uncomfortably excited and over-eager about the whole thing from the moment their instructors called his name on the roster.

Merlani doesn't know who their instructors will end up pairing them with first out of this year's batch of

Navigator prospects, but they're not sure it'll matter in the end. None of the bright young humans they ran sims with today particularly drew their attention, just like last year. It's not that the new Nav cadets aren't nice people or qualified for the role—thy wouldn't have been let into the program if they hadn't performed well in the trials. It's just that for one reason or another, Merlani can't see themself partnered with any one of the new Nav cadets any longer than they have to be.

Everyone *else* in Nav/Quan is off right now getting to know all of the new cadets, human and Florivan alike, at the usual welcome-to-the-department social dinner Entile Wyndi and Uncle Julian are holding at their house. Merlani, though, is *here*, about to meet Aunt Penny's best students for the first time. They haven't decided yet if they're disappointed about missing the social—they're waiting to see how this goes. They may still have time after the practice to make an appearance, in any case.

"Now," Merlani hears their aunt say as they put their uniform, shoes, and bag away in their newly-claimed locker, "since your co-captains have confirmed that everyone is here... Time for my traditional beginning-of-the-term motivational speech! Let's see who remembers all of it."

There's a pause, punctuated with a few muffled groans and chuckles.

"All right, quiet down..." Aunt Penny stifles a laugh herself. "Welcome back, kiddos! You'd better have been keeping up with your practices during the summer break. If you think I'm going to let you slack off when we have our first regional tournament coming up next month, you have another think coming. *Especially* you seniors! You're getting ready to graduate this year, so that slacking off rule goes double for you three. You know the drill; you don't keep on top of your coursework, I drop you like a supernova."

As Merlani enters the practice room, they see their aunt is now standing in front of the mirrored far wall. The six members of the team are gathered around her, most of them sitting either cross-legged or on folded knees and all of them wearing either their general athletic gear or the traditional garb associated with their discipline.

"Now, I know you're all probably missing your previous team captain, our dear recently-graduated Midshipman Wells... but I have *every* reason to believe that Vasquez and da Silva here will be able to keep you all in line in her place." Aunt Penny gestures to Reese and the cadet sitting next to her, then chuckles. "Assuming I continue to keep the two of *them* in line, that is."

Reese is off to one side of the group, wearing a white judogi tied with a black belt. Her hair is tied up in a neat folded bun instead of the ponytail she'd had it in when Merlani met her. The young man beside her, presumably da Silva, is wearing loose athletic trousers and red tank top. The armholes of his shirt are wide enough to show the edges of the geometric tattoos that flow across his chest from his upper arms. He's clearly much shorter than Reese even though the two of them are sitting, with a similar medium-tan complexion to her and a close faded style cut into his dark brown hair.

"And as far as making up our numbers goes, I think you'll find our newest addition to the team has a lot to offer." Aunt Penny waves to Merlani now and gestures for them to come forward. "Come up and say hello to your new teammates, kiddo."

Merlani hesitates, but only briefly, and then walks around the other cadets to stand next to their aunt.

"You *can't* be serious, Colonel." The young man sitting beside Reese looks incredibly confused now, if not outright shocked.

"What makes you say that, da Silva?" Aunt Penny tilts her head curiously.

"You had a Cadet *Barker* down on the roster."

"I did, yes. And here they are!" She chuckles and sets one of her warm pale hands on Merlani's shoulder. "Although I believe you use the Florivan name convention?"

"I don't really have a preference, ma'am," Merlani says. Their tail swishes with amusement.

"All right, then." She gives their shoulder a subtle but reassuring squeeze before releasing it and gesturing to the group of young humans sitting in front of her. "Cadet *Barker*; this is the rest of the team. Your co-captains here will introduce you to the others properly after practice. As for the rest of you: This is your new teammate. They're going to be filling Josie's spot for our Judo set and serving as an alternate for Capoeira."

"But they're..."

"They're *what*, da Silva?" Aunt Penny arches one of her white eyebrows pointedly at him.

Da Silva flushes and then shrugs and crosses his arms. "Well... there's no way *they're* competition grade—even with the advantage from the extra arms and tail."

Reese nudges the young man with her elbow, stifling a laugh. "Settle down, Toby, you're making a fool of yourself again."

"I agree, Vasquez." Aunt Penny turns to Merlani again. "You up for giving him a demonstration, Little Ocean?"

"Which discipline, Colonel Albright?" Merlani does their best to stand at attention throughout this exchange, trying not to show any irritation in their face or posture. They're used to being underestimated, but it still stings.

Their aunt looks back to the rest of the cadets, then grins broadly and cracks her knuckles. "Both, I think. After warm-ups, we'll run a few rounds with the different disciplines and see where everyone is since I last saw them. You can be da Silva's playmate in the roda, of course… and since our other co-captain has already seen you in action, perhaps *she'll* be up for volunteering to be your partner in shiai?"

"Of course, Colonel." Reese makes eye contact with Merlani and winks. "I'm looking forward to that already."

Merlani relaxes and gives her a small nod in return. Reese probably has no idea how much of a relief her presence is to them, especially with the way the rest of their day has gone.

"There we go!" Aunt Penny claps her hands together sharply. "Okay, folks, let's get to it!"

WHEN THE TEAM'S PRACTICE IS OVER AND
Merlani has finished changing back into their
cadet uniform, they're somewhat startled to see most of
their new teammates waiting for them when they open the
changing alcove's curtain.

"Hey, Ocean!" Reese waves to them from the bench
she's sitting on to tie her shoes. "You ready to go?"

"I... just need to get my bag down from my locker."
Merlani is somewhat confused by the collection of eager
faces around them. They look around for the stepladder,
then realize that da Silva is sitting on it. They approach
him with a genial twitch of their ears. "Mind if I borrow
that?"

Da Silva makes a show of hopping up from the stepladder and spinning it around on one leg. "Sure, Barker—I take it you got stuck with one of the high ones too?"

Merlani laughs. "Wasn't much to pick from." They take the stepladder over and climb up to get their bag. "But hey, I'm used to it."

One of the other cadets, a thin-framed young man with deep warm-brown skin and close-cropped dark hair whose accent marks him as being from one or another of the Alpha Centauri colonies, chuckles as he swings his own gym bag over his shoulder. "Hey, Toby—I couldn't tell earlier while the two of you were in the roda. Are you still our shortest? I need to send Josie a picture if you're not..."

Da Silva lets out a huff of mock annoyance. "Just because the rest of you are annoyingly tall, Kouassi, doesn't mean *I* have to be obsessed with whether people are shorter than me or not."

Merlani comes down the stepladder and sets their bag on the bench beside Reese. They tilt their head questioningly, making a motion with their third eye towards the teasing argument that's still going on between the two young men.

Reese laughs, seeming to pick up on what they're asking immediately. "Yeah, they're always like this. Don't worry, you'll get used to it."

"Ah. Okay, then." They wave their tail cheerfully and stride over to stand beside da Silva. "Are we counting my ears?"

"—And you have to admit that—wait, what?" Da Silva seems to have forgotten what started the argument already. He whips his head around to look at Merlani.

Merlani makes a vague measuring gesture with one of their upper hands. "If you want to see which of us is taller. Are you counting my ears in the measurement? I'd guess it's a lot closer if you do."

Kouassi laughs. "They've got you there, Toby—I'd say ears should count."

"Well… we'll see just how close it is." Da Silva turns his back to them with a beckoning gesture. "Come on, back to back so we can get this over with."

Merlani smiles and goes along with it, holding their tail out of the way and lining themself up with the young human so their teammates can measure them. It's hardly what they expected to be doing this evening, but somehow they can't help but be amused by the whole thing.

"Hey, now, Toby," calls Reese, clearly holding back a laugh, "play fair—off with the shoes."

"What?" Da Silva turns around and looks down at Merlani's feet.

They wiggle all eight of their long silver-striped toes at him. Their shoes and socks are still sitting beside Reese with their bag, after all. Merlani hopes this little exercise will be over soon; they don't mind having bare feet for practice, but they've started to get cold now.

"Oh. Fine, fine. Shouldn't make much of a difference…" Da Silva rolls his eyes and kicks his shoes off in Reese's direction, revealing a *dazzlingly* stripy pair of blue, white, and pink socks. "Satisfied, Vasquez?"

Reese laughs. "Yep! Carry on!" She makes a show of picking up his sneakers by the shoelaces and moving them further away from her perch on the bench.

Once the two of them are lined back up back-to-back, Kouassi spends several intentionally dramatic minutes circling them and humming as he makes the assessment. Finally, he sets one hand on da Silva's head, then pauses and looks down to Ocean with a vague gesture of his other hand. "Are you okay with being touched, Barker?"

"On this occasion? Yes, go ahead." Merlani smiles at him and twitches their ears softly. "But thank you for asking."

Kouassi nods to them and gently settles his other hand on top of Merlani's head. It's surprisingly warm. After a moment, he raises it up to the level of the tufts of silver fur on the tips of their ears. He laughs as he withdraws his hands. "Okay, folks, we have a verdict!"

"*Finally*," says the freckle-covered young woman with bright reddish, wavy hair who's currently lounging upside-down on the bench opposite Reese. "You took long enough, Kouassi."

"Patience, Martins," Kouassi chides, shooting a charming smile her way.

Martins rolls her eyes at him in response. "Will you just get it over with so we can be done here? Lavine says they and Katz have everything ready now and they're starting to wonder where we are."

"Agreed," says da Silva, turning to face Kouassi and crossing his arms over his chest. "Well?"

"Well," says Kouassi, grinning, "if we count from the tops of heads... congratulations, Toby. You're *not* the shortest anymore!"

"Woo!" Da Silva pumps his fist in the air. "Finally!" After a moment, he seems to force himself to recover his composure, although he can't hide the grin on his face. "Wait—And if we count from their ears?"

Kouassi laughs. "Then you and Barker here are the same height."

Merlani stifles a giggle. "I can live with that. What about you, da Silva?"

Da Silva nods, still grinning. "Officially, we're counting from *heads*... but sure."

"All right, then, you two," calls Martins, still upside-down but now pointing her pocket-com's camera at them. "Strike a pose so we can show Josie and *then* we're out of here."

Merlani finds themself stifling giggles the whole time they're posing with da Silva, halfway back-to-back again but this time with both of them crossing their arms over their chests in the most dramatic fashion possible. Merlani even curls their tail around in front for good measure.

"All right," calls Reese once the picture has been approved, tossing da Silva's shoes at him while Merlani reclaims their own. "Let's get out of Dodge. You have the blindfold, Martins?"

Martins pulls a black scarf out of her bag. "I hope it's enough," she says, handing it to Reese. "I wasn't expecting someone with a third eye."

"*Blindfold*?" Merlani looks to Reese with a hesitant curiosity.

"Don't worry, Ocean," she says, reassuringly. "It's just a silly little tradition we have. Nothing unpleasant or dangerous, I promise—Colonel Albright would have our hides if it was."

Merlani looks between her and the other three humans for a moment, then smiles and scoots over next to her on the bench. "Okay... but this had better not be anything *weird*."

"Remind me again what the Florivan definition of 'weird' is?" Kouassi asks while Reese is carefully fitting the scarf on around Merlani's eyes.

"I'll know it when I... well, hear it, at the moment." Merlani swivels one of their ears in his direction and makes a pointed swish of their tail. "But if I get a call from any of my entiles asking what's going on, trust me when I say *you'll* be the ones who have to explain it to them."

Kouassi laughs. "Fair enough."

"There we are," says Reese. Merlani hears her stand up from the bench and shoulder her gym bag. "Do you mind taking my hand so I can lead you?"

"Go ahead." Merlani reaches over to pick up their own bag, which thankfully is still next to them, then slips its carrying strap over their shoulder and stands. They hold out both of their left hands to the air in the general direction of Reese's voice. "Which one do you want?"

Reese's warm, very human hand wraps around their upper-left. "Let's go with this one. Come on, Ocean, I promise you'll like where we're taking you."

"Lead the way, then, Captain Reese." Merlani finds themself laughing as they let their new friend lead them out of the changing room and down the hall. They decide not to point out that their species has an innate sense of direction far better than that of a human. It would probably take some of the fun out of this for their teammates to know that they can recognize by sound and their sense of objects in space around them which way they're going and what buildings they're passing.

If they're honest, this is already the most fun they've had since they moved to Earth last year. It's worth playing along with the game to get to enjoy it for just a bit longer.

Half an hour later, Merlani finds themself sitting in the innermost spot of a corner booth table with Reese on one side and Kouassi on the other at what is arguably the *last* place they would have expected to be brought by their new teammates: an all-night 'breakfast themed' eatery a few streets over from the south end of campus. As it turns out, their 'initiation' as the newest member of the team consisted of little more than the blindfolded walk here and hanging out with the others while they all devour waffles. According to Reese and da Silva, the weekly post-practice meal is a core tradition of the team which presumably dates back to its founding.

It's not at all what Merlani expected when they allowed themself to be blindfolded and led from the athletic center—not that they really knew what to expect at all. Still, it's the *best* initiation ritual any humans have ever come up with, as far as Merlani is concerned. It's certainly better than what the former darter pilots in their life have told them being welcomed into a squadron was like; they're still not sure if they would believe Aunt Penny's story about the childish pranks she and her wing-sisters had pulled on their Uncle Julian when he first joined the Musketeers, if she hadn't shown them the pictures.

Waffles are *far* preferable to waking up to find one's uniform boots full of marshmallow fluff.

Of course, Merlani likes waffles to begin with—and they don't regret missing the Nav/Quan social at all now. *These* humans are more interesting, after all, and actually have something in common with them outside of their future career path. Maybe it's because Reese was the one to introduce them to everyone, but Merlani has found themself almost immediately at ease with their new teammates in a way that's always escaped them with the people in their own department. They're too caught up in the conversation going on around the waffles to really think about why that is, though.

"Okay, though, *seriously*," asks da Silva, gesturing to Merlani with the bit of blueberry waffle on the end of his fork, "why do you do everything with your lower arms held behind your back?"

"You're the one who pointed out they'd be an advantage," Merlani replies. "It's the same with my tail. My first sensei wanted me to focus on learning how to do everything with them held out of the way so I could play fairly with humans." They take a bite from their own pumpkin-and-cranberry waffle and then add with a cheeky smile, "I *can* use them for most techniques, I just don't during spars, usually."

"One of these days, Barker, we're going to have a match where you're not holding back on anyone and see what happens." Cadet Lavine, the light-skinned, sandy-haired martian who had introduced themself with neutral pronouns, grins at Merlani. "It's a pity you're not on the Tàijíquán side of things with me and Martins—I'd bet you'd be fun to push hands with."

Merlani stifles a giggle. "Well, I'm not nearly as proficient there... I can go through the forty-two form set pretty well now, but I've never done any of the competition style things."

Martins shares a look with Lavine, who's sitting next to her, and takes on their grin. "So... you're going to be our practice buddy now so we can have a few more eyes on our forms? That's what I'm hearing. Ooh! How do you feel about *swords*?"

"I..." Merlani hesitates, then finds themself smiling. "I'm pushing the limits of my nature as it is. I don't know if I could handle weapons."

"My competition jian isn't particularly dangerous... but I guess that makes sense." Martins makes an exaggerated teasing pouty face that reminds Merlani all too much of their sibling Miradyn. "Oh, well, it was worth a shot."

Lavine laughs, nudging Martins teasingly. "You get to stay our token pointy thing person, I guess." They look back to Merlani with a curious tilt of their head. "How would you feel about a folding fan, Barker? The ones we use for tieshan forms aren't the historic weapon sort they represent, and they make the *best* sound when you flip them open."

"You'll have to show me what that looks like first." Merlani takes a sip from their tea, twitching one of their ears to signal their amusement.

"Good grief, you two," says da Silva, pouring more coffee into his mug. "They've only been on the team for what… three hours? At least give them a couple of weeks to settle in before you go recruiting them for an extra discipline."

"You mean we should give you a chance for a rematch first, oh illustrious team co-captain?" Martins teases, playfully twirling a lock of her hair around one finger.

"Give me a break, Martins—hasn't my pride suffered enough today?" Da Silva rolls his eyes dramatically, taking on a mournful tone to match. "You never gave *Josie* a hard time…"

"Josie is *Josie*." Martins leans on her elbows on the table and lets out a dreamy sigh that may or may not be more of her teasing. "You're you."

Da Silva stares at her for a moment or two, then chuckles. "Fair enough."

"So, Barker," says Kouassi, midway through claiming another waffle from the sharing platter in the center of the table and arranging bits of cut fruit on top of it. "While there's a chance, I'm just going to go ahead and change the subject before those two go getting all syrupy again—no pun intended."

"What are you changing the subject to?" Merlani's tail swishes curiously under the table.

"*You*, if you don't mind—specifically, whether you're ever going to explain to us how you have a human name. Are we allowed to ask about that?"

"Oh, certainly. And don't feel bad, *that's* been confusing people since I was a kitten." Merlani can't help but laugh. That little personal detail of theirs has been driving all of their new teammates to distraction ever since the mix-up with the roster, apparently.

"More importantly," says Reese, pouring what must be her third helping of coffee out of the carafe in the middle of the table, "while we're on the subject, even if we don't get your origin story tonight, Ocean... you *really* need to tell us what you actually want us to call you so no one gets confused again or forgets outright."

"You mean so *you* don't forget, Vasquez?" da Silva grins at her broadly.

"Toby. I told you before, they didn't tell me their full name when we met. And I *did* remember the part I knew, so unless you happen to want coffee in your lap..." It's impossible to tell even with the wry smile Reese is wearing whether she's serious about that threat or not.

Da Silva makes an acquiescent gesture with both hands. "Fair, fair, I'll stop. For now."

Merlani, for their part, is reminded quite strongly of conversations they've overheard between the senior Nav/Quan cadets. They're not close to any of the upperclassmen, really, but they've observed a lot of the same sort of camaraderie there. They have to wonder just how long Reese and da Silva have been friends to be so close.

"Ocean is fine," Merlani says before any more arguing or questions can redirect the conversation. "That's my public name, same as any other Florivan has—but if you want to use my surname like you use each other's, I don't mind. It's kind of nice, actually, that it's getting used for a change."

Da Silva groans dramatically. "See, Vasquez? There's your answer: both. Take your pick, we all know who we're talking about by now."

"And do we get to know why you're listed in the registers with a human name, or is confusing hapless fools like Toby here during roll calls part of the game?" Martins pushes one of her reddish locks back behind her ear and looks at them curiously over the edge of her coffee cup.

Merlani takes a sip of their honeyed green tea. They've determined that they must have made a decent impression on these folks during the practice matches with Reese and da Silva—a close draw and a genial concession, respectively, but apparently enough of a show of skill and determination to win them the right to this so-called initiation by waffle. Likewise, this little set of humans has made a decent impression on *Merlani*. None of their classmates in the Nav/Quan department have ever shown much curiosity about their surname—it's barely acknowledged at all, though, since their instructors are family and everyone else there knows how Florivan names work anyway.

"You know," Merlani says, "the confusion is really more of a problem with the registry databases than it is with me. The system's set up to take our names the normal way, but since my littermates and I have a surname too, the computers assume *that's* supposed to be prioritized human-style. From what Sky and Storm told me, it was every bit as much of a mess out at AC-NW when they did their registrations—more, actually, because the two of them have the same initials and everyone gets them mixed up."

"You are very gracefully dancing around the question, Barker," says the final member of the team, a young man with lightly tanned skin and a short, tapered mass of loose dark curls under the small domed grey cap that covers the back of his head. This is the first thing Merlani has heard Cadet Katz say since he first provided his name. They aren't sure yet whether he's genuinely quiet-natured, or just can't get a word in edgewise against the others.

Merlani dips their head slightly to Katz in acknowledgment. "Forgive me. The Elder I apprenticed under is notorious for being cryptic... I suppose a bit of that must have rubbed off."

"So, does that mean you're going to tell us?" asks Lavine again, liberally coating their second waffle in a layer of syrup.

"It's not really that interesting," Merlani admits. "My parent died when we were kittens. Their Navigator legally adopted and raised us, that's all."

A chorus of intrigued and sympathetic 'oh' sounds and similar gestures of satisfied curiosity circles the table.

"It could actually be worse," Merlani adds with a chuckle. "If Dad had gone with the hyphenated name after he married our mother, the full thing would be 'Ocean Merlani Barker-Hämäläinen'—and I'm pretty sure that would have broken the registry database altogether trying to sort me out."

"Forget the registry database," da Silva quips, "that whole mouthful would have broken Vasquez and me *both* today."

Reese calmly sets one of the sugar cubes she's been dropping into her coffee onto one end of her spoon. In a smooth, well-practiced motion, she leans around Merlani and flips the other end of the spoon, launching the sugar cube across the table so that it lightly strikes da Silva squarely on the temple.

"Hey!" da Silva rubs at the spot where the sugar cube hit him. "What was that for?"

"You were being cheeky about her thing with names again," Lavine supplies.

"I said it would have gotten me *too*, though," da Silva protests. "It's memorable, for sure, but if I was reading it, I probably couldn't pronounce that last bit at all without having heard it first."

Reese shrugs and takes a swig of her coffee. "Sugar cube retracted, then. But I'm sure you'll deserve it again later."

"Probably," da Silva agrees with a chuckle. "Teasing you is too much fun to resist, *Docinho*." He tosses the sugar cube back to Reese, landing it with a neat little splash into her coffee just as she's setting the cup down.

"You two keep throwing food," Martins comments, doing her best impression of Aunt Penny's 'serious instructor tone' through a stifled giggle, "and I'm going to ping Josie regardless of what time it is on the *Mirzakhani* and tattle on you."

"Noooo," Reese says, half laughing, "*we're* the co-captains now! Josie doesn't get to lecture us for acting like children anymore."

"Just don't start anything that gets us kicked out, okay?" Kouassi shakes his head, doing his best to stifle any potential laughter in his voice. "I like this place."

"Who, us?" da Silva attempts to make an innocent face. "But we haven't gotten kicked out of anywhere in *months*."

"Yes," says Katz, solemnly, "and my mother still reminds me that I'm not allowed to bring any of you home for dinner the next time we have a match up at Luna 3."

"Don't worry, Simon," says da Silva. "I'm sure she'll forgive us eventually..."

"Toby, you got all of my nephews into a noodle-flinging match in *public*. She's never going to forget that."

"What can I say?" Da Silva grins, making an imperious gesture with the bite of waffle he's just speared onto his fork. "The noodles had it coming!"

Merlani looks between the two of them, and then turns their third eye to Reese with a curious twitch of their ears.

Reese giggles softly. "Yes," she says, leaning over to stage-whisper to them, "we're always like this. Great, isn't it?"

Merlani thinks about it for a moment, then smiles, nods, and returns their attention to cutting squares off of their own waffle and listening to the animated conversation going on around them. They couldn't be more pleased to have been accepted by this collection of humans—even if the lot of them could rival any group of Navigators they've ever met for delightful oddness.

THE NEXT MONDAY, MERLANI RETURNS TO THEIR flat from their afternoon crystallography class to pick up their gym bag and finds that the common area outside their room has been filled with piles of trunks and duffel bags in their absence. They don't hear any people, so they assume their new housemates must have dropped the mess off after they left this morning and haven't returned yet from their own classes to unpack. Merlani *had* received a note from the administrators of the Campus Accommodation Lottery over the weekend to expect four people to be moving in—but true to form, *that* was all the information they were given.

With a shrug, Merlani makes their way through the maze to their room. They have to climb over the piles to get through the small sitting area and shove one particularly heavy trunk out of the way so they can even get their door open. They've been looking forward to having other people in the flat again, though, so for the moment they don't mind the hassle.

They spent the whole summer term living entirely alone, after all, and the quiet of an empty living space has never quite settled with them. As a kitten, they'd always had Mir and Mel by their side and their Dad's nest to snuggle in so they wouldn't get cold at night. Even if they *did* have a private cabin on *Starbright* after their littermates left, Merlani had been right next door to both of the ship's Nav/Quan pairs—never far from companionship and the comfortable sounds of people moving about the ship. Their old cabin had taken some adjusting to in itself, but it hadn't been the sheer, empty loneliness of their room here after their first set of housemates had all graduated.

Merlani makes a mental note while they're changing into their cozy white-and-amber trousers and tunic and packing their judogi into their gym bag that they should bring some muffins back with them from the mess hall on their way home so they can properly welcome their new housemates. They're quite hopeful that these will be friendly people—perhaps even ones like Reese and the rest of their teammates who will have something or other in common with them so they'll be more than the cordial but barely-known acquaintances the folks who lived with them before were.

As Merlani closes their door and begins to weave their way back through the maze of housemate-belongings, though, any hopes they had for a pleasant experience with their new housemates pop out of existence like soap bubbles in a cactus garden.

"Oh! Hey, there!" calls one of the four young men now entering from the hallway in a far-too-familiar voice.

"…Hello, Cadet Lewis," Merlani replies, hesitantly. "And you too, Condrey, Maltbys." They wave to the dark-haired, ruddy-pale young man and the twin redheads with one of their lower hands. "What are the four of you doing here?"

"We're finally moving in, now that Commander Potts is done drilling checklists into us for the day," says Cadet Anton Condrey cheerfully. "I can't believe it took so long for the accommodation folks to finally have a place sorted for us."

Merlani shakes their head. "You're lucky. I had to bunk with the Commanders for a *month* last year before they finally got me a proper room."

"Wow!" says the Cadet Maltby with the short hair—Richard, if Merlani remembers correctly from their brief introduction last week. "Glad they didn't do that to us."

The other Maltby twin, the one whose hair falls all the way to their lower back—Robin—plops down onto the one empty spot on the sofa and looks up to Merlani curiously. "So, Ocean, are you a friend of Cadet Barker's or something? We saw the name on the door earlier, but we seem to keep missing them."

Merlani stifles a laugh. "Or something, I suppose." They swing their gym bag around to their back and head for the door. "I'll explain when I get back, if you budding Navigators haven't figured it out by then."

The Maltby twins share a look, then look at Merlani's door, then each other again. Robin turns back to Merlani with a giggle. "Okay. We *think* we know, but the explanation will so be worth waiting for!"

"Totally!" Richard echoes.

Merlani shakes their head again, almost looking forward to that now. They had a good impression of the twins when they first met—they both have an infectious sort of kitten-like enthusiasm. Condrey too; he'd struck Merlani as far more mature, but friendly enough.

Cadet Lewis, on the other hand? Merlani once again finds themself pushing away a sensation of annoyance at the sound of his voice.

"What's the rush, Ocean?" Cadet Lewis asks, leaning on the open door frame so one of his arms is obstructing it. "We missed you at the social—this'd be a great time for all of us to get to know you better, don't you think?"

Merlani holds in a sigh as they look up at him. They can't fathom why this particular human seems to *always* be getting in their way like this. "I have a class to get to."

"But you're out of uniform." Cadet Lewis raises an eyebrow.

Merlani rolls their third eye. "I'll change when I get there, after I'm done warming up."

"What's the class?" asks Condrey from across the room, where he's shoved someone's duffel bag out of a chair so he can sit.

"Judo," Merlani replies nonchalantly. "And I *do* need to get going—I promised a classmate I'd do warm-ups with her beforehand."

"Seriously?" Condrey almost falls out of the chair in surprise.

"Neat!" chorus the twins.

"That's cute." Cadet Lewis looks down at Merlani and laughs. "But really, Ocean Breeze, where are you off to?"

Merlani looks up to him with a disdainful flick of their ears and a swish of their tail to match. "My Judo class. And I'll thank you *not* to call me that."

"You can stop with the joke—It's a good one, I'll admit, but it's too funny to be true. Why would a *Florivan* need to learn Judo, anyway?" Cadet Lewis asks, laughing again. He doesn't even acknowledge the rest of what they'd said. "You'll have a Navigator to protect you soon enough—and as your training partner, *I'd* be more than happy to escort—"

"—You're not my training partner *yet*, Cadet Lewis." Merlani takes advantage of the difference in their heights and ducks under the annoying human's arm. "And I *don't* need an escort." They wave at the other three Nav cadets as they leave. "See y'all later, Condrey, Maltbys."

"Bye Ocean!" Condrey calls behind them.

"Have fun at Judo!" chorus the twins.

All Merlani hears of Cadet Lewis as they stride purposefully down the hallway and slip into the elevator is confused spluttering.

"Phew!" Reese plops down onto the bench beside Merlani in the team's locker room at the Athletic Center. "That was a long one."

"You said it, Vasquez." Kouassi steps out of one of the changing alcoves, now dressed in his casual workout clothes. "How are you holding up, Barker?"

Merlani turns their third eye up from tying their shoe. "Oh, I'm fine—everyone but you two seems to think I'm fragile or something... still feels like they're holding back on me."

"Don't worry, Ocean." Reese gives their shoulder a light pat. "They'll figure it out sooner or later."

Merlani smiles up at her. "Thanks. I hope so."

"Besides," says Kouassi, pulling his own sneakers out of his locker, "if anyone in the class is holding back on their opponents, it's *you*."

Merlani laughs. "Is that permission for me to not hold back on *you* the next time we spar, then?"

Kouassi grins at them. "You'd better not. I want to be able to beat you properly."

"Good luck with that," Reese teases.

"Hey there!" calls Lavine as they and Martins enter and set down their gym bags. "Y'all done with class already?"

"Yep!" Reese waves to them. "What are you two up to?"

"Getting in a bit of practice to clear our minds before we abduct Simon from the Engineering building and start our battle with homework." Martins sticks out her tongue in a mock-disgusted expression. "The three of us have a group project and it's going to be a *pain*."

"You up for playing with us, Barker?" Lavine asks, dramatically pulling a large red folding fan out of their locker and waggling their eyebrows over it in Merlani's direction. Somehow, they sound just like Merlani's littermates always do before pulling them into some bit of adventurous chaos.

"Well..." Merlani stifles a giggle. Considering who's waiting for them back at their flat, they don't mind the delay in going home at all. "Sure. Just let me put my stuff back in my locker. Is what I'm wearing okay?"

"Can you move in it?" Martins looks them over curiously. "That's all that matters for practice, really. Looks comfortable enough to me."

Merlani stretches and makes a show of displaying their full range of motion by elegantly standing and pulling one leg up in the air so their foot can almost touch the back of their head. Flexibility of that sort comes naturally to their species, of course, but it's still fun when they have occasions to take advantage of it. "Yeah, this is my normal workout outfit."

Lavine applauds teasingly. "Oh, that'll do. *Now* I see how you could leap circles around Toby even with your lower hands and tail out of the equation."

Merlani makes their most graceful bow as they come out of the stretch and wave their tail in a proper acknowledgment. "It's more fun when I can use them, of course..."

"Okay, I have to ask." Kouassi crosses his arms and raises an eyebrow at Merlani. "Dance or gymnastics? You *have* to have trained in one of them."

Merlani shakes their head. "Not any of the human forms or anything that formal... I'll admit that my Entile Jade is a Star-Keeper and taught me the basics of our old story dances during my apprenticeship, though." They smile at the memories. "I'm nowhere *near* as skilled as they are, of course, but there's a few of the moves that aren't all that dissimilar to what we do in martial arts."

"That sounds like it'd be neat to see," says Kouassi, "if you're ever in the mood to show us."

"Maybe." Merlani absently runs the fluff at the tip of their tail through the fingers of their lower set of hands for a moment. "Not tonight, though. I haven't done any of that in long enough that I'd have to practice before I'd be up for showing any of you—and Entile Jade would be disappointed if I didn't do whatever story I was telling justice."

They're not sure how well they could really show their new friends such a thing at all, particularly since the stories they know best are ones which need two or three people to perform properly. Merlani's not close enough to any of the other Florivan cadets they know to really ask them, and their Entile Wyndi might be fully trained as a Star-Keeper themself, but *they're* always so busy with their work.

"Well," says Reese, gently, "no rush or pressure on that. We just like having you around, Ocean. If you ever feel up to showing off some of your other moves, just let us know. Okay?"

Merlani looks back to her and smiles. "Okay."

"Speaking of moves!" Lavine taps their fan on their other hand. "We have some of those to go practice."

"Mind if we hang out and watch?" Reese gestures with her head in the direction of the practice room door. "Toby's still in class for another hour, and Kouassi and I had plans to study with him after that for our license exams."

"Fine by me," says Martins, pulling a tassel-decorated sword in its scabbard out of her locker before shoving her bag inside. "Lavine?"

"Same here!" Lavine fans themself dramatically and then snaps the fan closed with a swishing flourish. "And then we can *all* go somewhere and eat waffles while we pretend to study!"

"Lavine." Martins puts her hands on her hips and tosses them a teasing glare. "We *have* to at least *try* to get some headway made on our project tonight."

Lavine sighs. "Yes, yes, fine... but only because it's you and Simon I'm working with."

Kouassi takes a swig from his water bottle. "And because the Colonel doesn't like it when any of us shirk our coursework?"

Lavine shudders and then makes a point of scampering towards the practice area. "Point taken. She's scarier than the homework is! You coming, Barker?"

Merlani laughs, then scampers after them. "I'm right behind you."

Once Lavine and Martins are done practicing their Tàijíquán routines and walking through the full forty-two form sequence with Merlani, the five of them elect to head to the mess hall for snacks and studying. It's well past the dinner service rush hour by the time they get there, meaning that much to Merlani's delight, their favorite table in the corner is open.

This is the first time that they've ever had the table full of delightful humans to keep them entertained while they collate their notes from the day's classes. Merlani finds themself comfortably squished into the back corner of the booth with Reese beside them and Martins on the aisle side. Kouassi, Lavine, and Katz have taken up the bench opposite them, while da Silva had resorted to pulling over a chair from one of the central tables when he finally arrived.

"All right, Kouassi," says Reese, gesturing with the biscotti she's been nibbling on, "what's my next question?"

Kouassi flips through some pages of notes on his pocket-com's holoscreen. "Ah. Here's a good one. In the event you're coming in for a hot landing, what's the *first* thing you do once you make it to the ground?" He chuckles. "Assuming you don't crash badly enough that you pass out, that is."

"Activate fire suppression systems?" Reese takes another nibble from her biscotti before dunking it into her coffee.

"Mmm... *close*. Toby?"

Da Silva shrugs, leaning back in his chair so he's balancing on just the two rear legs of it. "That was going to be my answer—wait! Don't those activate automatically? Or is it supposed to be *confirm* that they're working and activate them if they haven't been turned on already?"

"Again, close." Kouassi grins. "Lavine? Martins? You want to cut in and best your upperclassmen?"

"Not listening, Kouassi," says Lavine, waving absently with one hand while they continue to tap through things on the datapad they're holding.

"Don't involve us in your flashcards," Martins continues. She nudges her own datapad across the table to Katz. "How about this, Simon? It looks like it *might* be a decent source..."

Katz takes the datapad and skims through it, then sighs, shakes his head, and hands it back to her. Martins and Lavine share a groan.

Merlani sets their own notes aside for a moment to pour themself another cup of tea from the pot they're sharing with Kouassi and Lavine. "It's shutting down the maneuvering engines to protect them and prevent additional fires, isn't it?"

Kouassi laughs. "Finally, someone gets it!"

Reese lightly smacks her forehead with the hand that isn't holding her half-eaten biscotti. "Ack, I *know* that one, too. We just did that simulation *last week*..."

"How in the stars did *you* know that, Barker?" Da Silva asks, giving Merlani a curious but somewhat suspicious look from across the table.

Merlani shrugs. "Dad started out as a darter pilot, and now he teaches Tactical Flight and Nav at AC-NW. I spent my entire kittenhood hanging out with him while he graded papers and things. Don't try to get me to *fly* or anything—that's my littermate Sky you want for that—but it's hard to forget the protocols when some of your first memories are of listening to your father drill his students on them."

Reese giggles and gives them a playful nudge on the shoulder. "Ocean, every time we get a bit of information out of you it just gets more and more fascinating. You *do* know this means we're going to beg you to help us study now?"

Merlani smiles and nudges her back with one of their lower hands, since their upper ones are still busy with their tea. "I *might* be enticed to take a break from my notes if some kind human or other could perhaps see if there are any more of those nice muffins in the automat and retrieve one for me?"

Da Silva laughs and bounces up from his chair, nearly tipping it over in the process. "Do you want that pot of tea refreshed too, oh great all-knowing one? I will stuff you *full* of muffins if it means we have a better chance of passing the license exam."

Merlani passes the teapot down the table to him. "You three are going to be *fine* and have your cute little pilot's wings pinned on you in no time even without my help, but sure. Tea and muffins, please, and I'll hold the flashcards for all of you when you get back."

Kouassi flicks the holoscreen of his pocket-com off and takes a sip from his own tea as da Silva leaves. "Thanks for the vote of confidence, Barker. It was bad enough getting through the provisional tests last year... but considering what everyone we know who's gone through it has said about the exam, it's a bit nerve-wracking."

Reese sighs, shaking her head. "I haven't been this nervous about a test since I was taking my final classification assessment in middle school..."

"Your exam isn't for a month or so, right?" Merlani smiles and gives their friend a reassuring pat on the arm. "You're all studying so well for the written portion, and I *know* you'll ace the practical. Colonel Albright brags about the three of you enough to make that clear. Try not to let it all get to be too big of an opponent in your mind. That just makes it harder to take down in the end."

Reese smiles at them. "Thanks, Ocean."

"All right," Kouassi says, cracking a smile himself, "Barker believes in us, now we have no choice but to pass! I vote we take a break from the flashcards until Toby gets back, though."

"Agreed," says Reese. She turns and gives Martins a curious look, angling her head to try to read the text on the younger cadet's datapad. "How's it going on your end?"

Martins looks up at her with a dramatically mournful expression and a tone that betrays genuine frustration. "This assignment is *impossible* and we are *doomed*."

"Commander Saleh is punishing us for something, I just know it..." Lavine chimes in.

Katz shakes his head, finally entering into the conversation. "They let the groups draw the assigned topic names at *random*. It's not punishment for how often you've been late to their class, Lavine, no matter how much you want to think it is."

"I *still* feel like they must have rigged it for some reason..." Lavine pokes at their half-eaten waffle.

"Simon's their favorite student," Martins points out with a giggle. "Why would they want to punish *him* just to get you?"

Merlani finally reaches the point at which they cannot hold back their own curiosity. "What's the assignment, then, that makes it so impossible?"

"So," Reese explains, gesturing with a new biscotti, "these three unfortunate friends of ours are in Commander Saleh's second-year History, Tactics, and Theories of Command class. A full third of the grade for the class is this group project where you have to research and give a presentation on someone who was at some level of authority in the Fleet during the War. They used to let the different teams *pick* who they wanted to do the project on as long as it met one of the criteria on their list... but now they put all the names of acceptable subjects in a hat and make the teams draw them at random."

"Yes, and whose fault is *that*, Vasquez?" Martins gives her a sideways glance and a teasing glare.

"Ooh, what's her fault now?" asks da Silva, now reappearing and unloading a teapot and a plate full of muffins from the tray he's carrying. "—Ah, I only pulled the ones that were marked Florivan-safe, Barker. No need to worry about hidden chocolate or anything like that. Take your pick!—Now, what did I miss and what are you blaming Vasquez for?"

Merlani shakes their head at the quick way in which he goes back and forth between topics, but happily takes a blueberry muffin from the plate when its passed down to them. It's sweet how thoughtful their new friends are about not poisoning them by accident.

"We're talking about the dreaded 'Command Personalities' project," Kouassi supplies. "And the fact that the *three of us* are to blame for Commander Saleh's change in tactics for assigning subjects."

Da Silva laughs, plopping back down into his seat and setting the tray aside with the collection of others the team has assembled since they arrived. "Oh, *that*... no, no, I'll agree that it's mostly Vasquez' doing. *We* just shoveled the manure."

Martins and Lavine share a giggle. Kouassi rolls his eyes.

Merlani twitches their ears curiously as they look to Reese. "Do I *want* to know what the three of you did?"

"Well," says Reese, cheerfully dropping sugar cubes into her coffee mug to go with the fresh coffee she's just poured into it. "It wasn't nearly as interesting as these two make it out to be. 'Squadron leader' was on the list, and one of the other teams had already called Colonel Albright... so I claimed someone I knew would actually show up if we invited him to campus."

"Commander Saleh gives bonus points if you can document first-hand accounts of the person, or interviews with them, or if you can get them to show up to your presentation if they're still alive," Lavine supplies.

"Ah." Merlani nods. "So, who did you pick, then?" They raise an eyebrow suspiciously. "One of your relatives who served with the Fleet, I take it?"

Reese grins. "Got it in one! Tió Esteban made us earn the favor, of course, just like all of the other pilots do... but hey, we got a perfect score with all of the bonus points!"

Kouassi grimaces. "By 'earn'," he says, making air quotation gestures with one hand for emphasis, "she means 'spend every free weekend we had leading up to our presentation mucking out stables so the old man would cooperate with us'."

"And mending fences. By *hand*." Da Silva shakes his head. "I still say that was all a scheme so we'd get roped into helping with your chores, Vasquez."

"Hey," Reese protests, "we passed the class! And Tió Esteban still likes you two even if he did have to keep rounding the horses up because *you* kept forgetting how to latch the gates—."

"—Who'd you draw, anyway, Lavine?" Kouassi asks, pointedly turning the conversation back to the younger cadets.

Lavine sighs dramatically. "The Fleet's Phantom."

Kouassi, da Silva, and Reese all wince in sympathy.

"Oof." Reese shakes her head. "That's a hard one."

"Wait," says Merlani, holding up one of their hands. "Who's the Fleet's Phantom? I've never heard of someone called that."

"Oh," says Martins, "That's... more what everyone who takes Commander Saleh's classes calls them, because it's *so hard* to find information about them and they just show up in the history right before Procyon and then vanish from the records entirely when the War ends."

Merlani gives her their most thoroughly perplexed look. "Does your phantom at least have a name?"

Katz nods. "That's all we have at the moment: 'Jade of Procyon'."

Merlani raises an eyebrow. "That's *all* your professor gave you?"

"Yep... Part of the assignment is that they give us a role or reference and we have to figure out who it is—one of our housemates is in the group who drew 'Squadron Leader: 2nd Darters, SCV *Athene*'." Martins giggles. "I'm waiting to see if they track down Colonel Albright on their own, or if we get to claim a favor for introducing them to her."

"That's why we're sitting here combing through our textbooks for scraps of information." Lavine sighs. "No one's ever made more than the bare minimum passing grade doing a report on the Phantom before, even the people who picked them *intentionally*."

"Like I said," Martins groans, "it is the impossible assignment of doom."

"Ah." Merlani nods. "Carry on, then, I suppose."

While the others are talking back and forth about theories and sources and getting sidetracked a dozen times, Merlani turns their attention to their pocket-com and pulls up a palm-sized holoscreen interface with their messages. They tap through their contacts until they find the one they're looking for. They're not entirely sure where *Starbright* is right now, but if they're lucky, their favorite uncle will be awake.

```
Good Evening, Uncle Rudy! Do you
think you can tell me where Entile
Ilmi is? I need to ask them a ques-
tion or two.
```

After a few moments, the screen lights up with a response.

```
Sure, Cinny. I'll pass word to them.
I think they're with Endeavor at
the moment. You okay?
```

Merlani smiles. If he'd asked them before their Judo class, they'd have had a much different answer—but right now? They glance around the table and the animated conversation their teammates are having. Right now things are quite nice.

```
I'm good. Made some new friends,
even! Aunt Penny has nice little
pilots. You'd like them.
```

It doesn't take long for their uncle to respond.

```
Glad to hear it! Don't let them get
you into too much trouble. Have to
get to work now. We'll talk prop-
erly soon. Love you, kid.
```

Merlani sends back one last message with a picture of their lower hands making a heart shape, then flips the small holoscreen off and turns their attention back to their teammates.

"Well, it's not *completely* impossible," Reese is saying, giving Lavine and the others her best impression of Aunt Penny's most encouraging tone.

"Yeah," Martins laments, "we *might* be able to find enough about them in the textbooks to pass…"

"Well, you'll probably have to content yourself with a listing of all of the hearsay like Nathan's group did when we went through it." Kouassi pauses thoughtfully. "But if you work at it, you might be able to get a second-hand account? Maybe the Colonel met them after the Musketeers were transferred to *Aegolius*?"

"She's on our list of people we might be begging for help," Katz answers. "But considering her policies on helping us with our homework…"

"Point taken." Reese pulls out her pocket-com. "Well, it's a long shot, but I can get you in touch with my Tió…"

Lavine pulls a face. "No, we'll save the manure shoveling for our last-ditch backup plan. We're desperate, Vasquez, but we're not *that* desperate yet."

Da Silva claims a muffin from the plate and begins unwrapping it. "Well, lucky for *you*, you've got what... a month before your presentation?"

"Give or take," Martins answers. "It's the week before fall break starts."

"Well," Reese starts to say, "that's plenty of time—"

She's interrupted by the bright pinging chime of Merlani's pocket-com announcing that they have a relay call coming in.

"Do we need to get up so you can go take that privately, Ocean?" Reese asks, already starting to nudge Martins towards the aisle.

"Well, I wasn't expecting anything..." Merlani looks at the notification, then laughs when they see that the call is tagged as 'private caller; MSS *Endeavor*'. "Oh! *Wow*, that was fast! No, no, don't get up—this is actually for you three." They make a vague gesture towards Lavine, Martins, and Katz with one of their lower hands while they're tapping through to accept the call and put it up on the holoscreen they have their notes on.

"For us?" Katz asks, raising an eyebrow.

"Yep!" Merlani replies cheerfully.

When the call connects, the loading screen is replaced by the cheerful face of a lightly greenish-blue Florivan in an amber tunic and shawl who's sitting in what seems to be the window seat under the viewport in a cabin on some starship or other. They have their long silver hair down, as if they were in the process of brushing it out before putting it back up into their usual set of looped braids.

"Hello, kitten! Rudy said you were looking for me? How's my favorite apprentice doing today?"

Merlani smiles and nods their head. "I am, and I'm doing okay—I wanted you to meet some friends of mine. Is that okay? Do you have a minute?"

Entile Ilmi laughs, spreading their lower hands wide. *"For you, kitten, I have all the time in the galaxy. Are your friends there with you?"*

"They are!" Merlani adjusts their pocket-com so it's transmitting an image of the whole table instead of just their face. "So, this is Miss Theresa Vasquez," they say, gesturing to each of their teammates in turn, "and these are Miss Antoinette Martins, Mr. Tobias da Silva, Mr. Simon Katz, Mx. Beck Lavine, and Mr. Paul Kouassi. They're my friends from the martial arts team."

"It's so nice to meet you all!" Entile Ilmi waves through the holoscreen. *"It's nice to see that Little Ocean has friends."*

Merlani's ears twitch in slight embarrassment, but then they smile. "Everyone? This is my entile, Jade Ilmi of Procyon and Elder Celadon Toreval's line—their proper titles are 'Star-Keeper' and 'Council's Agent.'" They look over to their friends, who seem a bit stunned for some reason. "They're the one I was telling some of you about earlier who taught me our story-dances. They're also probably the only Florivan alive aside from the Elders who really *does* know pretty much all of us."

"Stars, kitten, you're never this formal." Entile Ilmi twitches their ears in amusement. *"You make it sound like I'm supposed to be someone dreadfully important."* Their tail swishes into view on the screen, making a bright jingling sound from the little enameled bangles they wear on it. *"Your friends can call me Jade. I'm having to deal with enough needless formality at the moment with Endeavor's crew."*

Reese is the first to recover her composure. She laughs lightly, halfway covering it with one hand. "Nice to meet you, too, then, Jade."

"*That's better! So, kitten,*" says Entile Ilmi, tilting their head curiously, "*Rudy said you had questions for me?*"

"Well, *I* don't." Merlani pours a bit of fresh tea into their cup. "But Lavine, Martins, and Katz are working on a group project for a class they're in, and if it's all right with you, I'd like to listen while *they* ask you questions."

"*Oh, that does sound exciting. What's your group project about, then?*"

"Well..." Lavine looks to Martins, who's still staring wide-eyed at the screen, and then Katz, who gives them a smirk and a cheeky sort of a nod. "Um... how common is 'Jade' as a public name among Florivans?"

"*Oh, I'm sure Little Ocean could have answered that—not all that uncommon, when I was younger... offhands, I can think of maybe ten or twelve of us out in the stars right now. Why?*"

Lavine awkwardly rubs at the back of their sandy hair with one hand. "Well... how many of them served with the Fleet during the Novan War?"

Merlani shakes their head, stifling a giggle. They hadn't expected their friends to be so awkward about all of this.

Entile Ilmi, of course, is fully in their 'cheerful Star-Keeper educating the kittens' mode now. They think about it for a moment, tapping the index fingers of their lower hands together. "*Oh, I remember now. Officially there were two Volunteers: Jade Ria of Elder Aquamarine's line and Jade Yrin of Elder Topaz's line. They were with the starships Otus and Tyto. Does that help, Mx. Lavine?*"

Katz looks up from the notes he's been tapping onto his datapad and gives Lavine a nudge.

Lavine hesitates, then nods and looks back to the holoscreen. "It means neither of them are the person we're looking for. Are...? Well. There's supposed to have been a 'Jade' who served on Admiral Marvin's flagship, too... Is that...?"

Entile Ilmi shakes their head, their tail making another softly jingling swish. Their third eye turns to the direction that Merlani suspects their own image is being projected. *"Are your friends always so nervous and quiet when meeting new people, kitten?"*

Merlani absently runs a finger around the rim of their teacup. "Oh, no, usually they're all *much* more talkative than this—I think they're just a bit nervous about talking to 'the Fleet's Phantom', that's all." They make small air quotation gestures with one of their upper hands, unable to help smiling at the nickname.

"Oh?" Entile Ilmi almost laughs. *"Is that what the human kittens are calling me now? I'll have to tell Nida and Rudy that I've been issued a nickname. I'm sure that will amuse them."*

"So it *is* you?" Martins asks, finally breaking her stunned silence.

"Yes, Miss Martins. I... hmm. 'Served' isn't the correct word, but suffice it to say that I became involved in the War and spent quite a bit of time on Aegolius as a result." Entile Ilmi takes on a particularly familiar sort of softly sad tone for a moment before brushing it away with a flick of their ears. *"Now, what do you truly want to ask me? Whatever other duties I may have acquired over the years, I remain a*

Star-Keeper first, dears. Educating the young ones I meet and passing down the stories that have been entrusted to me is the work of my heart."

Something in Entile Ilmi's tone and gentle bearing seems to finally set the humans at ease.

"Well, our assignment is to put together a presentation about you and your leadership contributions during the War..." Lavine begins, back now to their usual cheerful and confident self as they explain the full extent of the project.

Merlani smiles, nibbling at their muffin. They're glad they could help their friends with their assignment in the end—and it seems they've made their entile happy, too, judging from their tone and expression as they answer questions from Lavine and Martins.

Even with the minor annoyance of having the Nav cadet they're not looking forward to working with living with them, they decide this has been a good day after all.

"*REALLY, THOUGH, YOU DIDN'T HAVE TO terminate the sim early again, Waves,*" says the almost pouting voice of Cadet Lewis over Merlani's earpiece. "*I would have fixed it—*"

"—There isn't any 'fixing it' if you break my concentration like that while I'm stabilizing the Drive for real," Merlani interrupts, glaring at the readouts from one of the computer interfaces in their simulation chamber. "And my name is *Ocean.*"

"*Aw, okay—I thought 'Waves' was a cute one, though. Don't worry, I'll come up with something better.*"

Merlani pushes off from the ceiling and floats over to the wall where the chamber's gravity control panel is and catches on to the anchor bar with their tail. They roll all three eyes, even though they know their training partner can't see it. "I don't want you to give me a nickname, Cadet Lewis. I like my public name just fine. Now, will you *please* just focus on filling out your paperwork? I'm done with mine and I need to take my earpiece out to run some checks on it."

If Cadet Lewis replies, Merlani doesn't hear him. They pluck the little ball of the earpiece out from their left ear and unclip its safety barrette from their hair. With a groan of frustration, they turn the little device off and tuck it into the breast pocket of their uniform jacket.

"*Stars*," Merlani asks the air, now that they know no one is listening, "why does he make this so *difficult*?"

This is the fifth attempt at a basic jump simulation they've made with Cadet Lewis today. In the two weeks since he was officially assigned as their training partner, the two of them have only successfully *completed* a simulation *once*. None of the Nav cadets Merlani had worked with last year had been so frustrating, not even the two who left the program altogether halfway through their time as training partners. Cadet Lewis, though, seems incapable of learning the first rule of Astral Navigation: *don't distract your jumper.*

Merlani floats there in their little simulation chamber for a few minutes in silence, trying to re-center themself so that they can be polite when they step out of it. They focus on the distant but comforting sensations of the system's star, Sol, and the various planets and moons that dance around it. With one carefully controlled breath after another, they release the frustration they've been feeling.

Thankfully, there's not enough time left in the class period for them to have to make another attempt. They're exhausted enough as it is that they're not sure they could manage to run another sim safely even if it was one of their *parents* on the other end of the intercom.

Once Merlani has found their calm again, they let out a deep sigh and tap the access panel to return the simulation chamber to Earth's natural gravity. They land gracefully on the floor beside the chamber door. A few taps of the analog buttons built into the door frame, and one by one the safety seals on the door disengage.

Unfortunately for Merlani, when the door opens, their training partner is waiting on the other side.

"Okay," Cadet Lewis says with a grin, "Paperwork's filed. I'm ready to walk home when you are, since we're out of sim time—here, I got your bag for you!"

Merlani holds in a grimace, although their tail swishes with annoyance as they accept the bag they carry their school-issued datapad and water bottle around in and slip it on over their shoulder. "Thank you, Cadet Lewis," they say, trying their best to remain polite, "but you really don't have to get it out of my locker for me when we're done for the day..."

"I don't mind!" Cadet Lewis laughs, reaching out as if to ruffle Merlani's hair. "Besides, Anton gets *Kingfisher's* bag for them all the time—"

Merlani catches his jacket sleeve to halt the motion of his hand and steps around him. "—You know I don't like it when you touch me without asking, Cadet Lewis. And Condrey is Kingfisher's *Navigator* now. If they've given him permission to open their locker and carry things for them, that's between the two of them."

"Aw, now, Seaweed, I'm just trying to be nice…" Cadet Lewis follows them out into the hall connecting the various simulation chambers with the rest of the Nav/Quan department's workspaces. "Besides, if I'm going to be *your*—"

"—Cadet Ocean?" Entile Wyndi interrupts, popping their head out of their office as the two cadets walk by. "You *do* remember we were going to chat once you finished for the evening, don't you?"

Merlani smiles, holding in the sigh of relief they desperately want to let out. "Yes, Commander Cerulean, I remember!" They turn to their annoying training partner with a polite but curt nod. "Don't wait for me, Cadet Lewis. I don't know when they'll be done with me."

"Oh… are you sure? I was hoping we could hang out later…" Cadet Lewis gives them one of those annoyingly pitiful looks he seems to think will make them *want* to be around him so he won't be sad.

Merlani, so far, has found it has the opposite effect. "I'm sure." They slip into their entile's office before he can say anything else. The door, thankfully, shuts behind them.

"Long day, I take it, Merlani?" Entile Wyndi asks, flicking their ears curiously.

"*Very* long day." Merlani sighs and plops down onto their entile's couch, grabbing one of the small pillows and hugging it. They're grateful for the unspoken permission to be informal. "Have you read my sim reports yet?"

Their entile sits down beside them. "That's why I called you in, yes. I thought you might need a hug after all that—and perhaps an excuse to take a break from your training partner?"

Merlani nods silently.

Entile Wyndi wraps them up in that hug they'd offered, lightly untangling a bit of Merlani's hair with one hand. "Better?" they ask after a minute or two.

Merlani finds themself relaxing into the familiar warmth. They absently run the tuft of their tail through their lower pair of hands. "Sort of. Thanks, Entile Wyndi."

Their entile releases them partway, settling back into a comfortable position with their upper arm around Merlani's shoulders. "That's what I'm here for, kitten."

Merlani is silent for a few minutes, just soaking up their entile's reassuring warmth. Finally, they look up from the tail-tuft they're still straightening over and over again. "Remind me again how much longer I have to work with him?"

Entile Wyndi shakes their head. "Not much longer, I promise. Sarge and I had to adjust the rotation schedule a bit, thanks to Kingfisher, but you *should* get to have a new training partner the week after the fall break. We'll give Cadet Lewis a final chance to see if Jay or Bunting can hear him then... and if they can't, he'll be returning to his previous course of studies and we'll sort things out to bring in one of our alternates from last year's trials." They twitch their ears teasingly. "Unless, of course, you decide you *want* to continue working with him for the rest of the year."

"I can *promise* you I won't," Merlani says dryly.

"That's fine." Entile Wyndi smiles. "Thank you again for giving him a chance, Merlani. I know he's not the easiest human to work with…"

Merlani sighs again, hesitating for a moment. "Entile Wyndi… I know it's probably wrong for me to ask… but how in the *stars* did he ever pass Nav trials? He can calculate hex points, sure, but the boy never lets me even get far enough to take them." All of the frustration they've been feeling begins to spill out as they speak. "And he's always acting as if I'm supposed to *like* the way he talks to me and like it's *mean* that I don't want him to be all touchy-feely with me when we barely know each other—and he *never* listens to me about *anything*…" They let out a groan, burying their face in their upper hands. "I'm trying to be nice, I promise. It's… just going to be a very, *very* long time until November."

"I know you are, dear." Entile Wyndi sighs lightly themself. "And I appreciate your patience with the situation. As far as how he passed Nav trials… his letters and qualifications are incredibly high, by the Administration's standards, and Elder Cloud and I were satisfied enough with his background check and our ability to hear him that we couldn't refuse when Assistant Chancellor Lewis insisted we give him a chance ahead of some of our other candidates whose scores were lower but personalities might have been more suitable." They shake their head. "Human politics is *frustrating*, even to me… but it's rare that I have to give in when someone tries pushing a Nav Cadet in like that."

Merlani looks up at their entile curiously. "Wait. Assistant Chancellor Lewis… as in the woman who *runs* the Accommodation Lottery and most of everything else around here? What's she got to do with... oh." Somehow they'd never made the connection between the two names before.

"His mother, yes, although I appreciate that *Cadet* Lewis is at least not the sort to go telling everyone that as if it should garner him special treatment." Entile Wyndi's tail swishes with annoyance. "Keep all of that between your ears, will you?"

"I will." Merlani nods. "It... does explain a lot, though."

"Mmm. It certainly does." Entile Wyndi shakes their head, then brightens and gives Merlani's shoulder a squeeze. "So, dear, how would you feel about coming home with me for dinner? It's been a while since we've got to have you around—I think Reba said something about bringing home *pie* from that bakery we like near the Medical Center..."

Merlani smiles. They're glad now that they don't have any other plans for tonight aside from studying, since it's their 'late evening simulations' day. "That'd be nice, Entile Wyndi. I could use a night off with family."

"You're *always* welcome to come over if you need a break from campus, Merlani." Their entile stands and stretches, heading back over to their desk and the holoscreens they have open on it. "Just give me a bit to get the last of my day's paperwork done, and then we'll go track down my Navigator and head home."

"Okay." Merlani makes themself comfortable on the couch with one of the bright-colored blankets tucked up around them and gets out their pocket-com so they can read through some of their homework while they wait.

★

It's starting to rain when Merlani and their instructors get out of the Nav/Quan building, and heavily storming by the time the three of them reach the small old-fashioned two-story house just outside the city where Entile Wyndi lives with their Navigator and his wife. Merlani finds themself properly soaked just from scampering between the carport where the flitter is parked and the front door.

"Ugh," says Entile Wyndi, peeling their own soggy jacket off. "Next time, Sarge, I am *not* letting you talk to anyone in the hallway when I know there's rain coming."

"Fair enough." Uncle Julian laughs brightly. "But hey, I got us home, didn't I?"

"Yes," Entile Wyndi teases, "and you didn't even get us lost..."

"Ye *both* had better dry off before ye catch a chill," calls the familiar strongly-accented voice of Auntie Reba from the kitchen. "And leave ye shoes at the *door*, Julian—I've set too many broken bones today to care to deal with ye slipping on the stairs again."

"Yes, Reba!" he calls back, still chuckling, and plops down on the storage bench by the entry to pull his boots off. "*Stars*," he mutters dramatically, "a man falls down the stairs *once* because of a puddle and no one ever lets him live it down..."

"To be fair, Sarge," Entile Wyndi says with a giggle while they're removing their own soggy shoes and socks and setting both by the door to dry, "she *had* just warned Heather and Mereday about tracking in puddles the first time you did that."

Merlani smiles through a shiver while they're peeling their soaked-through outer layers, shoes, and socks off. Their instructors might do their best to be formal out at the Academy, but it's always comforting being around them when they're just being themselves like this. They hadn't realized just how much they've missed spending time in this house before now.

"Here," says Uncle Julian, pulling a shawl down from the coat rack above him and passing it to Merlani. "Wrap up in this so you don't get too cold and head on upstairs. You still know the way?"

Merlani smiles and flicks a bit of the water off of the tuft of their tail at him. "Of course. Thanks, Uncle Julian."

"I think you still have a spare set of pajamas in Heather's closet," Entile Wyndi tells them, also accepting a shawl from their counterpart. "If they're not there, come let me know and you can borrow some of mine while your things are drying."

Merlani gives their entile a rather soggy hug on impulse and then scampers up the stairs to change. Their cousin's room hasn't changed since the last time they were here—it doesn't have a reason to, since Heather is still off-planet doing some sort of extended inter-species medical residency. Merlani's only met her twice in person, but they like her all the same. Back during their first year at the Academy when their housing situation was still being sorted out, hers had been the room they borrowed.

Once they're all dried off and changed into the cozy yellow flannel pajama top and trousers which had, in fact, been waiting for them in the closet, Merlani goes back down to the kitchen.

"Ah! I *did* hear a wee stray coming in from the storm, then." Auntie Reba laughs and gives Merlani a rather warm hug. Her bright reddish curls have come free of the braid she was wearing them in, framing her freckle-spotted pale pink face with a halo of hair frizz. "Good to have ye home, Little Ocean."

"Thanks, Auntie," Merlani hugs her back. "I missed you too."

A lightning strike somewhere outside echoes through the walls of the house, setting Merlani's skin on edge. They let go of their aunt and smooth some of the static sensation out of their hair.

"*Please* tell me ye be staying here tonight instead of letting me husband try to take ye back all the way into Houston?" Auntie Reba clicks her tongue, shaking her head. "This storm's supposed to stick around until *midnight* and I ain't having the two of ye out in it if I can help it."

Merlani stifles a giggle. "I wouldn't mind staying... I *just* got dry, after all."

"Good. Ye be a smart one." She ruffles Merlani's ears softly. "Now, come help me set the table?"

"Yes, ma'am."

Over the course of dinner and generous slices of the promised blackberry pie, Merlani enjoys the opportunity to properly catch up with this little segment of their extended family. Part of them still wonders why they were ever set on living on campus like the other Florivan students do—especially considering how lonely they'd been in the evenings all summer and how *awkward* their living situation has become now. The other part knows that they do genuinely enjoy being so close to their classes and—now that they *have* Reese and their teammates—their friends. They wouldn't change things now, but they're glad for the reminder that they do have this place to come to as a refuge when they need it.

"So, Little Ocean," Auntie Reba asks after they're all comfortably seated in the living room after dinner to listen to the rain and relax, "Penny tells me ye be doing well working with her other students?"

"I am, I think." Merlani nods happily. "The rest of the folks on the team are really nice... I wasn't expecting to have quite so much fun training with them. We have our first regional competition coming up next week, too." They pause to take a sip from the cup of tea they're holding in their lower pair of hands, then look over to their uncle. "Thanks again for letting me out of classes and simulations for the week so I can go to that."

"Hey," says Uncle Julian, "standard procedure for student athletes—but I'm excited for you. It sounds like your team has a good shot at winning a few titles, too, and I don't mind at all getting to brag to my buddies over in Sec/Tac about you." He absently strokes Entile Wyndi's long, still-somewhat-damp hair as he talks, since as usual they've curled up beside him and Auntie Reba and fallen asleep nestled across his lap. Merlani can already hear their entile's contented purring from where they're sitting in the cozy armchair across from the couch.

"Well..." Merlani feels themself blushing slightly. "Don't brag about me too much until we manage to come home with actual trophies for you to brag *about*, okay?"

"Okay." Uncle Julian grins at them. "Doesn't make me any less proud if you come home just with a participation ribbon, kid. I'm just glad you're getting to have fun doing something you enjoy that *isn't* your homework."

Merlani stifles a giggle. "Thanks, Uncle Julian."

"Same here," says Auntie Reba, taking on her 'doctor voice', "but do try not to get yeself hurt. I know Penny trains all of ye to take care of yeselves and not do anything too dangerous, but I've had *her* come to me enough times after one of her matches needing mending that I worry about ye."

"Yes, Auntie." Merlani nods as solemnly as they can. "I'll pass that on to the rest of the team, too."

Auntie Reba chuckles. "See that ye do. I like me champions best when they ain't showing up in my office."

"Now really," Uncle Julian says, stretching and setting his free arm around Auntie Reba's shoulders, "you and I both know that *Penny's* more likely to get into trouble next week than her kiddos are."

Auntie Reba seems to think about it for a moment, then smirks at him. "Aye. I'll drop by and give her me lecture on coming home uninjured and setting a good example for her students tomorrow."

Merlani shakes their head in amusement. Their Auntie always teases their Uncle and Aunt Penny about how much the two of them get into trouble. That stands to reason, though, since she was the doctor who took care of their squadron when they were all serving with the

Defense Fleet during the War and Entile Wyndi was just a kitten.

"Say, I meant to ask: are you rooming with Penny for the trip?" Uncle Julian asks, pointedly changing the subject, "Or has she put you in with some of your teammates?"

"Oh, I'm Reese's travel buddy—Cadet Vasquez, I mean. From what Aunt Penny said, it'll be the guys in one bunk room and me and Reese and Martins and Lavine in the other." Merlani laughs softly. "Hopefully those three are were only joking about staying up late playing card games, though, since we're going to be competing most of the time we're gone and all."

"I'd wager there's going to be a bit of sleepover mischief," says Auntie Reba. "If Penny's young pilots are *anything* like the ones I know, she may have put ye with them in hopes ye can keep them out of trouble for her."

Uncle Julian rolls his eyes teasingly. "You *do* remember who raised this innocent little nibling of ours, don't you, sweetheart? If trouble runs in the family..."

"Ye be one to talk, Julian." Auntie Reba playfully pokes him in the ribs.

Merlani takes a sip from their tea, then lets out a small sigh. "I'll take troublesome pilots over the fellow I have as a training partner any day, Auntie. Pilots at least make *sense* to me..."

Uncle Julian stifles a laugh at that.

Auntie Reba pokes him again and looks over to Merlani sympathetically. "Wyndi mentioned ye be having difficulties with him. How are ye holding up, then?"

Merlani hesitates, nodding slowly. "I'm managing. It's a bit frustrating, especially because he lives in the room next to mine... but I can handle him until November."

"November?"

"That's when their training partner gets his last chance to stay in the program," Uncle Julian supplies. "The boy's a bit of an odd duck, to say the least—not that I'd go saying that outside the house—but we can't do much about him until then, thanks to certain meddling administrators..." He shakes his head. "I've been meaning to ask you if you want me to talk to him about boundaries and such, though, Little Ocean."

Merlani looks down into their half-filled teacup for a few moments. "I wouldn't mind if you did... but maybe you could just... talk to *all* of the Nav cadets about that again, so it doesn't come across as me complaining to you and him getting singled out? I don't think Cadet Lewis would take being pulled into your office alone very well."

"Okay. I'll add that to my schedule for while you're out of town, then." Uncle Julian nods, taking on a genuinely sympathetic and concerned tone. "But remember, you can *always* come to me if he keeps making you uncomfortable. It's my *job* to protect you and the other young jumpers, you know."

"I'll remember." Merlani looks up and makes a point of smiling at their uncle. "Thank you."

"Well, I'm glad ye be working to resolve all of that," says Auntie Reba. "Now, I seem to recall ye were going to tell me more about ye teammates and the people ye *do* get along with? Maybe ye can start with that Vasquez girl—she sounds nice."

Merlani smiles genuinely now, grateful for the change of subject. "Oh, Reese is wonderful. She's *incredible* at Judo, for one, and she's going to be a Fleet captain someday." They giggle softly. "She always teases that she's going to recruit me for her ship's jumper when that happens—which I wouldn't mind, really, even though I'm not specifically aiming to join the Fleet... You'd like her, I think, Auntie! She's a lot like Aunt Penny, actually."

"Oh, is that so?" Auntie Reba shakes her head. "I can see why ye like her, then." She looks up to Uncle Julian with a teasing smirk. "Maybe ye should have *Penny* help pick ye new Navigators next time instead of the Administration. She has better instincts for folks."

Uncle Julian laughs. "Now, there's an idea... and then we can just have *all* of our Nav cadets cross-trained as pilots, just like most of us were during the War." He strokes his beard thoughtfully.

"Oh, dear, and then me poor students will have twice the chance to practice patching them all up when they go and get themselves in trouble..."

"Or they'll be better off with nice counterparts to keep them out of trouble?" Uncle Julian grins. "Like me!"

"Have ye met yeself, Julian?" Auntie Reba raises her eyebrows at him knowingly. "Poor Wyndi's spent their whole life trying to keep ye out of trouble, and ye *still* manage to find ye way into it more often than not."

"Heh. Point taken."

Merlani's not sure they get the whole joke passing between the two humans, but they can certainly agree that they like Aunt Penny's students better than most of the Nav cadets they've met.

"So, ye friend Reese is wonderful," Auntie Reba says, clearly stifling laughter herself now as she redirects the conversation. "What about the rest?"

"Oh, they're great too. It actually turns out I have a class with Katz, since he's minoring in geothermal engineering..."

Merlani spends the rest of the evening chatting with their Aunt and Uncle about their friends and their classes and the latest news from the scattered members of their extended family. As they curl up into their borrowed nest in their cousin Heather's bedroom and listen to the now-gentle sounds of the rain outside, they feel more at ease than they have in a long time. They make a promise to themself as they drift off to sleep to make sure that they come to visit their family more often. They hadn't realized just how *much* they needed a night like this before now.

ANOTHER LATE NIGHT IN THE MESS HALL NEARLY a month into the term, and Merlani is once again sitting in their usual spot. This time, though, they have something far better than homework up on the holoscreen of their pocket-com. The long distance between star systems and differences in schedules mean that they only get to call their family over the relays once a month or so. It's a wonderful feat of combined human and Florivan technology that allows real-time video calls between Earth and the Alpha Centauri-New West Space Station where they were raised.

Tonight is one of those special occasions when Merlani's been able to arrange just such a call.

The ruddy-pale human man with the dark, graying beard and short-cropped hair on the other side of the call has just finished telling them about the goings-on in his little corner of the galaxy. He takes a long sip from the little cup of coffee and steamed milk he's been holding all this time and smiles at them. *So anyway, Cinna-bun, that's all of my gossip. How's it going with the new Nav cadets?*

Merlani resists the urge to roll their third eye. "They're... okay, I guess, Dad. Kinda standard-issue this year."

"No one's caught your eyes yet, then?" Their father arches an eyebrow at them teasingly.

"Not really... the Commanders paired me up with this really... well, *enthusiastic* guy for the current rotation, but I don't have much hope for that working out."

"Oh?"

"How do I put this, Dad... he's just..." Merlani struggles for a few moments to find an appropriate word. "Well, *irritating*. One of those ooh-I've-always-wanted-to-be-friends-with-a-Florivan-can-we-braid-each-other's-hair sort of people who *also* seems to think he knows everything about Nav/Quan even though he just transferred in from *Command*... and he's never even been off-planet before."

"I know the type. Sounds like a challenge for the two of you to work together, then."

Merlani makes an unimpressed face. "He's been my training partner for all of a month and I was already sick of him after the first week—and he keeps trying to give me *nicknames*..."

"Well, Mer, at least you aren't obligated to keep him." Dad strokes his beard thoughtfully. *"Hopefully one of the others will be a better fit for you."*

Merlani lets out a small groan. "That's the thing, though. Even if I do get to switch out for one of the other Nav prospects for the next rotation, I'm *still* stuck with the guy."

"*How so?*"

"Remember how I said the accommodation folks had finally placed new humans with me in the flat? This Cadet Lewis person is one of them." Merlani twitches an ear in annoyance. "The other three Nav cadets I live with are nice, really, but he's just... too much."

"*Seems like you're going to have to figure out how to deal with him one way or another, then.*"

"I know, Dad, I know." Merlani sighs. "Doesn't mean I have to like it, though."

"*No, it doesn't.*" Dad shakes his head and smiles at them. "*Things are going okay with your team, though?*"

Merlani is more than grateful for the change of subject. "Oh, definitely! They're really nice folks, Dad—you'd like them. There's even a few pilots in the mix! And they're all absolutely *brilliant* to practice with..."

Merlani is halfway through telling him all about the details of their first regional competition with the team when they spy Reese heading their way from the automat service line. It's her usual time to appear from one of her late-night workouts and give them an excuse to take a break from their studies—and to share whatever sort of baked goods she's happened to find to go with her coffee.

Merlani stands for a moment to wave to her. "Hang on a sec, Dad, I have one of them here to introduce to you!"

Once Reese is installed in the seat next to Merlani at their table, they look back to their father's image on the video call.

"So, Reese, this is my Dad—Lt. Commander George Barker, if you want to be formal about it." Merlani sets a hand on their friend's shoulder. "And Dad, this is the future Fleet Captain I've been telling you about."

"*Vasquez, right?*"

"Yes, sir," says Reese, smiling. "Nice to meet you."

"*Cinny here tells me you're aiming towards tactical pilot on your way to that captaincy?*"

"I am, sir."

"*Good choice! I flew darters myself, back in the day—*" Dad snaps his fingers the way he does whenever he's remembered something important. "*Say, speaking of darter pilots! You wouldn't happen to be related to a Colonel Esteban Vasquez who used to lead the 6th Squadron on SCV Gymnasio, would you?*"

Reese laughs. "That's one of my great-uncles, actually, sir."

"*Such a small galaxy we have here!*" Dad grins. "*Figured it was something like that—there's a good family resemblance. Good man, that uncle of yours. Saved my hide a time or three back when I was a greenhorn, even. He still around causing trouble?*"

"Oh, he is." Reese nods. "Retired to the ranch just before I came to the Academy—I'll be sure to tell him you said hello the next time I go home to visit."

"*You do that! And tell him there's a bottle of Centauri's finest with his name on it if he ever decides to darken my doorstep again, will you?"* Dad chuckles, stroking his beard again. *"I do still owe him one, I think."*

"I'll do that, sir."

Merlani is about to ask about this connection between their family and Reese's that they've never heard about before, but a door chime on their father's end of the call interrupts them. In a few moments, they find themself unexpectedly introducing their littermates to Reese as well. Both have appeared still in their academy uniforms; Miradyn, as usual, has a large matching bow tied behind their bright sky-blue ears, while the more grayish-blue Melbryl seems to have come from one of their secondary classes, since they're wearing their cream-colored nurse-in-training outfit.

"So," asks Mir, looking curiously over Dad's shoulder from where they've draped themself over the back of the couch, *"you've finally got a Nav trainee worth introducing to us?"*

"You must be someone special, Miss Teresa," Mel adds, grinning at the two of them through the holoscreen and winking their third eye at Reese. *"Cinny never introduces us to their training partners."*

"Ooh, are you planning to keep this one, Cinny? Is that it?"

Merlani lets out a small groan. They love their littermates dearly, but sometimes the two of them can be entirely too much. "Sky. Storm. She's not in Nav. Reese is my friend from Judo and the martial arts team Aunt Penny leads. I *told* you about her."

"Oh? Right!" Mel imitates Dad's snap-of-remembrance gesture with two of the light grey-blue fingers on each of their left hands. *"The human girl you play warriors with!"*

Reese laughs at that. "You mean the best friend they just took a regional competition *record* with—did Ocean tell you yet that we qualified for Earthwide?"

"*They did!*" says Dad, rescuing the conversation. "*Which reminds me, I need to pass that on to Taimri. She's still pleased as punch the powers that be are letting you compete, you know.*"

"How's Äiti doing, then?" Merlani asks.

"*Well as ever, far as I know. Last I heard, she and River are headed your way for some headquarters thing or other. I don't know when, but if I know those two, they're going to make a point of dropping by to see you right when you least expect them.*"

Merlani smiles. It'd be nice to see their mother and entile again for sure. "Well, I'll keep an eye or two out for her, then." They take a good look at their family and then ask, "And y'all have plans tonight you need to get to, don't you?"

"*We're dragging the old man out to dinner with Joy and Merek,*" Mir says, playfully messing with Dad's hair.

"*Since he only has a few more months before he's on his own again and all—and since my poor innocent Merek is still trying to get back on his good side,*" Mel adds.

"*It's not my fault that Ranger of yours is failing my class, Storm...*"

"*...Sure it's not, Dad. Sure.*"

Merlani shakes their head. From what they understand, Mel's counterpart is only taking a few refresher units because he's been on semi-sabbatical assigned to AC-NW while Mel finishes their studies and needed something to do. They're certainly looking forward to meeting Merek again, too, when he and Mel come to Earth next spring so Mel can go through their required new Ranger training. They've only really talked to the Ranger in calls like this, of course, since they can't remember all that well when the three of them were small kittens and he was a trainee assigned to their mother and entile. From what they've seen, though, he seems like a good match for Mel. Merlani never *has* figured out quite why Dad puts on such a show of acting like he disapproves.

"I'll let you go, then," Merlani says, somewhat reluctantly. "Wouldn't want to keep you from a family meal."

"*All right, sweetheart. Goodnight,*" says Dad, smiling that sad but affectionate way he does every time a call ends.

"*We love you Cinny!*" Mel and Mir chorus, making their usual adorable hand-hearts. "*Goodnight!*"

Merlani mimics the gesture. "Goodnight, Sky, goodnight, Storm. Love you too."

"Nice meeting you all," Reese chimes in now that Merlani's family has said their goodbyes.

"*Same to you, Vasquez. Thanks for keeping my Little Ocean out of trouble.*"

"You say that as if *she's* not a troublemaker herself, Dad." Merlani chuckles and then looks over their family fondly. "Talk again next time you get a chance?"

"*Of course. Love you, Cinna-bun.*"

"Love you too."

After the call ends, Merlani switches off the holoscreen and reaches over to where they left their tea. It's gone cold again, but there's not much left in it anyway.

Reese is still sitting beside them. "Your family's lovely, Ocean."

"They really are…" Merlani finishes the remainder of their tea slowly.

Reese sets a warm hand on their lower arm that's nearest to her. "You okay?"

Merlani nods, setting down the empty cup but not releasing the grip their upper hands have on it. "Yeah. I just miss them, you know? Especially because they're all together and I'm… *here*."

"I know." Reese leans in and gives them one of those brief but warm and reassuring hugs she's so good at knowing when to offer. "Want some tea and distraction somewhere that isn't so public?"

"…Yes, please."

Merlani couldn't be more grateful to have someone to distract them from the maelstrom of feelings that always threaten to overwhelm them after they have to say goodbye.

"All right, here we are! *Mi casa es tu casa*."

Merlani has been friends with Reese for a while now— long enough for them to happily allow her to claim them as her 'best friend,' at least—but this is the first time she's ever brought them to her apartment. It's small, of course, since she doesn't share it with anyone, but it's a *comfortable* sort of smallness.

Reese taps the panel by the door to turn on the lights and then gestures to a low couch covered in layers of striped blankets. "Have a seat, I'll put the kettle on. You like jasmine tea, right?"

Merlani nods and makes their way to the couch.

To get there, they have to walk around a positively enormous blue ceramic pot holding some kind of overgrown cactus. The whole sitting area seems to be trying to turn itself into a greenhouse, really. A row of cacti of different sizes are arranged along the windowsill, each in a bright-colored pot of its own. Two equally bright-striped hanging planters take up the far corners of the room, one with a massive trailing spider plant and the other with some sort of succulent that looks like tiny strings of green beads.

Somehow, this was not what Merlani had pictured as a living space for Reese to occupy. They'd always assumed she had more utilitarian tastes, for some reason.

"Here we are." Reese comes back into the room and hands them a steaming mug of lightly floral-scented liquid. "Jasmine green tea, courtesy of Lavine and Kouassi—I don't really drink it, of course, but I still have some on hand from the last time the team descended upon my house."

"Thank you." Merlani scoots a little to one side on the couch so there's more room for her to sit down with her matching cup of coffee.

"So! Introductions!" Reese grins and gestures to her collection of plants. "The big girl here by the couch is Miranda—she's an angel wings cactus, and even though she doesn't *look* spiky she can still bite with those little white spots, so try not to get too friendly with her unless you're ready to get prickled. The ones along the window are the old ladies—Rebecca, Doris, Karen, and Gillian— and then Charlie on the end there is my hairy old man. Up in the baskets, we have Edwin and Godfrey—Godfrey is the spider plant."

"You've given them all names?" This is another delightful detail Merlani certainly didn't expect.

"Sort of? It's more they just came in with personalities so I found names that suited them."

"I see." Merlani nods. "Is that usual? I don't really know much about keeping plants, really. My old housemates left a couple of leafy things with me, but... well, there aren't any plants in the flat now for a *reason*."

"If you like, I'll pick you out a nice succulent for your room sometime. These don't need all that much tending—they're adapted to desert conditions."

Merlani smiles. "I don't know how well that would go, but I wouldn't mind trying."

Reese smiles back and takes a sip of her coffee before her curiosity comes back. "Now, Ocean, I have to ask... your family calls you *Cinna-bun*? Like the pastry?"

Merlani chuckles. "I was wondering if you would remember that one. But yes, although it's just Dad who takes it all the way to pastries. 'Cinny' is the nickname that stuck when we were kittens and Sky and Storm were still learning to use my public name—and you didn't get a chance to see him in action, but Dad's a fiend with puns."

"Well, it suits you."

"You can use it if you like, Reese. I don't mind." Merlani smiles softly. Nicknames are special, after all, meant for family and close friends—and Reese certainly qualifies for that.

"Thank you, then, *Cinny*." Reese says the name with a particularly warm tone, shifting into a grin. "This one

I'll remember—It won't be hard. I can definitely see where your dad was going with the whole cinnamon roll thing."

Merlani shakes their head. "I never did get it, aside from him thinking it was cute when I was a kitten... but I have to say, it's nice you got to meet them all."

"So, why were you having the family call in the mess anyway? Even this late at night, it's hardly the most private place."

"Too many housemates that I didn't want to have to introduce." Merlani takes a cautious sip. The tea's still a little too hot to drink properly, but it smells wonderful and somewhat purple from the jasmine.

"Ah... *still* haven't come to an understanding about personal boundaries with the boys, then?"

"I thought I had, but it's been a long day and I was stuck in sims with Cadet Lewis for most of it..." Merlani's ears droop, but they try to force a laugh anyway. "Besides, well, you met my family. Even if the boys and Robin had behaved and *not* been awkward, Sky and Storm would have probably done something even more embarrassing."

Reese raises an eyebrow. "So either way it would have been more uncomfortable than being in the back table of the mess where *anyone* could have overheard you?"

"Got it in one." Merlani takes another careful sip from their tea.

"Sounds familiar." She sips her coffee for a moment and then settles back into a more comfortable position against the armrest, facing Merlani and crossing her legs underneath her. "Just wait 'til you have a chance to meet some of my older cousins—they raise being embarrassing to an *art*."

"If we put your cousins in a room with my littermates, then, they might create the galaxy's first black hole of embarrassment."

"Most likely!" Reese laughs for a moment and then tilts her head slightly to one side. "It's okay if you don't want to talk about it, but out of curiosity... I don't think you've ever told me how you ended up signing to the Academy *here* when they're all out at Alpha Centauri."

"Oh, that..." Merlani pauses and swirls the tea around in their cup, considering the question for a moment. "No, I don't mind. It's because our mentor kept me as a provisional apprentice longer than the two of them. By the time Elder Celadon decided I was ready to release, there was an opening here and there wasn't there... and the geology program here is better anyway, you know?"

"That explains it, then." Reese nods and gestures vaguely with her coffee. "And why they're both getting ready to graduate and you just started here last year."

"Yeah. Even if I had managed to click with someone last year, I'd still be a few years behind the two of them." Merlani takes another small sip of their tea. "Granted, it's just Storm that's actually graduating; Sky's got a two-year junior assistant post on ACS *Bell Burnell* first."

"Why the difference?"

"Storm's counterpart isn't a Nav Cadet—Rangers have a different system, and Merek's already fully trained anyway."

Reese looks at them for a moment as if something incredibly confusing has just clicked into place in her mind. "Wait... so your sibling who's a *nurse* is the one paired with a Ranger, but *you're* the one who could actually hold your own in a fight if you had to?"

Merlani shakes their head, stifling a giggle. "Funny how that worked out, isn't it? Apparently, Storm imprinted on him while he was recovering from some job-related injury or other in the AC-NW Medical Center… or rather, *re*-imprinted on him. None of us really remember much of it, but according to my parents, Storm was pretty insistent about trying to claim him back when we were kittens."

"I'm adding that to the list of things I don't understand, for sure." Reese pauses for a moment and then smirks at them. "But hey, if this year's run of Nav cadets don't work out, we can always take a little trip up to Waco and go Ranger-hunting for you."

Merlani can't help smiling at that. "You sound like my Entile River. If it was that easy, I'm pretty sure my instructors would be sending me up there *gift-wrapped* at the end of the year."

Reese bursts into giggles. Merlani doesn't quite understand why until she catches her breath again.

"Sorry, Cinny, it's just…" Reese stifles another laugh, trying to regain her composure. "I got this image in my head of you being delivered to Ranger Headquarters in a big basket with a bow tied behind your neck or something like that."

Merlani can't help giggling a bit themself. This is part of why they like Reese—she has just a touch more developed imagination to her than most humans they've met.

"Dad has a family portrait from when we were kittens like that, actually."

Reese's eyes go wide and sparkling. "*Please* tell me I get to see this someday."

"I'll ask him to send it," Merlani says, laughing. "Just don't expect me to recreate the look. Ribbons are *Sky's* thing, not mine."

"I won't," Reese promises. "So, going back to what we were talking about before I interrupted... it's not as easy as just letting you pick out someone qualified that you can work with, then?" Her curiosity has returned, if it ever really left.

"Yes and no..." Merlani shrugs and takes another sip from their tea. "It's more than just picking someone to work with, you know? I can *train* with anyone whose voice I can hear—I could probably run jumps for anyone who knew how to give landmarks, even, if I had to. But there's a lot more to it than that."

"Oh?"

"Yeah... it's..." Merlani turns their eyes down to their mug. They've never tried to talk about this with anyone before. They stare into the tea, trying to find the right words to explain it to her. "It's trying to find someone who's going to work with me for the rest of my *life*, really."

Reese stays quiet, giving them space while they look for those words.

"There's this whole... *thing*..." they say at last, "with needing to choose a human that clicks right, that you can imprint on as strong as family... because they'll be your anchor when you're in the Strange and that stronger imprint makes everything *safer*. But also because we're all..." Merlani trails off for a few moments, still unable to find an adequate word to express the feelings. "... *Alone,* otherwise. Spread out. And space is *cold* when your family isn't there."

Reese sort of nods and sips quietly from her coffee. "That explains a lot."

"Sorry," Merlani says, "I don't know how to make that make sense."

"It made sense enough. You're supposed to be a semi-eusocial species, right? I always found it a little odd that most starships only have one or two Florivans in the crew at a time, considering that."

"There's not really enough of us to do otherwise anymore." Merlani shrugs. "It's not something we really talk about much—even with the Nav prospects. I don't think any of them really get it until someone's already at the point of wanting to be their counterpart."

"So that's why it's a problem that you don't fit with any of the Nav cadets, then?"

"Pretty much. I'm going to be hanging out in the program until someone comes along who *does* work out... and so far there's not been anyone who even came close." Merlani goes silent for a moment before sighing and taking a longer sip of their tea and then looking to Reese again. "If I could click with the Nav folks the way I do with you and the rest of the team, it'd be a lot easier all around. I don't know why it's so *hard* for me to even begin to imprint on them... but it *is*."

"Well, then, Cinny," says Reese, nudging their leg with one of her red-socked feet, "at least you'll have friends to keep you company for however long you end up being here waiting on your Navigator to show up."

Merlani smiles. "I suppose you're right."

"And while we're waiting…" Reese gives them a teasing grin now. "I will gladly trade 'little Reese in a lacy fiesta dress' pictures for 'Cinny and sibs as kittens' ones, if that's not too embarrassing for you."

Merlani sets down their tea and reaches for their pocket-com. "Deal."

7

ON A RATHER NICE MORNING SEVERAL DAYS later, Merlani is sitting in the Nav/Quan department's central meeting room with the rest of their classmates waiting for their instructors to appear and issue the simulation assignments for the day. They're in their usual spot in the back row of long table-desks, thankfully *alone* for the moment. They have one ear swiveled to half-listen to the chatter going on in the room, but most of their attention is focused on the environmental geology homework assignment they're working on to pass the time. Merlani always does their best to come in early so they can claim their preferred chair and study a bit while they wait.

"Here you are!" Cadet Lewis plops himself down into the chair beside Merlani. "I was looking for you in the Mess Hall earlier, since you didn't answer when we knocked on your door this morning."

Merlani turns their third eye over to him, resisting the urge to roll it. They keep the majority of their mind focused on the images of rock formations they're studying. "I have a class at eight on Wednesdays."

"Really? You never mentioned it to me."

"Really." Merlani's tail twitches with subtle annoyance beneath the table. The fact that they're not officially enrolled in the early morning beginner's Tàijíquán class that Lavine and Martins have helped them arrange to attend so they can come into their weekly full day of Nav/Quan simulation training with a clear mind isn't any of their training partner's business.

"Huh. I'll try to remember that so I can be up in time to catch breakfast with you next week, then!"

"Please, don't feel like you need to get up early on my account."

Cadet Lewis laughs entirely too cheerfully and makes a move as if to pat Merlani on the shoulder. "Oh, it's no trouble, Ocey—"

"—I thought we discussed this, Cadet Lewis." Merlani scoots their chair out of his reach just before his hand can make contact. They try to keep their tone as polite and even as possible.

Cadet Lewis looks at them with nothing but confusion in his tone. "Discussed what, Ocey?"

"*Ocean*." Merlani holds back a frustrated sigh. "And I prefer if people *ask* before they touch me."

"Aw, but we're friends now, aren't we?" He almost looks hurt for a moment, then chuckles and scoots his chair over back closer to them. "Besides, if I'm going to be your—"

"—Good morning, Ocean!" the Maltby twins call as they arrive and take their usual seats on Merlani's other side; Richard in the chair and Robin cross-legged on the table with their back against the wall.

"Good morning, Maltbys," says Merlani, grateful for the interruption. "Did you have fun at the mixer with the Command-track students last night?"

"We did!" says Robin excitedly. "Would have been more fun with you there, of course—that miss Vasquez of yours is an *amazing* dance partner." They give their twin brother a bit of a playful nudge on the shoulder.

For some reason, this makes Richard *blush*.

"Well, she's not 'mine'," Merlani says, smiling and making appropriate little air quotation gestures with their upper hands, "and I've not gone to any of the mixers to see her in action, but if she dances anything like she spars? I'm sure Reese is good at it."

"Oh she is!" Robin laughs brightly. "Especially when they put the swing dance songs on—I let her lead when she danced with me, and let me tell you, getting picked up and twirled around in the air by someone that strong is *fun*."

Merlani stifles a laugh. "I can see her doing that. Hopefully next time I won't have a field trip going on the same evening so I can come and dance with all of you."

"Speaking of your miss Vasquez, do you know if she likes guys who—"

"—Birdie. *Please*, not now…" Richard looks up to his twin with the most embarrassed look Merlani's ever seen him wear.

"Aww…" Robin giggles, then reaches over and pats their brother on the head. "Fine, I'll be good and wait to ask them until we get home."

Richard groans softly, then turns back to Merlani. "Sorry about that. They're still wound up from the mixer, I guess. How was the field trip, then?" He's still blushing for some reason, although he seems to be recovering his composure.

"Oh, it was lovely," Merlani replies, now flicking the holoscreen with their homework off and slipping their pocket-com back into their jacket pocket. "I've never seen *anything* like all of the bats flying out like that—and the tour we took of the caverns in the afternoon was great too."

"It sounded neat when you told us about it," says Richard. "Say, what if we organized something with Condrey and Kingfisher and their sibs and we could all go up there some weekend? Maybe sometime during fall break? It'd be fun for all of us 'juniors' to do something together for a change."

Merlani finds themself smiling. Aside from their training partner, they do like the idea of getting to know their classmates better. "I wouldn't mind that, if you don't mind listening to me babbling about rocks the whole time."

"Ooh!" Robin interjects, "You could invite your miss Vasquez to come with us, Ocean!"

"*Robin*." Richard lets out a dramatic groan and covers his face with both hands. "Why must you be like this?"

"What? I didn't say anything…" Robin tries to put on a pouting tone, but they're trying too hard to stifle giggles for it to come out that way.

"I'm sure she has more important things to do," says Cadet Lewis, with an edge on his voice for some reason that Merlani doesn't quite understand. "Isn't Cadet Vasquez one of the graduating seniors or something?"

"She is," Merlani replies, confused still by his tone of voice. They've never heard a tone *like* that from him before. "But Reese did grow up in this region, and from what she's told me she does like hiking and outdoorsy stuff." They shrug and turn their eyes back to the Maltbys. "Plus, she'll have her full pilot's license by then, so if she wants to come with us it makes transportation a lot easier—and I won't be surprised if some of my other teammates want to come too."

"Even better!" says Robin. "I've been hoping to meet your friends properly ever since we came to watch your team's demonstration at the Academy expo."

Merlani twitches their ears in amusement. Robin's enthusiasm for the world could rival most *kittens*, sometimes. "Well, we'll see about that." They pause thoughtfully for a moment. "You know, we *could* ask Commander Cerulean if they want to come along as a chaperon, in any case. They're a proper caver and everything."

Both of the twins' eyes widen. "Really?" they ask in unison.

Merlani stifles a laugh. "Yep. It's their hobby. They took me with them a few times last year as their caving buddy, since Commander Potts doesn't like being underground."

"That's so neat!" says Robin. "I vote we ask them!"

"Wait. You want to take one of our *instructors* on a trip with us?" Cadet Lewis asks, raising an eyebrow. "I mean, we're all adults now, aren't we? I wouldn't think we need a chaperon for something we're organizing ourselves."

Merlani is about to say something, but the timely appearance of their instructors interrupts them.

"Good morning, cadets!" Uncle Julian crows, knocking loudly on the wall near the door to quiet the chatter in the room. "Raise your hands if you had a bit too much fun at that mixer with Command last night and need me to lower my voice."

A handful of the senior Nav cadets raise their hands, as does Condrey as he slinks into the room and flops down in the empty seat next to Kingfisher in the first row. He's wearing sunglasses, for some reason. Kingfisher gives him a comforting pat on the hand instead of their usual bouncy hug of greeting. He reaches up and ruffles their bright blue ears in return.

"See?" Cadet Lewis whispers to Merlani, nodding his head in the direction of their classmates, "are you just the only Florivan in the galaxy who's not tactile-affectionate or something, Ocey?"

"Shh," Merlani hisses as quietly as they can. "And stop calling me that."

"But—"

"—Those two are *counterparts*. It's *different*."

"Is something the matter back there, Cadet Ocean?" Entile Wyndi calls, looking up in Merlani's direction to the back row where they're sitting.

"No, Commander," says Merlani, flushing lightly with embarrassment.

"Okay, then... See that it stays that way." Entile Wyndi's tail swishes in a gesture that's more sympathy than amusement before they turn their eyes back towards the rest of the room. "Now that you're all settled down, I have a stack of simulation assignments for you! Seniors first, you know the drill—come up and get your data chip for the sim computers as I call your names. Cadets Indigo and Nghiem?"

Halfway through their entile's calling of pairs of upperclassmen, Merlani feels their pocket-com vibrating with a silent message notification. They ignore it, since they're officially in class now, grateful that they remembered to set its pings to silent this time when they first arrived in the meeting room.

"Mist and Perkins?"

Merlani feels *another* message notification in their pocket. Again, they ignore it.

"Raindrop and Nolasco?"

A third notification, then a fourth.

Merlani finally glances over with their lower two eyes to see that, as usual, Cadet Lewis has *his* message interface out under the table. He looks to them expectantly.

Merlani sighs and shakes their head.

"Okay, and now for our first-year pair and training pairs: Kingfisher and Condrey?"

Cadet Lewis gives them his best attempt at a cute pleading expression.

Merlani does roll their eyes this time, pointedly pulling their pocket-com out where he can see them turn it off altogether.

"Jay and Mx. Maltby?"

Robin bounces off of the desk to join their training partner, waving to their twin as they pass in front of Merlani.

Cadet Lewis holds his message screen out towards Merlani under the desk. They pointedly fold all four arms on the table in front of them and rest their chin on their upper pair of hands, looking away from him and towards their instructors at the front of the room.

"And last but not least... Bunting and Mr. Maltby?" Entile Wyndi holds up the last data chip from their pile.

"See you later, Ocean, Lewis," Richard says as he slips behind the chairs the two of them are sitting in.

"See you later, Richard," Merlani whispers in reply, not taking their eyes off the front of the room.

"Um, Commander Cerulean?" Cadet Lewis asks, raising his hand, "What about me and Ocean?"

"Ah! Don't worry, I'm not leaving you out." Entile Wyndi waves their tail cheerfully. "You'll be working with me today—The Elder of Cadet Ocean's family has requested they be excused to attend to a household matter." They turn toward the door and beckon with both left hands. "Come along, Cadet Lewis. Don't dawdle, I've already got the conditions loaded for us in sim chamber eight."

"Yes, Commander." Cadet Lewis reluctantly stands from his seat, turning back as he leaves to look at Merlani and give them a disappointed wave.

"A household matter?" Merlani asks, tilting their head curiously as they come down to meet their uncle, since he's still leaning on the wall near the door like he always does while Entile Wyndi is handing out assignments. "Is everything okay?"

"Yeah, I think so." Uncle Julian smiles and gives Merlani a reassuring pat on the shoulder, since all of their classmates are gone and he doesn't have to pretend to be formal. "But 'household matter' is about as much as Wyndi told *me* this morning when they asked me to help with it."

"Ah." Merlani nods, stifling a chuckle. "So they've caught a case of cryptic from Ai-Nida Celadon today, then?"

Uncle Julian laughs. "Seems like it! Come on, let's get your things and head out—I've got a shuttle warmed up and ready to go, but I'd assume you need to stop by your flat and change clothes first."

"*Shuttle*?" Merlani asks, startled.

"Yep! Whatever we're handling is waiting for us up at Luna Orbital, apparently."

Merlani follows their uncle out into the now-empty hallway, then looks up at him with the most innocent face they can manage without giggling. "Did they *really* ask for me specifically, Uncle Julian? Or am I coming along to make sure *you* have someone to keep you from getting lost again?"

Uncle Julian laughs long enough at their teasing that he never does get around to answering.

When Merlani climbs up into the shuttle after their uncle, they're surprised to see a pair of *very* familiar faces waiting for them inside.

"You three all set with the pre-flight checks?" Uncle Julian asks, nodding his head towards the access ladder up to the shuttle's cockpit from the small passenger cabin.

"Yes sir, Commander Potts," says Kouassi, saluting crisply. "Cadet Vasquez is confirming our flight plan with the control tower right now."

"All cargo is stored, sir," da Silva chimes in, mimicking the gesture, "and we double-checked the fuel charge and backup power cells as you requested."

"Good." Uncle Julian sets his small flight bag down on one of the passenger seats and takes off his uniform jacket, draping it over the back of the seat. He pulls his well-worn Darter Pilot's jacket out of the bag and shrugs it on, grinning at the two cadets who are still standing at attention in front of him. "There! Now we can get this show on the road. Help our passenger settle in, we'll take off as soon as Vasquez and I have our flight clearance."

"Yes, sir!" chorus Kouassi and da Silva.

With that, Uncle Julian climbs up the ladder to the cockpit, leaving Merlani standing somewhat confused with their two teammates.

"So, Barker," says Kouassi, making a broad and teasingly polite gesture with both arms towards the selection of open seats around them, "do you prefer an aisle or window seat?"

Da Silva stifles a chuckle, doing his best to mimic Kouassi's tone. "And as our only passenger, feel free to ask one of your cabin attendants if you need any assistance..."

Merlani giggles, shaking their head. "You two are the *best* sort of silly, do you know that?"

"We do try," says Kouassi, breaking out of his formal tone with a laugh.

"That's why we're friends, isn't it?" da Silva asks with a chuckle, plopping down into one of the seats.

"It is," Merlani agrees, taking the aisle seat opposite him and setting their bag down beside them on the floor. "Now, what in the *stars* are you doing here?"

Kouassi sits down cross-legged in the aisle between them. "Special training assignment—Colonel Albright called the three of us in this morning and told us we'd be going up to Luna Orbital as a shuttle crew with an experienced pilot buddy of hers as preparation for the practical portion of our license exam. Vasquez is flying us out, and I'm flying back."

"Meanwhile, *I'm* getting to credit all of this as hours towards my 'Security Personnel Practical Experience' unit," da Silva tells them.

"Oh?" Merlani twitches an ear curiously at him.

"Yep!" He grins. "I'm your bodyguard for the day."

Merlani raises their third eyebrow at him teasingly. "Even though I could probably best you in a fight if I wanted to?"

"Hey!" Da Silva holds a hand over his chest dramatically, as if wounded. "No need to point *that* out to anyone." He smirks at Merlani after a moment. "Besides, thing one: we've only ever gone to a draw, so jury's still out on whether you *could* beat me. Thing two: it's better tactics for people to assume you're the sort of Florivan who *doesn't* know how to defend themself."

Merlani shakes their head, stifling giggles. "Okay, both points taken. I don't see how I'd need a bodyguard if we're just going up to Luna Orbital, though—it's not exactly a dangerous place."

Da Silva shrugs. "All I know is that I received orders to protect and assist you for 'the duration of your mission'." He makes little air quotation gestures with both hands for emphasis. "It's good practice, either way."

"*Get yourselves secure back there, kids,*" calls Uncle Julian's voice over the intercom. "*We're cleared for take-off now.*"

Kouassi reluctantly gets up and takes one of the other aisle seats while the shuttle is making its way up into the planet's atmosphere. The shuttle's internal gravity and inertia controls keep it comfortable and level-feeling inside, of course, but safety protocols are safety protocols.

Merlani finds themself somewhat disappointed that this model of short-range shuttle doesn't have viewports in the passenger area so they can watch the scenery. At the same time, they're grateful that their teammates are with them so they have something more interesting to think about. This is *certainly* a better way to spend the day than cooped up in a simulation chamber trying to deal with Cadet Lewis, that's for sure.

"What *is* your mission, anyway, Barker?" Kouassi asks as soon as the green 'safe to move' light comes on and he can unbuckle his safety belt and get back into his apparently-more-comfortable spot on the floor in the aisle.

"No idea." Merlani tells him. "Elder Celadon just had word passed to me that I needed to go up to Luna Orbital to handle some household business or other for them."

"That's... cryptic." Kouassi looks up to them curiously. "I take it 'household business' is also the explanation for why you're not in uniform?"

"Elder Celadon is *notorious* for being cryptic." Merlani smooths the amber-embroidered white silk of their long-sleeved tunic over their lap with their lower hands. Underneath, they have a pair of loose trousers in amber with a wide white ribbon embroidered along the outer seams to match the translucent sash they're wearing around their waist and the warm bead-fringed shawl over their shoulders. "But yeah. Household business calls for family clothes."

"The look suits you," Kouassi says with a smile. "Not that different from the outfit you wear for workouts, actually."

"Same sort of thing," Merlani replies, "just shinier. It's more comfortable than you might think... and *warm*, thankfully, since we're going up to Luna Orbital and all."

Da Silva tilts his head curiously. "Any particular reason for the colors? I feel like you're *always* wearing some variation on that when I see you out of uniform."

"Oh, they're family colors." Merlani gestures to the edge of their shawl. "The amber is Elder Celadon's, and the white is for my Ai-Nida. Those of us who had to be adopted into other households after the War wear our line Elder's color too."

Both of their human friends nod. Thankfully for Merlani, like Reese, these two have been through enough classes about the Novan War to understand why they and so many others among their people have cause to wear two colors and not need to ask too many questions about it.

"Well," says Kouassi after a small silence, "they're colors that look good on you."

"Thanks," says Merlani. They giggle softly. "Hopefully in a decade or two I'll have a different color to wear, though."

"Oh?" asks da Silva. "And that's... good, right?"

"Oh, yes!" Merlani nods. "That would mean that one of my littermates had grown up to be an Elder and I'll be part of *their* household instead—which will be a *very* good thing if it happens." They mean this from the fullness of their heart, too. They know it's impossible that *they'll* ever have kittens and take on that role, but Mir and Mel would both make wonderful parents, in Merlani's opinion.

"Well, then," says da Silva, grinning even though he probably doesn't understand the context. "I'll look forward to seeing you in whatever color that turns out to be."

Merlani dips their head to him in agreement.

"So..." Kouassi pulls his ever-present deck of cards out of his jacket's innermost pocket. "Go Fish, anyone?"

Da Silva nods, taking the cards the other man has already begun to deal out to him and Merlani. "I *swear* I'll manage to beat you this time, Paul."

Merlani waves their tail happily as they accept their cards. "Has that ever happened before?"

"Nope," says Kouassi, grinning, "but I suppose there's a first time for everything..."

S EVERAL HOURS LATER, MERLANI STEPS OUT OF the docking ring access corridor and into the central atrium of the Luna Orbital Space Station with a smile, pausing to stretch a residual bit of shuttle stiffness out of their arms. "Ah," they say to no one in particular, "I always forget how nice it is up here—reminds me of home."

"This is smaller than AC-NW, though, isn't it?" Reese asks, no small hint of excitement coloring her voice.

Merlani nods. "About half the size, but I still like it here."

High above them, beyond the reinforced polyglass dome of the atrium, there's a magnificent view of Earth's Moon itself and the galaxy beyond. This time of day, the station's orbit is bringing it into line so that Earth is rising over the horizon of the gray expanse of the lunar surface. The lights of two of the Moon's five domed cities are clearly visible too, shimmering like stars that have been somehow misplaced among the ancient craters and plains.

Around the atrium, in between all of the hydroponic plantings of decoratively-arranged food plants, four levels of refreshment stations, entertainment facilities, and station operations offices are busy with the bustle of people from all of the different ships docked here. There's even a few Florivans in the mix, from what Merlani can see, along with the distinctively different bodies of a handful of multi-eyed, feathered-serpent-like T'irsh-fel on one of the upper levels. Space stations like this one are always full of interesting goings-on.

"So," says da Silva, "where do we go now, Commander Potts?"

Uncle Julian chuckles. "You and Cadet Vasquez should stay with Ocean while they sort out the household business. Ping me if you wind up needing me for anything. Cadet Kouassi?"

"Yes, sir?"

"You're flying us home, so you're sticking with me. Once we get ourselves some coffee and stretch our legs a bit, the two of us will head back to the shuttle and make sure we'll be ready to go once they're done."

"Yes, sir!" Kouassi salutes and follows Uncle Julian as he strides off towards his favorite place on the station to get coffee. As they disappear into the crowd, Merlani catches Kouassi asking their uncle if he's permitted to get tea instead—and, naturally, Uncle Julian getting a good laugh out of that.

"Well, Barker," says da Silva, putting on his most formal 'bodyguard tone', "I believe that means *you're* in charge now. Which way do we go to sort out this household business of yours?"

Merlani shrugs. "Well, since all I was *actually* told was that I needed to come up here, your guess is as good as mine, da Silva." They glance around. "We might go check with the cargo office first to see if there's something listed for me to pick up."

"Lead the way, then, oh noble agent of the Florivan Council of Elders." Da Silva makes an elegant—if dramatically exaggerated—bow. "I'll guard your tail with my life if need be."

Merlani and Reese share a look, both of them desperately trying not to crack up. Merlani stifles a giggle. "Okay, oh fearless bodyguard..." They gesture with said tail in the direction of the cargo office. "We're going this way."

Reese walks beside them through the atrium, da Silva making a point of staying precisely a step behind and to Merlani's right. That's even funnier somehow than his tone of voice had been, but they do appreciate that he's practicing for protecting *actual* dignitaries.

"I'm not exactly an agent of the Council today, you know," Merlani tells him, casting a glance over their shoulder. "Just a member of Elder Celadon's household running an errand for them, that's all."

"You make it sound like your grandparent's just handed you a basket and asked you to scamper off to the market for peaches, Cinny." Reese grins, lightly nudging them with her elbow.

Merlani shakes their head, twitching their ears with amusement. "In my world, this is the closest it gets to that." They pause, unable to stifle a laugh this time. "Granted, knowing Elder Celadon, there's always a chance that I *am* going to end up with a basket of peaches or something by the end of this little 'mission'."

"Wait," says da Silva, just as the three of them arrive at the doors to the cargo office. "Barker, you're *not* up here as the Council's agent?"

Merlani turns to look at him with a curious swish of their tail. "No, I'd have been told if this was Council business. Why?"

Da Silva looks between them and Reese with confusion still obvious in his tone. "My orders were to escort and assist the 'Council's Agent'—when you showed up on the shuttle, I figured that was you—but if it's *not*, then who...?"

Merlani's eyes widen as they make the connection. "They said it was the *Council's Agent*? Not me? They didn't give you a name?"

Da Silva nods.

"That means something specific?" Reese asks.

"It means *me*!" answers a bright, cheerful Florivan voice from above. "You're right on time, kittens!"

Merlani and their two human friends look up. Merlani can't help laughing when they see that it is, in fact, their Entile Ilmi sitting at table on the next level up, waving down at them. As usual, they're dressed in their casual amber tunic and trousers and have a set of bright-colored enameled bangles jingling on their tail.

"Entile Jade!" Merlani calls up, still delightedly surprised. "No one told me *you* would be here!"

"Now, really, Little Ocean." Entile Ilmi leans on the railing beside their table and winks their third eye. "When have Nida and I *ever* told anyone where I was going to be before I was there?"

Merlani shakes their head mirthfully. "*This* is why people call you a Phantom, Entile Jade."

"Maybe so! Come on up, kitten, and bring your friends—we can go pull the surprise on your uncle once I've finished my tea." With that, Entile Ilmi turns back to their table and the cup of tea in question.

Merlani laughs again and motions for da Silva and Reese to follow them to the nearest crew lift.

"I think 'Cheshire Cat' might be an even better description for them than 'Phantom'," says Reese, eyes still a bit wide.

Merlani's ears twitch with amusement. "You have no idea how right you are, Reese..."

Once they've made it all the way back around to the refreshment station where Entile Ilmi is sitting, Merlani finds themself the happy recipient of a long-overdue hug. They can't help clinging to their entile for an extra moment or two, if only because it's been nearly two years now since they've both been in the same place.

"I missed you too, Merlani," Entile Ilmi whispers into their ear before letting them go and sitting back down in their chair beside the railing. They gesture to the other chairs around the small table. "Now, sit down for a moment, all of you, so I can finish this and refill it before we leave—oh, that travel cup there is tea for you, Little

Ocean. I didn't know what sort of poison your friends here prefer." They tap the button on the table to pull up the menu interface. "Go ahead and order your coffee, Miss Vasquez, Mr. da Silva, but be sure you have it delivered in a travel cup so you can take it back to the shuttle. We have some time to spare, but I'd rather we were early than late."

Reese and da Silva share a look that's equal parts overwhelmed confusion and amusement before sitting and tapping through the menu to place their orders.

"I thought you were with *Endeavor* the last time we talked, Entile Jade," says Merlani, taking a sip of what turns out to be their favorite variety of lightly sweetened green tea. "Somewhere off around Teegarden's Star?"

"I was!" their entile smirks over the edge of their teacup at Merlani. "But since I had an appointment on Earth today... well, I made my way here. *Endeavor* was only a brief bit of Council business to get them back to the shipyards while our dear cousin Cornflower was under the weather, thankfully—although I *do* need to talk to Cerulean while I'm hear about recommendations for a secondary Nav/Quan team for Cornflower." The smirk becomes a soft hint of a genuine smile. "It's about time they had one... You have some folks graduating from your program this year, don't you?"

"We do," Merlani says, catching the unspoken good news hidden in their entile's words: Cornflower has survived catching their first litter of kittens, and next year when those kittens open their eyes and are publicly announced to the world as existing, they'll be acknowledged as a future Elder of the Council. That, of course, means that there *has* to be a secondary team on their ship now, both for their sake and the ship's. "Is that why you're here, then? Scouting for people to recommend?"

Entile Ilmi takes a sip from their own tea and then shakes their head. "No, that's just convenient. I'm here on *personal* business for once, instead of some errand of the Council's."

"Ah." Merlani nods. They don't bother asking any further. They know their entile well enough to know that they'll be told what's actually going on sooner or later.

"Now," says Entile Ilmi, turning their attention to the two humans at the table, "as I should have said already, I'm *so* pleased to finally meet you both in person. Mr. da Silva? I hope you don't mind my requesting to borrow you while I'm here. If the Council has to insist on me having a companion of some sort when I'm between ships to 'protect me', I prefer it to be a human I'm at least *somewhat* familiar with."

"I'm honored," da Silva replies, clearly doing his best to remain professional even though his voice still sounds a bit like he's not sure whether to be shocked or excited. "My assignment wasn't explained to me in detail, sir, but I'll do my best to keep up."

"I'm sure you will—and you've either forgotten or you're uncertain about it, but you're welcome to call me Jade." They turn to Reese with a genial dip of their head. "Same goes for you, Miss Vasquez."

"All right, Jade." Reese nods, then tilts her head curiously. "May I ask you a question, then? No need to answer if it's too personal."

"Oh, please do." Entile Ilmi drains the last of the tea in their little ceramic cup. "I *like* curious human kittens."

Reese smiles. "Well, you said your Council of Elders insists you have a human companion... do you not have a Navigator to travel with you, then?"

Entile Ilmi shakes their head. "I never have, and I doubt I ever will." They pause for a moment before adding, "well, I suppose that's not *entirely* correct; I borrowed my Nida's current Navigator for a few months at one point, but his compact has always been with them."

"Ah." Reese nods thoughtfully. "I didn't realize there were any Florivans outside the Academies who *didn't* have counterparts of their own."

"As far as I'm aware, there aren't others, anymore," Entile Ilmi replies. "My situation is a bit unique in general, though."

Before either human can ask more questions, the hovering multi-limbed service robot arrives with a tray bearing three travel cups, each one marked with its contents, and a paper sack full of pastries. It sets all of this down on the table, then buzzes off to collect its next delivery from the kitchen.

"There we are, then!" Entile Ilmi gets to their feet and shoulders their travel bag, picking up their newly-acquired travel cup of tea in one lower hand and the paper sack in the other. "Come along, kittens, we have places to be—where is that uncle of yours docked, Little Ocean?"

"We're on outer ring A, airlock sixteen," Merlani replies, scampering to catch up with them.

Reese is right there at their side in moments, while da Silva slips into his precisely-one-step-behind-and-to-the-right position behind Entile Ilmi.

"Now, really, Mr. da Silva," says their entile, turning to look at him and beckoning with their tail as they walk. "I know you're assigned as my bodyguard officially, but I like my companions where I can see them. I'll tell you if we get into a situation where I need you to act formal."

"As you wish, then, Jade." Da Silva chuckles and moves to walk beside Entile Ilmi instead. "Why do I get the feeling this is going to be even more of a 'learning experience' than Colonel Albright made it out to be?"

Entile Ilmi smirks at him. "Oh, I'm not doing my job as a mentor right if it's not. Now, kittens, tell me all about your team and what's been going on at this Academy of yours?"

"Well," says Merlani, happily accepting one of their Entile's free upper hands to hold while they're walking, "I went on a field trip yesterday to see some amazing caverns and meet the bats who live in them..."

They arrive back at the Academy just in time for Merlani, their teammates, and their entile to slip in through the back door of the big lecture hall where Commander Saleh's second-year History, Tactics, and Theories of Command students are about to give the major project presentation that's worth a full third of their grade for the term. The five of them take the empty seats in the back row and make themselves comfortable.

Twelve presentations later on people ranging from the head of Fleet supply services to Admiral Marvin and back again, and it's finally time for Merlani's friends to have their turn. It seems fitting, somehow, that they would be going *last*.

"Now, class," says Commander Saleh from their chair at the side of the stage, their dusky, lyrical voice echoing over the room's sound amplification system, "our last group drew a bit of a *challenge* for their assignment... but I'm sure they've done their best researching their subject. I know it's late in the day, and you're all probably eager to get down to the mess hall before it fills up, but I expect you to give Cadets Katz, Lavine, and Martins your full attention." They clap their hands sharply together once and then hold an arm out to the three cadets standing behind the lectern in the center of the stage. "Cadets? You have the floor."

"Thank you, Commander Saleh," says Katz, dipping his head respectfully. He turns his attention towards the rest of the class. "Our group drew the name 'Jade of Procyon.' They're more properly known as the Agent of the Florivan Council of Elders, Star-Keeper Jade Ilmi of Procyon and Elder Celadon's household..."

Merlani has to admit to themself as they listen to their friends describe their entile's involvement in the Novan War that there must be even more the adults in their family have never told them about all of that. For one thing, while they've heard the story before about how their Ai-Nida Celadon had been injured at the battle of Procyon and Elder Navy and their Entile Indigo had taken over most of their duties with the Defense Fleet until they could recover, they'd never realized just how much responsibility had fallen on Entile Ilmi's shoulders—even though they were never *officially* part of the Fleet.

The sheer scale of the War and the tragedies their own family suffered during it are hard for Merlani to comprehend, even though the shadow of it all has been part of their life for as long as they can remember. They can only imagine what it must be like for Entile Ilmi and the handful of visiting Fleet officers and veterans in the room to listen to these presentations, having *been* there and part of everything. They give their entile's hand a squeeze when their friends come to the section of the presentation Merlani knows must still be the most painful for them to remember—the part about how the Novans destroyed the Sanctuary planet at Procyon *itself*, and with it the majority of their species, even though Entile Ilmi had managed to get out without the Novan invaders noticing and bring the Defense Fleet to their people's aid in time to bring an end to the occupation.

Entile Ilmi looks over to them with a gentle but still sadness-tinged nod. They scoot their chair closer and wrap an arm around Merlani's shoulders. "I'm okay, kitten," they whisper into Merlani's ear, quiet enough that even Reese and da Silva probably can't hear them. "The story hurts, but it has to be told. Your friends honor our people by telling it so well."

Merlani nods, snuggling up next to their entile for the rest of the presentation anyway.

At the end, Commander Saleh leads the whole audience in a well-deserved round of applause for Lavine, Martins, and Katz. Entile Ilmi stands to add their hands to the sound, and continues clapping loudly long after everyone else has stopped.

Everyone in the room turns to look at them. Still clapping, Entile Ilmi slips out of their seat and walks down the center aisle of the room to the stage, hopping up onto it with an easy grace. "Saleh, old friend," they say, offering a nod of greeting to the instructor, "I'd like to congratulate your students *personally* for the excellent job they've done with their presentations. Do you mind?"

"Of course not, Jade," says Commander Saleh, shaking their head in what seems to be amused amazement. "Feel free to talk as long as you like. I'll be posting their grades next week after I've had a chance to read through all of their written reports on the project."

"Thank you—Don't worry, kittens," Entile Jade calls to the class as they take the lectern, "I promise I won't take too long talking so you can make your escape before all of the good pastries disappear. Hello, by the way! I'm Jade; I'm told most of you probably know me better as the 'Fleet's Phantom'."

A murmur that's mostly scattered giggles and soft gasps passes across the room.

"As you just heard," Entile Jade begins, "I was the same age that a lot of you are now when the War began. I was the youngest of my people's Star-Keepers—our story-tellers, the ones tasked with keeping our history alive in memory so that its lessons and truths would be passed down to those who came after us. On the day the peace talks concluded, I was the *only* Star-Keeper left." They pause, the bangles on their tail jingling softly as the deep sadness they're keeping out of their tone is expressed in its long, slow swishing. "In the years since, I have done all that I can to continue the work that was entrusted to me, not only with *our* stories and traditions, but with the stories of our human friends and the lives that were touched by what I hope with all my *soul* is the last war either of our peoples will ever know."

Merlani finds themself brushing unbidden moisture out of the corners of their eyes. Reese sets her hand on theirs. Merlani looks up at her, then accepts the silent hug she's offering. They're grateful their best friend knows them well enough to recognize that they need one.

"On behalf of those of us who've been the subjects of your presentations, I'd like to thank all of you," Entile Ilmi continues, "for being willing to listen to and gather our stories, for doing your best to learn from us, and for *telling* our stories and helping to keep them alive. Not all of us who live through such days can talk about them easily; some cannot talk about them at all. So many more no longer live, and it is only in the stories we carry with us that we can ever hope to know them." They dip their head for a long moment.

The whole room is silent save for the soft jingling of the bangles on their tail as it swishes to a thoughtful, even rhythm.

When Entile Ilmi raises their head again, they're smiling. "I'm *proud* of you, cadets," they say, "for the work you've done here and the stories you've come together to tell. You are the future of the world we share. I look forward to seeing how you shape it."

With that, Entile Jade turns to Merlani's three teammates who are still standing on the side of the stage. They walk over and give each of them a hug in turn before hopping back down and striding back to their seat in the back of the room next to Merlani.

"Thank you, Jade," says Commander Saleh, breaking the long silence that follows. "I couldn't have said it better myself. Class dismissed."

“There you are, O-zone!” calls Cadet Lewis as Merlani, Entile Ilmi, and da Silva pass the stand-by break room in the Nav/Quan building on their way to pick up Entile Wyndi now that all of the days classes should be over. He strides over with his usual overconfident enthusiasm. “Are you done with your thing now? I’ve been trying to ping you all day.”

Merlani holds back a sigh. “I’ve had my pocket-com on *silent* all day, Cadet Lewis—and please, I’ve *asked* you use my public name.”

“You should check your messages, then!” Cadet Lewis laughs. “Don’t worry, I’ll wait—already made the reservations, though, since I *knew* you’d be excited about it.”

Merlani does sigh audibly now, pulling out their pocket-com with a distinct sensation of dread for whatever it is he's planned without waiting for them to properly turn him down.

Cadet Lewis finally seems to notice the other Florivan standing with Merlani now and offers his hand to them, still with that same bold as brass self-assuredness. "And in the meantime, I should probably introduce myself to you! Astral Navigation Cadet Bennington Lewis of Earth—I'm Ocean's counterpart."

"My *training partner*," Merlani corrects quickly, looking up from the string of barely understandable messages. "You're not my counterpart until I *say* you're my counterpart, Cadet Lewis, we've been over this."

"I see." Entile Ilmi's tone is cheerful and polite, but their tail makes a jingling swish of disapproval. They fold all four of their arms behind their back. "Forgive me, Cadet Lewis, I've never been one for shaking hands as a form of greeting. I'm Jade, an agent of the Florivan Council of Elders; the gentleman here is my companion, Cadet da Silva."

Cadet Lewis makes a vague, disinterested nod in da Silva's direction. "We've met. I take it you're here to meet with Commander Cerulean? They just went back to their office—I've had the honor of working with them today while Ocean here was busy."

Merlani is *shocked* to hear him use their public name correctly. They can't tell if he's doing that because Entile Ilmi introduced themself the way they did, or if it's because he's run out of supposedly clever nickname ideas for today.

"I am," says Entile Ilmi. "Cerulean was my first apprentice; I make a point of stopping by to visit them whenever I'm in the neighborhood." They turn to da Silva with a genial flick of their ears. "Speaking of which, Tobias, would you mind waiting here with Ocean for a few minutes? Cerulean and I have some private matters I'd like to discuss while I have the opportunity."

"Yes, Jade," says da Silva in his most official tone. "Call if you require my assistance."

Entile Ilmi's tail swishes in jingling amusement this time as they stride off in the direction of the instructors' offices. "Of course. I'll be back shortly, Little Ocean."

"So, what do you think?" Cadet Lewis asks, now stepping over into Merlani's personal space and leaning over to look at the holoscreen of their pocket-com.

Merlani flicks their ears with annoyance and looks up at him. "I haven't finished reading yet. You didn't *have* to send me so many messages, you know."

"I thought maybe you'd just set your 'com down somewhere and couldn't hear the pings." He lets out a laugh that *might* be interpreted as self-deprecating. "Well, go on, finish reading so you can be excited about it."

"Why don't you just *tell them* whatever it is you've been messaging them about and be done with it?" da Silva asks, rolling his eyes. He takes a seat on one of the small cream-and-grey striped couches in the break room and nonchalantly relaxes his posture so his legs are spread out a bit and one arm is loosely draped along the back of the couch over the other seat cushion.

To anyone else, it probably looks like he's just casually taking up space while he waits for his charge to return.

Merlani knows their teammate well enough to recognize both the invitation meant for them and that he's meaning to make it clear to Cadet Lewis which of them is the 'more dominant male.' The latter part wouldn't catch Merlani's attention normally, but they've listened to too many of their friend's explanations of his theories of 'manly body language' not to notice.

Merlani gratefully accepts the unspoken invitation and takes the seat beside da Silva, although they can't bring themself to relax. They absently run the fluff at the tip of their tail through their lower set of fingers, looking up to their frustrating training partner as they slip their deactivated pocket-com back into the hidden pocket of their tunic. "I *would* appreciate if you did, Cadet Lewis. I know you meant well sending me the messages, but it'll be much more efficient if you sum them up for me."

Cadet Lewis makes a disappointed face for a moment, his eyes turned more towards da Silva than Merlani themself. "Well... fine. But it was a bit of a *personal* thing for the two of us."

Merlani once again finds themself perplexed by the odd edge in his tone. They shrug. "I consider Mr. da Silva a close friend. I don't mind if he hears."

Cadet Lewis looks at them for a moment, then shrugs. "Suit yourself—so, what I've been *trying* to tell you all day is that we're attending a formal dinner the Academy Administration is holding tonight. It's the 'tuxedos and evening gowns' sort of thing, and I wanted to know what color your formal wear is so we can match. Oh! And I need to know whether you're wearing a suit or a gown so I can pick up the right type of floral accessories for you."

Merlani stares at him for a long moment, unable to find words to express their internal reaction to that at all.

"You're inviting them to something like *that*," da Silva cuts in, echoing one of the many overlapping thoughts in Merlani's crowded brain, "and you didn't bother telling them until the day of? That's cutting it a bit close."

"I received the invitation this morning." Cadet Lewis shrugs dismissively. "Anyway, it's a great honor for the two of us—we're to be introduced to a number of people who will be on the selection committees for captaincies of the new *Nautilus* and *Otus Novae* class starships being built out at Teegarden."

"What for?" asks da Silva, raising an incredulous eyebrow. "Last I heard, *you* weren't on the Command track anymore."

"It's always good to network with people in positions of authority." Cadet Lewis says this earnestly, but with a tone that suggests that he's quoting something that's been said to him entirely too often. "Not to mention that we'll be graduating with perfect timing to potentially be chosen as a secondary Nav/Quan pair for one of those ships, which would be quite a prestigious appointment."

Merlani's frustration with being *told* things rather than *asked* finally forms into words. "The Elders have more to do with starship assignments for jumpers than human administrators do, Cadet Lewis." They pause, narrowing their eyes even though they're trying their best to remain polite. "Also, *I* don't know when I'll be graduating yet. I *haven't* made a compact with a Navigator, and I'll need to stay two years after I do to complete the partnered section of the program with them."

Cadet Lewis is about to say something else, but he's interrupted by the appearance of Kingfisher, their littermates, and the three other Nav cadets who live in Merlani's flat.

"Ocean!" calls Kingfisher, bouncing over and leaning on the armrest of the couch beside them. "Hi! We haven't seen you here all day! Ooh, and you're in your family clothes—special occasion? Who's your friend?"

Merlani finds themself giggling. Kingfisher reminds them entirely too much of how their own littermates were when they were all young kittens. They set a hand on the younger Florivan's head to stop them bouncing for a moment. "Settle down, will you? Yes, I had to run an errand for Elder Celadon. This is Cadet da Silva from the Security track—well, and Tactical Piloting, he's a double-focus." They turn to da Silva with a smile, gesturing at their classmates in turn. "This bundle of energy is Kingfisher; Condrey over there is their Navigator. Jay and Bunting are Kingfisher's siblings, and Richard and Robin Maltby here are our other two un-partnered Nav cadets. Robin uses 'they' pronouns."

"Nice to meet you all," says da Silva, nodding cordially.

"Oh! I recognize you, da Silva!" Robin comes over and perches on the armrest next to him, bouncing much the same way Kingfisher had. They grin. "You're the one with the *awesome* chest tattoos from Ocean's team who did all of the dance fighting stuff at the Academy Expo, aren't you?"

Da Silva chuckles. "I am indeed—and as much as I'd *love* to give you a capoeira demonstration right here and now, Mx. Maltby, I'm here in an official capacity." He shoots a smirk at Cadet Lewis. "Perhaps next time I visit, *you* could help me in that demonstration, Lewis?"

"Now *that* I'd like to see," Condrey says dryly. He's still wearing his sunglasses. "Can I put my bet on you in advance, da Silva?"

Richard laughs outright. "No one in their right mind would bet against him, would they?"

Cadet Lewis looks to Merlani with a stunned look of horror. They shake their head, doing their best not to show how much the thought of him trying to keep up in a roda at all amuses them. "I don't think Colonel Albright would appreciate *either* of us giving unscheduled demonstrations," Merlani says, giving their friend a look which they hope he interprets as a request to at least try to be nice.

Da Silva seems to get the message. "Point taken."

"Anyway, Seastar," says Cadet Lewis, clearly trying to change the subject, "about our outfits for tonight—"

He's interrupted again, this time by the appearance of Merlani's entiles.

"Ah! Such a nice group of students you have, Cerulean," Entile Ilmi says as they approach, "making sure my companion doesn't get all bored and lonely waiting for me and all."

In an instant, da Silva is on his feet and back in his bodyguard's posture. "They've been quite welcoming, sir," he says, saluting to Entile Wyndi primly.

"I'm glad to hear that," says Entile Wyndi, clearly amused even though their tone doesn't show it.

"Cousin Jade!" calls Kingfisher excitedly, bouncing up from their perch next to Merlani. "We didn't know you were here!" They take Condrey by the arm and guide him over to the two older Florivans, their tail swishing with pride. "This is my Navigator! He's *wonderful*."

"Well, hello to you, then, Navigator 'Wonderful'." Entile Ilmi waves their tail with jingling amusement. "I'm glad to see that Kingfisher's found someone who can keep up with their energy."

Condrey chuckles at that. "We balance each other out, it seems... and the name's Anton Condrey." He pulls down his sunglasses halfway, looking over them at Entile Ilmi with a wry smirk. "But if *you're* going to call me 'wonderful', I'll take it."

Entile Ilmi looks back to Entile Wyndi. "I see what you meant now. Elder Lake is going to *adore* this one."

Jay and Bunting both giggle at that. Merlani is tempted to join them. They've met Elder Lake's counterpart before, and Condrey bears an incredibly strong resemblance to her personality-wise—especially when his cheeky streak is showing like this. It's no wonder that Kingfisher was immediately drawn to a young man who's similar to the woman who helped raise them and their littermates, really.

Jay comes over and takes the Maltbys each by a hand, leading them over to Entile Ilmi too. "And *these* are Robin and Richard Maltby—Bunting and I are training with them right now."

The twins half bow in unison. "Nice to meet you."

Bunting scampers over and leans down to whisper in Entile Ilmi's ear, since they're nearly a head and a half taller. They keep their voice quiet enough that the humans can't hear it, giggling softly again. "We *know* we want to keep them, but we don't know yet who's taking which one. We're going to let Ocean have a chance to play with them for a while first, though, so they don't have to spend *all* year with someone who doesn't respect their boundaries."

Merlani shakes their head. They appreciate the sentiment, but Bunting's characteristic bluntness is probably best kept where Cadet Lewis can't hear it. He's *twice* as annoying when someone's wounded his pride or offended him by pointing out things like that.

"Well," says Entile Wyndi now that everyone has been introduced, "cadets, you're dismissed for the day. Good job with your simulations." They turn to Entile Ilmi. "I'll see you at the house, then?"

"Yes—and don't worry, your Navigator already has my bag." Entile Ilmi beckons to Merlani. "Come along, Ocean, we have household business to attend to for the rest of the evening."

"Yes, Entile Jade," says Merlani, smoothing the fabric of their tunic as they stand and join da Silva at their entile's side. They look to Cadet Lewis with what they *hope* he will interpret as a sympathetic but unwavering expression. "Please extend my apologies to your hosts for having missed the event you planned for us to attend tonight."

Cadet Lewis gives them his most pleadingly disappointed look in return. "If you're *sure...* next time, you should tell me you have plans before I commit us to things."

Merlani flicks their ears at da Silva in a warning for him to *not* say whatever it is that he's bristling to say on their behalf. Luckily, he knows *Merlani* well enough to read their body language and stand down. "I will be sure to do that, Cadet Lewis."

They mean that, too: they will *always* say they have other plans if he ever tries to commit them to something without asking them first like that again.

"Goodnight, cadets," says Entile Ilmi, starting out into the corridor. "See you later, Cerulean." As Merlani and da Silva follow them, they turn back briefly with a cheerful jingling swish of the bangles on their tail. "Oh, and Mr. Lewis? Do say hello to your mother for me at that shindig of yours tonight, will you? And tell her *I* apologize for keeping her from getting to meet your *training partner* and talk politics with the two of you."

"Ah. I..." Cadet Lewis flushes, hesitating noticeably. "I'll be sure to do that."

Once the three of them are outside, da Silva looks over to Entile Ilmi in awe. "Okay, Jade, you have *got* to teach me how you do that."

"Do *what*, Tobias?"

"Put people in their place and shut them up without even changing your tone of voice. I think you could beat the *Colonel* for intimidation factors if you wanted to—you practically had that Lewis guy shaking in his boots there."

Entile Ilmi smirks at him, twitching their ears with amusement. "Ocean's grandparent taught me that one... it takes a lifetime to perfect, I'm afraid. One learns the technique through observation and practice."

"Fair enough." Da Silva chuckles. "I know that guy's mostly bluster, but *boy* was he getting on my nerves." He gives Merlani a light nudge with one of his elbows. "No *wonder* you come spar with us whenever you've had classes with him—I don't know how you stand it, Barker."

Merlani sighs. "I do my best to be nice and *firm* about correcting him when he crosses a boundary I've attempted to set... but to be honest, I don't know either."

Entile Ilmi lightly sets a reassuring hand on their shoulder for a moment. "Your best is all you can ever do, kitten." After a moment, they shake their head. "I will say, that boy has the making of an *excellent* station operations manager—but I like the counterpart you've found for yourself better. She's *far* more suitable."

"What?" Merlani looks over to them, confused. "But I don't have a counterpart."

Da Silva laughs, sharing an annoyingly knowing look with Entile Ilmi. "What do you call Vasquez, then?"

Merlani shakes their head. "Reese is my best friend, that's all. She's not even *in* Nav, remember?" They lightly poke his arm. "Don't go teasing about things like that, da Silva. Compacts are serious things."

"Fine, fine..." He's still grinning at them. "Do *you* get to tease them about it, Jade?"

"I'm their entile." Entile Ilmi smirks at him. "But *subtlety* is an art you'd do well to learn, I think."

Merlani groans. "It's just as bad as when Sky and Storm are after me..." They waft the irritation out of themself with a wave of their tail. "So, Entile Jade, what household business do we have tonight, anyway? Thank you for giving me an excuse to skip *whatever* it was he wanted to show me off at, by the way."

"Oh, a family dinner, of course!" Entile Ilmi says with a satisfied flick of their ears. "I *do* want to spend some time with you and all of my human kittens, after all... we're meeting your Aunt Penny, and she'll fly us out to Sarge and Wyndi's house once we collect the rest of the people you've made your home."

"That sounds wonderful," Merlani says, impulsively hugging their entile for a moment as they walk. "And I don't even have to get out my ballgown..."

"We'll bring you to the graduation formal so you can still get some use out of it," says da Silva cheekily. "I have to ask, though... *'Aunt Penny'*? Seriously? You've gone this long without telling us you're related to the Colonel?"

"Subtlety is an art," Merlani quotes, laughing. "But yeah. She belongs to our household too."

"Oh," says da Silva, "neat. Makes sense, I guess... am I allowed to tell the team?"

"Sure," Merlani replies. "I trust you all well enough to know you won't treat me differently because of it."

"My 'big sister' is one of the people who normally occupies your current post, Tobias," says Entile Ilmi nonchalantly. "But she's so busy herding human kittens around and attempting to educate them that she's not really an option anymore."

"Noted." Da Silva is quiet for a moment, then looks back to Entile Ilmi with a smirk. "So... when we meet up with the rest of the team, would you be offended if I asked Kouassi to measure officially which one of us is taller?"

Entile Ilmi genuinely laughs at that. "Sure—but only if I get to count my ears."

Merlani cracks up. As a fellow former survivor-smallest kitten, their Entile Ilmi is all of two centimeters taller than they are.

As the three of them walk across campus, Merlani finally finds themself relaxing. Their entile's description of their teammates as the 'people they've made their home' sticks in their mind. It's true, in a lot of ways. For the first time since they came to this planet—for the first time since they were separated from their littermates, really—Merlani feels at *home* here. Even though they still don't have a real counterpart, and they know they'll still have to deal with Cadet Lewis for a while longer to some degree or other, none of that matters at the moment. They have both real family and friend family here, and right now they're happy as can be with that.

Somehow, with that realization coloring their thoughts, Merlani can't help but feel like things are finally starting to work out for them.

Part 2: The Pirate Queen and the Fugitive from Justice

On the Friday afternoon before the two weeks of the Academy's fall break officially begin, Merlani is hanging out in their bedroom working on their term paper for crystallography. It's a crisp fall day outside their window, and Merlani is pleased to be spending it cozily bundled up in their nest of blankets with a whole list of interesting articles to read.

They've set their pocket-com up on the small bedside table next to their mug and teapot so that the projected screens are arranged around their nest for easy access without leaving the warmth of their blankets. It's chilly in their quarters anymore regardless of the weather outside; their flat's central climate controls affect all of the bedrooms equally, and the four humans Merlani shares it with prefer cooler ambient temperatures. Merlani has learned to live with that, for the most part, but some days they can't seem to find enough layers of clothing to feel properly warm.

It's been a nice quiet day so far for them. Only one of their instructors had bothered to hold class today, and that was the environmental geology course they and Katz have first thing on Friday mornings. The rest of the day Merlani has had to themself. All of their teammates are attending some party or other this evening that's being held in the mess hall, too, so they've already secured plenty of snacks and have their dinner waiting on their desk in a stasis box. They're quite content with their plans for the night, and for the rest of the next two weeks. With any luck, they'll have a big chunk of their major assignments for the term sorted out and *finished* by the end of the break.

Merlani's contented contemplation of the structure of different fluoride-containing minerals is interrupted by a rather insistent-sounding knocking at their bedroom door. They sigh, getting up and slipping their shoes back on so their feet won't get cold on the tile floor even through their socks. The knocking doesn't stop until Merlani finally opens the door.

"Ah! There you are! I was starting to think you weren't home yet." Cadet Lewis laughs, holding out a garment bag on a hanger. "Here. This is for you!"

Merlani looks at him for a moment. He's out of his uniform, dressed instead in some sort of medieval-era noble costume in blue and white satin with a crown perched on his head and a short cape pinned to his back.

"Ah. You're going to one of the Halloween parties, I take it. What are you supposed to be, then?"

Cadet Lewis strikes what he must think is a dashing pose, still holding the garment bag. "I'm Prince Charming. Like from a fairytale."

"...Ah." Merlani doesn't have a better response for that. Their eyes turn past him, to the bustle of activity going on in their usually-quiet flat's common area. Their other housemates and several of the senior Nav cadets who live in the two neighboring flats on the same floor are busy hanging artificial spiderwebs from the walls and ceiling and arranging pumpkins and other decorations on every available surface. They step past the posing 'prince' and close their bedroom door, staring at the chaos. "What exactly is going on here?"

"Oh, you're going to *love* it—"

"—Hi Ocean!" Robin bounces over from the spiderwebs they've been securing over the doors to their and Richard's bedrooms. They're dressed all in pine green: tights, pointed cloth shoes, fitted long-sleeved medieval-style tunic falling to their mid-thigh, and pointed cap sporting a long pheasant feather. "What do you think of the decorations?"

Merlani's third eye scans the room while their lower two continue to assess their classmate's outfit. They can't quite place what Robin's costume is supposed to be, but they have more important things to ask after at the moment. "I suppose they're... festive... although I don't understand why they're *here*."

"They're for the party!" Robin replies, gesturing grandly at the collection of spiderwebs and pumpkins.

"Once Richard gets the fog machine working, it'll be even better."

Merlani tilts their head to one side, confused. "What party? I thought the three of you were going to the one the senior Nav cadets are holding in *their* flats."

"We are!" Robin grins. "Remember? Since we're all on the same floor, the party's going to be spread across all three units: karaoke and such in A, dance floor in B, and then *we've* got all of the refreshments and card games and such here. We've been planning it for weeks."

Merlani's eyes narrow. "No, Robin, I *don't* remember anyone telling me about any of that."

Robin looks up to Cadet Lewis now, startled. "You told us they said they didn't mind!" They set both hands on their hips. "I know they've been too busy to help us, but I *thought* you were supposed to be keeping them in the loop."

Cadet Lewis chuckles. "Calm down, will you, Birdy? They must just have forgotten that I mentioned it."

"How many times do I have to tell you that my *brother* is the *only* person who gets to call me that?" Robin rolls their eyes, then turns back to Merlani, softening to a more apologetic tone. "Sorry, Ocean. The rest of us really *did* think you'd consented to hosting with us—we never would have gone through with this otherwise."

Merlani sighs. "It's okay, Robin. I appreciate that you tried..."

"So, now that that's settled!" Cadet Lewis thrusts the garment bag into Merlani's hands. "Here! I got your costume for you—go ahead and get changed. I *promise* you're going to have fun tonight."

Merlani looks to Robin, raising all three of their eyebrows.

Robin shakes their head and pushes Cadet Lewis gently in the direction of the corner where their twin and Condrey are busy with what Merlani presumes is the fog machine they'd mentioned. "Why don't you go see if my brother and Anton need your help? *I'll* help Ocean get their costume sorted out."

With that, Merlani and Robin quickly slip back into Merlani's bedroom before Cadet Lewis can protest.

As soon as the door shuts, Robin leans against it and lets out a groan. "I *swear*, Ocean, I don't know *how* you put up with working with him. He's been driving me crazy all day just because I said he had to leave you alone until your classes were supposed to be over for the day."

Merlani plops down onto their nest, shaking their head. "I just... do my best to be patient? That was part of my training as an apprentice, though, because Elder Celadon has to handle a lot of humans like him for the Council." They sigh. "But I won't deny that I'll be glad after the break when Cadet Lewis *isn't* my training partner anymore."

"You and me both, friend." Robin crosses their arms across their chest. "And before you open that bag, small disclaimer? You weren't available to go with us when we all went to get our costumes, and Cadet Lewis told us that the two of you had already talked about what you were going to wear. Jay and their sibs and I *tried* to tell him that you'd probably get cold in what he picked... but he wouldn't listen to us. So, if you decide you want to wear something else that's—oh, I don't know, *comfortable?*—I'll back you up."

Merlani looks down at the black garment bag in their hands, then back up at Robin. "You *really* know how to make a person wary of opening something. You know that?"

"*I'd* be wary of anything that boy picked out for me." Robin shrugs. "But there's no talking to him when he gets set on something."

Merlani shakes their head, then cautiously unzips the bag and withdraws two perplexing purple and gold garments from it. One seems to be little more than a narrow shawl decorated with netting, shells, and glass pearls, while the other is a long, confusing tube skirt covered in large sequins and beads with two floppy triangles hanging down from the bottom of it. Merlani looks up to Robin with a curious tilt of their head. "Okay... I'll grant that it's *shiny*... but what *is* it?"

"*That*," says Robin, laughing, "is supposed to be a wrapped and tied 'shirt' and a *Mermaid's* tail. Be glad that Richard helped me talk him out of getting you the stupid seashell bikini top."

"A mermaid. Seriously?" Merlani's tail swishes in annoyance. "Let me guess—he thought it would be a cute pun on my name?"

"Got it in one." Robin shakes their head. "And he wanted the two of you to match like all of the senior Nav/Quan pairs do. Apparently *The Little Mermaid* was his favorite fairytale as a kid." They make a vague gesture with one hand towards the cloth in Merlani's hands. "I have to admit, it makes me feel better that you *didn't* know about this. I couldn't for the life of me figure out why you'd have agreed to it."

"I most *certainly* didn't agree to this." Merlani zips both pieces of the costume back into the garment bag and sets it aside. A thought occurs to them, and they tilt their head curiously at their friend. "Wait, I've read that book—doesn't the mermaid *die* at the end of it or something?"

"Yeah, but not in the version *he's* familiar with." Robin rolls their eyes. "We tried to tell him, believe me. There's just no talking to him."

"I've noticed." Merlani flops back on their nest of blankets and stares up at the ceiling. "Well, since I seem to be attending this party now... do I *have* to be in costume?"

"No, not if you don't want to be." Robin stifles a giggle. "I *did* pick up a spare of the costumes Jay and Bunting are wearing, though, in case you didn't like the mermaid and wanted to join my band of merry folks instead."

Merlani looks back to them. "Your 'band of merry folks'?"

"Yep!" Robin strikes a pose, pantomiming firing a bow and arrow. "I'm Robin Hood! Jay and Bunting are my merry folks this year, and Richard is, well, *King* Richard—we've dressed as our namesakes every year since we were *babies* pretty much. Never gets old." Robin laughs brightly. They've told Merlani before about their parents being an archaeologist and a literature scholar, and the somewhat non-standard nature of their upbringing. This must be part of that. "We even seem to have a 'Prince John' around this year, although he refuses to admit he fits the role."

Merlani stifles a laugh themself. "Cadet Lewis *does* bear a bit of a resemblance, doesn't he?"

"He really does." Robin takes on a dramatic tone as they take off their feathered cap and hold it up towards the ceiling. "And I swear to you, Ocean Merlani Barker, most noble warrior-geologist of the kingdom, the merry folk of Sherwood Forest will not rest until we have forced this Prince John to follow in the footsteps of his *historical* counterpart and sign a Magna Carta of the apartment declaring that he will never again attempt to make decisions on your behalf—or to try to give nicknames to *either* of us!"

It takes Merlani several minutes to stop laughing long enough to reply. "Thanks, 'Robin Hood'... I'm sure that will go down in legend if you pull it off."

"Well, I can dream, can't I?" Robin grins at them. "So, want to join my merry band? The more the... well, *merrier.*"

Merlani stifles another giggle. "Thanks for the invitation, but no... I think I'll just go as the resident 'warrior-geologist', as you put it."

Robin raises an eyebrow. "So... your uniform, then?"

Merlani nods. "Seems appropriate."

"Works for me." Robin shrugs. "I can't wait to see the look on Cadet Lewis' face when he sees you, though."

"Hey," Merlani quips, "if he wants there to be a mermaid at this party, *he* can be the mermaid."

Robin is the one to crack up this time. "Oh, now there's something I *never* want to see, Ocean—why'd you have to go and make me think of that?"

"Sorry, Robin." Merlani grins back at them now. "Try imagining him as a duck instead. It helps."

Robin giggles. "Yeah... he'd make a *good* duck." They pause for a moment, returning to a more serious tone.

"Really, though, Ocean. I'll talk to Richard and Anton—we'll make sure you're not stuck alone with Cadet Lewis tonight. I know you weren't planning to come to the party... or to have it come to you... but we'll try to make it so you can have fun with the *rest* of us, okay?"

Merlani nods, standing and going to their closet to retrieve their clean uniform. "Thanks, Robin. I appreciate that." They smile softly at their housemate. "You're going to make someone a fine Navigator, you know?"

"You think so?" Robin brightens.

"Yeah. Whichever of Kingfisher's littermates claims you in the end is going to be a lucky jumper."

"Thanks, Ocean. That means a lot, coming from you." Robin smiles back at them, pausing at the door. "Don't worry, we'll all help you find someone nice for *your* counterpart too, once you're done with your duty to the department of handling Cadet Lewis."

Merlani nods. "At least I'm not the only one who has problems with him... it makes it feel less like I'm losing my mind."

Robin laughs as they depart so Merlani can change. "Oh, you're not. He's got a *lot* of growing up to do if he's ever going to survive outside the Academy."

Once they're fully dressed, Merlani glances over at their cozy nest and arrangement of holoscreens and lets out a sigh. It seems their assignments will have to wait until later—but considering how loud the sounds from outside their room are already, they probably wouldn't have been able to get anything done tonight anyway.

"Oh, Halloween's my favorite human holiday," says Mist, the ash blue senior Florivan cadet who's sitting next to Merlani on the counter top in their flat's kitchenette, swinging their feet lightly. They reach behind them with their upper pair of hands to readjust the bright green fairy wings that are attached to the bodice they're wearing over their costume's blousy yellow shirt. They have a matching pair of fitted trousers on as well, and an apron of yellow and green petal shapes tied around their waist. "It's of the only times during the year when most of human society *encourages* imaginative silliness—what Florivan wouldn't want to be part of that?"

"It's nice to see them all having fun, I guess..." Merlani shrugs, absently running the tuft of their tail through their lower set of fingers. "I was looking forward to having some time to myself to work on my assignments, though."

"Don't worry, Ocean," says Mist's Navigator, looking up from the cauldron-styled punchbowl of questionably green liquids she's stirring. This is the short, pinkish-tan young woman known as 'Dix' Perkins—if she *does* have a legal first name in addition to her nickname, Merlani has never heard anyone use it. "Come tomorrow, everyone will be so partied out that they won't have the energy to bother you for *days*." She pauses to tuck a stray lock of her dark brown hair out of her face, then turns to her counterpart. "Pass me those bottles of tequila, Mist? I think it's safe to add it in now."

Mist shakes their head as they hand her the first of two large glass bottles. "I'd say 'safe' would be *not mixing the death juice* in the first place, sweetheart."

"The title of Nav department alchemist was passed down to me from the ages and I *cannot* ignore my duty to my fellows!" Perkins laughs, popping out the cork from the bottle and unceremoniously dumping the whole of its contents into the punch bowl. "I promise I'll keep to my half-glass limit tonight, though. I don't want to be hungover going out on the water tomorrow if I can help it."

"I'd appreciate it if you weren't." Mist passes over the other bottle with an amused swish of their tail. "Your parents will never let me hear the end of it if I have to carry you onto their boat again because you can't remember how to walk."

"Hey, now, it was just that one time—"

"—Dix. *Sweetheart.* Please. I spent half our first year together carrying you out of parties." Mist's teasing is affectionate, more than anything. "It's more fun now that you can *remember* them, isn't it?"

Perkins sets down the bottle and nods, smiling at her counterpart. "It is. And I *promise* I'll be good tonight... but I hold no responsibility over everyone else." After a moment, she tilts her head curiously at the now-empty bag sitting beside Mist on the counter top. "Did I forget to pack the rest of the bottles?"

"Looks like it," says Mist.

"There's *more*?" Merlani asks, staring dumbfounded at the half-filled punchbowl.

"Yep!" Perkins bounces over towards the door. "Guard the witches' brew for me, Mist! I'll be back in a bit!"

"Don't take too long, Dix! It might set itself on fire!" Mist calls after her. After a moment, they shake their head, turning back to Merlani. "Navigators. She's *brilliant,*

Ocean, truly... but I'll be glad when she finally grows out of her partying phase."

Merlani nods. "Entile River has told me a few things about what Dad was like when he was younger... I suppose they *must* all grow out of it eventually?"

Mist giggles. "Sooner or later—but your Dad's a darter pilot. From what Nida tells me, they make my Navigator look tame in comparison."

"Well, Elder Cloud would know, wouldn't they?" Merlani stifles a giggle of their own. They've met Elder Cloud's Navigator before—he's also a former darter pilot, and one who'd served in the same squadron as their father and Nida during the War.

Mist grins at them, nodding. "Yep!" They pause, looking over to where Merlani's housemates are still fighting with the fog machine. "I'm sorry things aren't working out for you this term, Ocean. I'd really hoped we'd get someone nice in who clicked with you this time around."

Merlani shrugs. "I've made my peace with it. Condrey and the Maltbys have turned out to be decent housemates, thankfully."

"I'm glad you have them, at least." Mist flicks an ear curiously. "And those teammates of yours—are any of them coming tonight so we can meet them?"

"No. I... wasn't aware that I would be attending tonight."

"Ah." Mist nods. "Pity. I've been curious about having a proper introduction with your Miss Vasquez ever since Dix came back from the last mixer with the folks from the Command track talking about what a good dancer she is."

"She's not *mine*," Merlani says with a laugh. "But I think you'd like her."

Mist gives them a curiously knowing look for reasons Merlani can't begin to fathom. "I'm sure I will, if you do. You seem to have good taste in humans."

"If I do, Mist, it doesn't seem to be helping me find a counterpart." Merlani turns their eyes back towards the bustle in the rest of the room. Someone's turned on a playlist of 'spooky' music at just the right volume to be a bit grating to their sensitive ears. There's far more people milling about now, too, setting up the last of the decorations and rearranging the furniture. Most of them are the other Nav/Quan pairs, easily distinguished as a costumed Florivan and the human who matches them. Merlani continues absently straightening the fluff at the tip of their tail. "How do you even know when you've found one worth keeping, anyway?"

Mist gives them a brief, reassuring pat on the shoulder. "You just know, Ocean."

"That's hardly helpful advice, cousin." Merlani sighs, rolling their eyes. "The only thing I can ever tell with Nav cadets is that they're either not suited for the job in the first place or better suited for someone who isn't *me*."

"Well, at least that's a start?" Mist giggles. "I don't know what to tell you, really. I just got on with Dix so well when we met that it wasn't long before I realized that I couldn't imagine having anyone else for my Navigator." They nod their head in the direction of said Navigator as she returns from her own flat bearing a rather heavy-looking bag that clinks as she walks. "Even if she *is* a bit flighty sometimes and prone to getting both of us into odd situations."

Perkins grins and sets the bag down on the counter beside Mist. "What, bragging about me again?"

Mist reaches out and pats her head affectionately, being careful not to mess her hairstyle up too much. "Always, sweetheart. Did you get the rest of your dubious liquids?"

"Yep!" Perkins laughs and withdraws two large bottles, one with a gold label bearing text in what appears to be Chinese and the other with rather ominous-looking flames painted on it. "Can you get the dry ice out of the freezer for me and break it up? I should be ready for it in a bit."

Mist hops off the counter. "You mean the freezer in *our* flat, right?"

Perkins grins at them silently.

"Of course you do." Mist shakes their head. "Do me a favor, Ocean? Keep my Navigator out of trouble until I get back."

Merlani giggles. "Okay, Mist. I'll try."

Perkins sticks her tongue out teasingly at Mist before they depart, laughing, and then turns to Merlani with an authoritative gesture of the flame-covered bottle. "All right, then, Ocean, see if you can get this open for me—the screw caps on these always give me trouble."

"I'll see what I can do." Merlani takes the bottle from her with an amused shake of their head. "I have to say, being an alchemist's assistant was not something I planned on today…"

B Y THE TIME THE PARTY IS IN FULL SWING, Merlani does have to admit—if only to themself— that their classmates *have* done a good job in their decorating efforts. The vast quantity of artificial spiderwebs draped from the ceiling and onto most of the other furniture looks almost realistic enough to make one wonder just *where* the spiders responsible are lurking. Pumpkins are strewn among the spiderwebs in every conceivable spot one could be placed, many of them carved with toothy grins and lit with small electronic candles.

The high counter top in the residence's small kitchenette area is covered with dishes of festive foods and a selection of bright colored beverages. Central to these is Perkins' cauldron full of questionably viscous green liquid with large chunks of dry ice floating in it which produce a passably sinister fog effect billowing down over the edges of the bowl. That fog spills down all the way to the floor, where it mixes with the knee-high clouds produced by the machine Richard Maltby had spent several hours convincing to work. The fog is illuminated by both the tea lights from the pumpkins and the colored overhead lights Condrey and Kingfisher had set up, producing what Merlani has been assured by their housemates is a *delightfully* spooky atmosphere.

Merlani swishes their tail, sending the fog under their chair billowing in all directions. They would *almost* be enjoying themself, if it weren't for the fact that so many people are milling about between their flat and the other two that are hosting the event. They suspect, even, that no less than two thirds of the costumed humans they've seen tonight weren't explicitly invited and have simply wandered in on their way to or from one of the other parties going on across campus. None of the Nav cadets seem to mind that, but Merlani finds it a bit annoying—particularly when people who are clearly unsteady on their feet bump into them or step on their tail.

It's loud, too, from the music just as much as the people. They're not sure how anyone ever gets used to this sort of event, even if the senior Florivan cadets have assured them that it's possible. Granted, the seniors also all either came prepared with muffling earplugs to tone out some of the noise or have taken a sip or two from their counterparts' strong-smelling beverages to dull down their senses just enough to make the noise levels tolerable.

Merlani wishes Mist and the other senior Florivans hadn't all just gone off to the other two apartments where the noise is *louder* to participate in the karaoke and dancing, if only so they could ask just how long it's supposed to take that to kick in. They can't tell if the single unpleasant sip they'd taken from Perkins' brew while she was fine-tuning the mix of it has actually made a difference, or if the volume around them has just *increased* since they did. The taste wasn't worth it either way.

They're also not sure how they let Condrey and Kingfisher talk them into participating in the current hand of "Truths and Drinks" with a few of the other Nav cadets and a handful of people they don't even know who have wandered in since it started. Merlani has never come to any of the social events with the rest of their department, much less played the game with them, but somehow they've wound up sitting with a shot glass full of Perkins' "death juice" in front of them and a small stack of face-down playing cards beside it. They *also* don't know how it happened that Cadet Lewis is sitting next to them—or how he seems to be the worst at the table at this game, considering that he's had to have his penalty glass refilled *twice* since he appeared and sat down.

"Okay, Condrey, your turn..." Perkins, the table's designated dealer, chuckles and turns over a card from the deck in her hands. "Aha! Two of spades. If you'd washed out of Nav, what was your plan B going to be?"

Condrey laughs, running a hand awkwardly through his well-oiled and coiffed hair. Aside from his hair, he's dressed much the same as he usually is when he's out of uniform: worn blue jeans, red shirt, fitted black leather jacket and boots. According to Robin Maltby, he claimed it's a costume tonight because *Kingfisher* is wearing a historically inspired costume to match: white shirt with the bottom portion tied in a knot rather than buttoned, pink handkerchief tied around their neck, fluffy white socks, black-and-white saddle shoes, and long pink circle skirt with a poodle on a leash appliqued on one side of it.

"I honestly don't know, Dix. Planning that far ahead isn't really my style, you get me?"

Kingfisher begins giggling.

"Hmm..." Perkins raises an eyebrow and turns to Kingfisher now. "Why do I suspect that your Navigator is *lying through his teeth* about that?"

Kingfisher tries to look innocent as they turn their eyes to Condrey instead. They barely manage to stifle their giggles, but their tail is still swishing mirthfully under the table and sending up plumes of fog.

"Aw, Dix, now, that's just not *fair*." Condrey lets out a self-deprecating laugh. "Let a man have his secrets and leave his poor poker-face-lacking counterpart out of it, will you?" He reaches for the nearly full glass in front of him and takes a swig. He makes a disgusted face as he swallows, then sets the glass down with a triumphant clink. "There, fine, penalty taken preemptively. Move on, nothing to see here."

"Touchy tonight, aren't you?" Perkins laughs and turns back to Kingfisher. "Conveniently, it's your turn now! Ready?"

Kingfisher twitches their ears in amusement. "Sure."

Perkins dramatically turns over the next card in her hand. "Ooh! Joker! Excellent." She grins at Condrey. "So,

Kingfisher… since that's dealer's choice, I just *have* to know. What *is* your Navigator here hiding from us?"

Kingfisher looks over at Condrey's pleading face, then back to Perkins. "What's the penalty again if I don't want to embarrass him yet tonight?"

"Same as ever," Perkins says, gesturing towards the glass in front of Condrey. "One of you has to taste the death juice."

Kingfisher turns back to Condrey with a questioning flick of their ears. "Anton?"

"I'll take the hit for you, buddy. Please?"

"Deal." Kingfisher giggles again. "Sorry, Cadet Perkins. You'll just have to remain curious."

"Fine, fine. Pay up, Condrey—I'll get an answer out of you yet, somehow." Perkins teases. "I can always get *Mist* to find out for me when they come back from dancing with their sibs."

Condrey gestures dramatically with his glass before taking his requisite swig. "You'll never make me talk."

Merlani shakes their head at the whole exchange. They've figured out how the game is played, by this point, but it still makes very little sense to them. Granted, the game is more for the Navigators; Florivans who participate are usually on a team with their Navigator so the penalties are easier on them. Merlani's playing on their own, having refused outright to be considered as Cadet Lewis' teammate for the game. So far, Perkins hasn't asked them anything worth taking a sip from their penalty shot glass to avoid answering.

"Kingfisher!" calls Jay as they and Bunting scamper over in their matching 'merry forest folk' costumes. "Come on!

We're stealing you and Anton so you can sing with us and the Maltbys—it'll be fun!"

"Sounds good to me!" Kingfisher stands, offering one of their lower hands to Condrey with a grin. "Anton? It's as graceful a way as any for us to get out before our beloved dealer starts asking about your *really* embarrassing stuff."

Condrey laughs. "Agreed—but *I* get to pick the first song." He turns to Perkins as he stands and lifts his glass high. "We're out, Dix. Good game." With that, he drains the remaining liquid in the glass and sets it on the table upside-down before departing.

"I'll get you next time, then, Condrey!" Perkins calls to his back teasingly. "One day, your secrets shall be mine!"

"Will you stop flirting with the underclassmen already and *deal*, Dix?" asks the young man sitting beside her—a tall, dark-complexioned fellow in a toga whose name Merlani has yet to hear, as he'd not been introduced to them when they joined the game with Condrey and Kingfisher.

"Fine, fine." Perkins sticks her tongue out at him briefly. "See if I ask *you* any juicy questions now, mister impatient."

"As long as you turn a card over and ask me, I'm happy." The young man leans on his elbows and flutters his eyelashes pointedly at her. "And maybe later you could—"

"—Not a chance, babe." Perkins laughs. "I promised Mist I'd not be making any *stupid* mistakes tonight." She turns over a card and sets it in front of him. "Ah, Ace of Diamonds... speaking of stupid mistakes, what's the stupidest one *you've* ever made?"

"Cheating on you, hands down." The young man sounds *insincere* somehow, even though his tone is trying to be earnest.

"Water under the bridge by this point, mate." Perkins rolls her eyes. "But I'll make you take the penalty on *principle* for bringing that up."

"Fair enough." The young man takes a pointedly long swig from his glass. He doesn't change his expression at all.

Merlani, needless to say, is *perplexed* by the whole exchange. They had the immediate impression when they met Perkins' apparent former lover that they didn't particularly like him, and as the game has progressed they're now to the point where they're wondering *why* he's still at the table at all—or, for that matter, who invited such a person to the party in the first place. If Perkins is bothered by his presence, though, she doesn't seem to be interested in showing it. They make a note to ask Mist about all that for clarification later.

Perkins turns to Merlani now, brightening. "Okay, enough of that. Your turn, Ocean! You still playing with us?"

"I suppose I am," Merlani says, shrugging.

"All right! Here we go... Ooh! Queen of hearts! That's a juicy one!" Perkins giggles as she lays the named card down in front of Merlani. She pauses to readjust the bright pink fairy wings tied to the back of her costume. "Okay, since asking about your romantic entanglements is *obviously* pointless... hmm... Oh! I've got it! If you had to pick one of us for your Navigator *right now*, who would it be?"

"I am *not* answering that one, Dix. Pass." Merlani turns the card over and takes a tiny sip from the glass of questionable green liquid sitting in front of them. They grimace at the texture of the drink almost as much as the taste. Everything about it is just *wrong* somehow.

The bothersome human next to Merlani nudges them with his elbow before they can stop him, taking on a teasing pout in his tone. "Come on, Sea-breeze, it's just for *fun*—"

"—I *told* you not to call me that, Cadet Lewis. And I *don't* appreciate being touched without warning." Merlani scoots their chair over a bit so that they're out of his reach.

"But it suits you! And you *promised* you'd actually make an effort to socialize this time, Breezy—"

"—That's it, I'm out." On impulse, Merlani throws back their head and swallows the remaining portion of the drink they'd been issued, leaving the glass upside-down and empty on the table as they stand to make their escape. They may have never played along with the others before tonight, but they know the supposed rules of the game well enough from watching.

"What? *Why?*" Cadet Lewis stands as well, nearly knocking over his chair as he does.

"I'm leaving," says Merlani, turning to head towards the door. Being outside in the quiet and the fresh night air is *far* preferable to being subjected to their training partner any longer. "Y'all have fun, I'm *leaving.*"

"Really, now, Merlani, how am I supposed to be your Navigator if—" Cadet Lewis sets a staggering hand on Merlani's shoulder, gripping it tightly as he tries to turn them around to face him.

Before Merlani even realizes what they've done, Cadet Lewis is on the ground under the fog. The blur of motion, sharp snap, and loud fleshy thud as he hits the floor silences the entire room at once.

"I told you to *leave me alone*! You have *no* rights to my name, Bennington Lewis. You are *not* my Navigator." Merlani reaches over impulsively to the nearest full-size glass left on the table. They drain the entirety of the foul-tasting green liquid in one go, gesturing with a sweeping motion at the rest of the room with the empty glass. "And I don't care *what* you've been telling people—you will *never* be my Navigator."

The rest of the party-goers stare at them, too stunned to do anything.

"Is that enough truth for your game now, Cadet Lewis?" Merlani's hand holding the glass is shaking too much now for them to keep their grip on it. It shatters when it strikes the tile floor under the fog that is now completely obscuring their former training partner.

"Ocean?" Perkins begins to ask, "what just—"

"—I'm leaving. *You* explain that to him." Merlani's frustration turns to a sheer, undeniable urge to get out of the noisy, oppressive room. They stride through the fog and out into the hallway, their long tail swishing behind them with all of the agitation that's making them want to run into the night and never turn back.

No one comes after them.

MERLANI HAS BEEN LAYING ON THIS COUCH in the darkness with their eyes closed for long enough that they've almost forgotten how it was they ended up here.

Almost.

It's hard to focus on the regrets when they're not entirely sure whether they still *exist* at all. They can't feel the stars anymore, or even the echoes of the Strange in the back of their mind to tell them where they are.

Everything else is dulled and faraway and *cold*.

They can't tell if they're asleep or not. Merlani wishes they had dreams of their own to begin with so they could slip into one if they are. If they're awake, in the darkness there's no real difference.

A light turns on somewhere on the other side of Merlani's eyelids. They take this as a sign that they must be awake after all, but they don't want to open their eyes. It's just not worth the effort.

A voice breaks through the static in their ears: clear and bright and laughing with citrus and spice. "What? No, I don't have any housemates, I told you—why?"

"... ... ..." There's another voice, but it's so dim and indistinct that Merlani can barely tell that it *is* a voice.

"Oh! No, they don't live with me."

"... ... ..."

"Just... wait for me in the bedroom, will you? This will only take a minute."

"... ... ..."

Giggles. A door opening and shutting. Soft footsteps.

The back of an alien hand, soft and gentle and *warm* brushes against Merlani's cheek.

"Hey there, Cinny."

Merlani cracks open their third eye. The human face looking down at them is the one that belongs to the voice that cuts through the darkness—and, for some reason, she's wearing an eye patch and an extravagantly feathered black hat with a bright red bandanna tied around her hair underneath.

"...Hey."

"You okay?" She flicks up the eye-patch to look at them. Her voice is gentle and concerned.

"...What are you supposed to be?"

"Old Caribbean pirate queen."

"Mm... suits you, Captain Reese."

"So, what's going on?"

Trying to remember the sequence of events in enough clarity to explain to her what's actually *happened* is too hard."...Too much party in my place... couldn't think of anywhere else to go... Can I stay? Please?"

"Sure." Her hand settles behind Merlani's ear now and ruffles their hair in a familiar, soothing sort of way. The warmth pulls them a little further back from the darkness. "Want a blanket?"

Merlani nods, but the motion is half an instinctive move closer into the warmth of the hand that's now anchoring them to reality. Their eye slips back shut, because *warm* is the only thing they can process aside from their friend's voice—warm and *safe* in a way that stirs up memories. There's a dim thought somewhere near where the sensations of stars and Strange usually reside inside them that it would be nice to be close to that warmth forever.

In a moment, though, the warmth is gone.

It's soon replaced by the weight of a blanket being lightly tucked over them. The smell of dark roses and cinnamon is all around. Somewhere in the depths of their memory, Merlani knows this smell—it belongs to the voice too.

"Get some sleep, okay?" The warm hand returns to brush a bit of Merlani's hair back out of their face again and then pats their shoulder through the blanket. "Looks like you need it. We can talk in the morning—I'll put some music on so my date and I don't disturb you."

"...Okay."

It's easy for Merlani to drift off into the dreamless darkness, now, knowing that they have someone who will never turn them away—no matter *what* mistakes they've made.

★

Uncharacteristically, Merlani sleeps through the next morning.

When they *do* finally wake, the first thing they see is Reese in one of her casual athletic outfits standing on the far side of the room with her back to them.

After a moment, it registers that she's arranging bundles of bright orange marigold blossoms on the coffee table that she's moved over to the far wall under her hanging plants. She's draped one of the bright striped blankets that normally cover the back of the couch over the top of the table and has the solid computer display screen from her bedroom desk set up on it with images of smiling human faces displayed as a collage. Merlani's eyes are blurred enough that they can't make out the details more clearly than that. A few little tea light candles in bright-colored glass votive cups are sitting in a row under the screen. There's a smell in the air alongside that of the flowers and candles—something yeasty and sweet, although Merlani isn't sure quite what it is or where it's coming from.

They don't know what's going on, but they're relieved to find that their senses are at least *beginning* to return. Blinking to try and refocus their eyes, Merlani eases up into a half seated position. "Good morning?"

"More like good *afternoon*, Cinny," Reese teases as she turns around.

"Oh." Merlani dimly recognizes from the light streaming in through the window that she's right. "Good afternoon, then."

Reese comes over and takes a long, close look at them. "Glad to see you're up, finally. I was starting to worry."

"Sorry for the intrusion..." Merlani hesitates, their tail twitching with embarrassment under the warm blanket that's still draped over most of their lower body.

"No, no, don't go apologizing. You didn't disturb my evening at all." Reese pauses to reach out and brush that same stray bit of hair that's fallen down from Merlani's braids back out of their eyes and then smiles, letting out a small laugh. "You *did* scare my date a little, but that's okay. He's a bit flighty to begin with."

"Is he still here?"

"Oh, no." Reese shakes her head, still with that same enigmatic smile. "He was fun to play with, I'll admit... but it isn't anything serious enough to warrant asking him to stay for breakfast, you know? Especially since I'm not planning to invite him back anytime soon."

"I don't," Merlani says, "but I'll take your word for it."

Reese has explained to them before that she's the sort of human who likes having "intimate playmates" from time to time—to use her phrase—but isn't actually drawn towards people romantically and doesn't have an interest in being in that sort of committed relationship with anyone. Merlani can't say they really relate to any of the alien concepts of desire and attraction themself, but they appreciate that such things tend to matter to the humans in their life. If anything, their best friend's aromantic nature was one of the things that made it easier for her to understand how things are for *them*.

Reese chuckles and goes over towards the little kitchen area on the other side of the dividing wall. "You like hibiscus tea, right? I have a pitcher with ice all made up. I'm sure you'll feel better with some fluids in you."

"Yes, thank you."

A few moments later, Reese has returned with two tall glasses of reddish liquid and ice. She hands one to Merlani and then takes her usual spot on the other end of the couch, being careful not to accidentally sit on their tail in the process. "So, Cinny. I've been waiting all day to ask: what in the *stars* happened to you last night?"

"Well..." Merlani takes a sip from their tea. It's cold and sweet and has a bright fruity-floral sort of taste; somehow, this is exactly what they need to help clear the last of the cobwebs out of their head. "...Nothing happened to *me*, really."

"You usually at least ping me before you drop by, Cinny—I don't think you've ever just manifested on my couch like that before." Reese looks at them with pointed concern. "*Something* must have happened."

"Ah... sorry about that." Merlani sighs. "At the time, I couldn't see the com display at the door to ping you."

"You couldn't?"

"Mm..." Merlani nods, ears drooping in embarrassment. "You know how I told you once that there were very good reasons why Florivans usually don't drink?"

"Yeah?"

Merlani makes a vague gesture at their eyes. The lower two are still giving them fuzzy halos of color around the edges of everything. Reese's big cactus next to the couch looks like it's covered in sharp rainbows, thanks to that. "Losing the ability to perceive holoscreens is part of that."

"Ah—wait, why were *you* drinking at all, then?"

Merlani groans softly. "Stupid party... trying to be social with the rest of Nav/Quan for once in my life since they were *all in my quarters anyway* and brought half of the student body with them... They run these stupid truth-or-dare sorts of games with penalty sips if you don't answer the question, and somehow I let Condrey talk me into participating." Merlani looks down at the ice in their glass for a few moments. "That would be mistake number two of the night."

Reese raises an eyebrow. "Do I *want* to ask what the other mistakes were?"

Merlani hesitates. "Oh... actually tasting the Nav death juice when Cadet Perkins was mixing it was probably the first one—*stars*, that stuff is vile—"

"—Wait," Reese interrupts, holding up two fingers on one hand to make air quotes. "'Death juice'?"

"It's this horrible sort of a liquid... *thing* that the Nav folks make when they want to torture each other. If I remember right, it's absinthe and melon liquor as a base with tequila or something like that thrown in and topped off with this... sweet bubbly flower stuff?" Merlani shakes their head. "There may be something else, too. I gave up on trying to keep track after Perkins realized she'd forgotten to bring whatever the other ingredients were and had to go back to her place to get them. I think it's something to do with cinnamon and rocket fuel?"

"And I thought *pilots* had odd traditions." Reese stifles a laugh, then raises an eyebrow at them. "So you were a barely-coherent mess hiding out on my couch because of a few sips of that?"

"Well... no," Merlani admits, taking another slow sip of the sweet red tea. "One shot and a nearly full doubles glass—that was mistakes three and five."

"And mistake four?"

"I..." Merlani hesitates to answer, needing a moment to banish the sounds of the memory out of their mind. "...I *might* be a fugitive from justice, actually, because of that one."

"What?" Reese raises her eyebrows. "Why?"

"Well... you remember Cadet Lewis?"

"Um..." Reese shrugs. "It sounds *really* familiar, but you know how I am with names."

Merlani sighs. "The tall guy who showed up at practice looking for me a few days ago? Blondish, not-so-successful attempt at a goatee—I think you said he was attractive? Lives in the room next to mine?"

"Oh! *Him*! That's your annoying training partner, right?"

"...Probably not anymore."

"Why not? I mean, I remember everything you've told me about him now, and that he's probably going to wash out after the break when your instructors rotate the un-partnered folks because no one else *can* work with him..." There's a visible concern in Reese's dark brown eyes now that matches the tone of her voice. "But it sounds like that's not what you're talking about?"

"Yeah... it's not."

"So something happened with *him*?"

"...Yes." Merlani turns all three eyes down at their tea again, unable to bear their best friend's gaze any more than they want to see her reaction to the truth of what they've done. "I got to a point where I wanted to leave. He tried to get me to stay—held me back, even, or had his hand on me to stop me, at least. I... sort of reacted *badly* to that. Or to something he said. It happened so fast I... I don't really know which."

"How badly?"

Merlani lets out a sigh. "Ippon-seoi-nage badly."

"*Ocean*. Really?"

Merlani swirls the remaining tea around and watches the ice chips clink together, trying not to replay the feeling of the shoulder throw they'd used to break Cadet Lewis' grip on them over again in their mind—or any of the rest of the party memories, for that matter. They're only partly successful. Their ears droop further. "I'm pretty sure I broke his arm doing it, too... I just *reacted* with my full strength before I even realized what was happening."

"I wouldn't be surprised if you did." Reese shakes her head. "And you just left him like that?"

"...Yeah. I just... had to get out of there... and then I couldn't think of anywhere else to go that I could actually *find* on foot in the dark with all my senses starting to dull or go out." What Merlani doesn't say is that they'd gotten as far as the green area in the middle of campus before realizing that they needed to go *somewhere* other than just away from their flat—and the only thought that came to them then was that Reese's couch was *safe* and adjacent to warmth.

"Wow. No wonder you slept so long." Reese takes a small sip from her tea. "I'm kind of shocked no one's come looking for you by now, Cinny."

"I don't think any of the people at that party would know *where* to look for me." Merlani absently begins straightening out the fluff at the tip of their tail to stop it from twitching under the blanket. "And it's a weekend... *and* we have the next two weeks off for fall break... kind of gives me a head start, if I was going to run away."

"Do you plan to?"

Merlani shakes their head again and takes another sip of the hibiscus tea. "I don't really have anywhere to go."

"Well, unless you want to turn yourself in today—"

"—I don't. I will after the break, I just..." Merlani sets one of their upper hands over their face, closing their eyes for a few moments in an attempt to get them to refocus. "I really don't think I can face anyone right now about this."

"I figured as much." Reese just watches them with that same calmly concerned look and takes a long swig from her own tea before setting it down on the floor next to her largest cactus. "I know you said you planned to stay on campus over the break and work on your assignments while everyone else was off home or traveling or whatever, but my offer to take you out to the ranch with me when I go tonight still stands."

Merlani considers it and then nods, slowly. They can't exactly go back to their flat now, after all. "If *you're* willing to harbor a fugitive... then I'd be glad to accept."

"Cinny." Reese reaches over and pats the blanket over their foot, since it's the closest thing she can reach. "If you'd come in here last night and asked me to help you hide this Lucas's... wait, that's wrong. Lucius? No... Listin?"

"Cadet Lewis."

"Right. That. Him." Reese's eyes meet theirs with the sort of intensity she has when she's sparring. "Well, *whatever* his name is. If you'd come in last night and asked me to help you hide his body, I'd have been right there with a bag of quicklime and a shovel, you know?"

Morbid as it is, that statement is incredibly comforting in a way Merlani can't even begin to explain.

"Thank you, Reese." Merlani doesn't say it, but they know they'd do the same for her if she asked. They're pretty sure she knows them well enough that they don't *need* to say it, though.

The bright ping of the kitchen timer interrupts the conversation.

"Ah!" Reese bounces up to her feet. "That will be the *pan de muerto*. We can figure out all the travel things once I finish with it, okay? I promised my little cousins *I'd* bring some for them this year, now that my mother's sabbatical is over and she's back out in space with the Fleet. Her recipe's sort of the gold standard for them, even if my tía makes perfectly good ones every year herself."

Merlani takes another sip from their tea and watches their best friend through the doorway of the little kitchen area. Reese lives off-campus, after all, and out of the jurisdiction of the Accommodation Lottery. While she does come through the cadet mess regularly, she still has facilities in her small apartment for making simple meals if she's ever home and needs to.

Reese busies herself with taking a tray of small round buns out of the oven and setting them on a counter to cool. That bright yeasty-citrus smell is everywhere in the air now.

"I didn't know you actually baked things," Merlani comments when their friend reappears and returns to the couch.

"Only on special occasions—I normally don't have time."

"What's the occasion, then?"

Reese gestures at her decorated coffee table against the far wall. "Old family tradition for Dia de los Muertos... we honor the spirits of the dead with gifts of food and drink and set up their pictures so they aren't forgotten and know where to come and visit—family and ancestors, you know? I've never decided if I believe for sure that they come back, but the traditions are comforting."

Merlani nods lightly. They look towards the flowers again—the petals are almost same color as the Elder's robes their Ai-Nida Celadon wears on special occasions. "Elder Celadon and their Navigator do something like that for the Procyon anniversary every year," they say, "but I think it's more of a personal ritual the two of them just settled into doing."

"Florivans don't have this sort of thing?"

"We do, kind of, but it's not a formal holiday with traditions like this." Merlani's never ended up on this subject with anyone before. Reese is one of the few humans they know who can ask a question like that without coming off as prying in the first place.

"Oh?"

"It's more... when our families are together, we take time to sit with the stars and remember the people who've gone. Tell their stories, if we can, but it's all small things, really. Little personal rituals that grow out of who they were to us, if that makes sense. Entile River—that's my Nida's littermate—they always lit candles with us when they were visiting." Merlani sighs softly at the memory. "They had a lot of family to tell us about, too, since the four of us are all that's really left from our family line."

Reese nods and picks her drink back up to take another swig. "If you have a picture of any of them, I can put it up with the rest of the family if you like."

"I can tell you how to find one." Merlani sighs. "You'll have to do the search, though, I couldn't see the screen on my pocket-com if I tried."

"Okay." Reese fishes through her pockets and pulls out the little device, then presumably activates its holoscreen—not that Merlani can see it. "Who am I looking for?"

"Let's see..." Merlani has to think about it for a moment. "Ah. Easiest way to find a good picture is 'Defense Fleet personnel, Novan War era... SCV *Gymnasio*. You're trying to find 'Lt. Ocean Marbree of the Eldest's Line and the household of Fleet Elder Celadon Toreval, secondary Quantum Space Drive Engineer and adjunct officer to the 6th Darter Squadron.'"

"Okay..." Reese taps at the air where her holoscreen interface must be for a few minutes before turning back to Merlani triumphantly. "Aha! Counterpart: Lt. George Barker?"

"That's the one," says Merlani with a nod.

"All right, then, I think I found them! Here, I'll put their picture up on the screen so you can see it." Reese goes over and fiddles with both devices for a few moments before the picture she's found pops up on the screen in its large form over the top of her collage. "Is this the right person?"

"Yeah," says Merlani, smiling with a touch of sadness. "That's my Nida."

In the image, a very young-looking Florivan is standing at attention and looking directly into the camera—Merlani recognizes it, even with their eyes blurred, as the personnel registration photo that was taken when their parent first volunteered for the Defense Fleet. If it weren't for their hair being a long complicated braid pulled up halfway into a bun and the fact that they're wearing a war-era green and ivory Fleet uniform, Merlani knows that it could easily be mistaken for a more recent photo of themself.

Reese considers the image for a while and then looks back to Merlani with a soft smile. "I can see the resemblance." She sets the photo to the same size as her other images and adds it into the collage before coming back to sit down on the couch with them.

Merlani nods. "That's why I was given 'Ocean' for a public name. They'd already planned names for Sky and Storm… but since *my* eyes didn't even open until after they were gone and I turned out to have inherited their coloring when I finally started to shed my kitten fur, Dad picked mine to honor Nida."

"That's sweet, really," Reese says. "My family does something like that too. I was named for one of my grandmothers." She gestures at a picture of a woman in an even older-styled Fleet uniform next to the image of Merlani's parent. "I never got to meet her, of course, but I've heard so many stories over the years, I feel like I know her."

"I know what you mean, Reese." Merlani sets their tea down and rearranges themself to fold their knees up and wrap their lower arms around them. "I never really got to know Nida for myself either. My littermates have a few memories of them, here and there, but for me it's only a dim echo of a voice in the darkness—and that's probably just wishful thinking on my part. I just... I always regret that I can't remember them, you know?"

Reese scoots over next to Merlani. She doesn't say anything, just settles in and offers an arm for them to lean into.

Merlani accepts the gesture, snuggling up against her. This human friend they've made is safe and *warm*. Being close to her feels like being with their littermates—just *comfortable* all around. Reese is also the first person they've ever felt comfortable talking about their parent with at all, aside from their family. They're not sure if any of the other Nav/Quan cadets are even aware of their family history. The rest of their teammates only know the bare basics. If they're honest, Merlani doesn't know if they'd even *want* any of their classmates to know the things they're telling Reese.

"They'd probably be disappointed in me, now," Merlani says after a long silence, not sure at all why the words come out aloud instead of staying between their ears where such thoughts usually lurk.

"Oh, I don't think so. Maybe a little concerned about the whole breaking-a-guy's-arm thing, of course, but not *disappointed*." Merlani doesn't have to look up at Reese to hear that she's smiling gently when she says this.

"You *know* I come from a species of instinctive pacifists, right?"

"Well, yeah, but that's what makes you neat!" Reese laughs lightly. "You didn't take up judo and such to learn how to hurt people—this one little incident hardly makes you a vicious killing machine, Cinny. I mean, self defense *does* mean defending yourself from people."

"Maybe…" Merlani can't help but sigh. "I took up judo because I couldn't keep up with my sibs and Dad thought it would help me focus, actually, since none of the usual Florivan solutions were working."

Reese is now occupying her hands with taking down what's left of the braids Merlani wears to hold their hair back out of their face so she can re-do them. The gesture is appreciated, and they know she's aware that it has a calming effect. A good portion of their growing closer as friends had to do with helping each other sort out their hair before the various practices and classes they have together, especially leading up to the regional competitions the team has been to recently.

"Oh? Is that why you don't tell people your origin story, then?"

"Yeah…" Merlani nods slowly. "There's this thing that happens with litters sometimes, where one kitten ends up being born—well, *smaller* than the others?—and then that one doesn't grow as fast or as much, and usually doesn't live long enough to open their eyes, much less be given their public name... and in my family, that's me. That's why my entiles Jade and Cerulean and I are all short even compared to other Florivans, actually. My Entile River's like that too, but you haven't met them."

"That explains a few things. You turned out really well for someone who wasn't supposed to live, then."

"Thanks... From what I've been told, if we'd been born before the War, I'd have been taken on by my Ai-Nida to be trained from the start instead of having to try to keep up in lessons with my littermates—but as it was, with all of us so scattered as a species, no one wanted to separate me from Sky and Storm until *they'd* finished their apprenticeships, so..." Merlani trails off, making a vague gesture with their free upper hand.

"So you did your best and you managed to become awesome at judo and capoeira at the same time—I'd say that'd be an accomplishment regardless of how you started off." Reese pauses her process of braiding to poke the back of one of Merlani's ears as punctuation.

"If you say so." Merlani finds themself smiling in spite of everything. Reese tends to have that effect on them.

"I do! Say, not to change the subject too much, but does this mean I get to know the capoeira origin story too?"

The darker tint to Merlani's thoughts is quickly flitting away simply from the tone of their friend's voice. They giggle softly at the question. "Oh, that one's easy. *Starbright*'s head of geosciences got me into it after I asked him about the music he keeps on in the background of the lab all the time. He said it was a more graceful way of practicing for self-defense on field sites than just throwing rocks at people—well, combined with the Tàijíquán sequences, but I only really started learning those properly once I got here and met Lavine and Martins, you know?"

Reese chuckles. "Well, then. That'll do it. Remind me never to underestimate geologists."

"I don't think I'll have to."

After a few more moments of quiet warmth, Reese nods her head towards the kitchen. "So, care to lend me a hand with getting the sugar dusted on the pan de muerto? They should be cool enough now."

"I'll lend you four if you like." Merlani grins. "We *do* get to eat these pastries of yours later, right?"

Reese stands and pulls them to their feet, laughing. "Naturally!"

IN ALL THEIR WONDERINGS ABOUT WHAT LIVING on Earth would be like, Merlani had never considered there would be an occasion where instead of their cadet's uniform they'd find themself wearing a borrowed red and black striped poncho over an equally borrowed red sleeveless athletic undershirt with a dusty old wide-brimmed black cowboy hat set precariously behind their ears. Neither had they imagined that they would be wearing such an outfit while sitting in the autumn sunshine perched on the cool silver bars of a corral fence.

But then, Merlani's assumptions about what their life on Earth would be like had never taken into account becoming friends with Teresa Vasquez. Somehow, being Reese's best friend makes it perfectly reasonable to be sitting in such a place watching her riding a grey-spotted horse in circuits around a wide oval arena studded with blue and white barrels and jumping fences.

As Merlani has recently learned, Reese's extended family has operated the same small Texas horse ranch for literal centuries. From what Merlani has been told, no less than three distinct lines of her ancestors had been taming and raising horses for as long as the beautiful creatures had been on the continent. The majority of the family might be spread around the stars serving with the Defense Fleet, but they all have this place for an anchor—the family agri-specialists and cultural historians keep it running, and all the various children and cousins are either raised here or brought to visit as often as can be arranged. Reese herself is one of the former.

Merlani has only been enjoying the hospitality of the ranch for a few days now, but the place is already starting to feel a bit like home to them too. There's something compelling about the mesquite-tree-spotted canyon lands surrounding them, the wide, seemingly endless expanse of blue sky above, and the *quiet* of being away from Earth's major cities. Merlani's spent the majority of their life out in space, and they know that's where they belong, really, but being welcomed by a little piece of a planet like this is its own sort of wonderful.

Reese's family had barely blinked when she brought them in. What is Merlani, after all, other than one more stray child to help with the horses, as Reese's great-aunt had pronounced upon meeting them. The word of the clan matriarch is law on the ranch, according to Reese, and

Tía Anita has no shortage of chores to keep even visiting children occupied.

The Quail Ridge Ranch is half run with modern technology, but as a cultural history preservation site, a lot of things are still done the way they had been when the first stones were hauled out of the canyon to build the original rock-walled ranch house. That building has since been converted to a small museum to occupy the steady stream of visitors who come in to experience what Reese had described as 'a little bit of living history in the middle of relative nowhere'.

"She's really flying today, eh?"

Merlani looks down from their perch with their lower two eyes to where Reese's great-uncle Esteban is leaning on the pipes of the fence below them. The man twirls the end of his long white mustache with two fingers before reaching up to adjust his grey felt cowboy hat. The parts of his hair that stick out from under the hat are silvery-white too, in stark contrast to his warm, sun-calloused brown face and hands. If they didn't know better, Merlani would almost have thought he'd spent his entire life here in western wear rather than out in the stars in a Fleet uniform. He may not fly *professionally* anymore, but there's still a pilot's wing pin fixed onto the front of his woven green and ivory hatband—and, although it's warm enough that he's not wearing it over his blue check western shirt at the moment, an ivory Darter pilot's jacket hanging on the coat rack in the house that bears the 6th Squadron's unmistakable horse head insignia.

"Yes, sir."

He laughs, brushing some dust off of his jeans. "I'm *retired*, Little Ocean. How many times do I need to remind you? I only pull rank on family if they're getting too big for their britches."

"Sorry, Tío Esteban," Merlani says with a giggle, "force of habit."

Another thing in the list of things Merlani had never expected: being told in no uncertain terms that they were to consider themself one of Colonel Vasquez' niblings just like Reese and her cousins. Apparently, although Merlani had only heard his name in passing all their life, he'd been far closer to Dad and Nida during the war than they'd ever realized.

"Don't worry about it, you'll learn." The old man gestures out towards Reese, who's now bringing her horse into slower circuits on her way to easing it back into a cooling-down walking gait. "So, are we getting *you* back into the saddle today?"

"Um... possibly? If one of the horses agrees to it?" Merlani shrugs. "*Definitely* not going that fast."

Merlani has an appreciation for the beauty and grace of horses from a safe distance, but the idea of being on the back of such a large mammal running at high speed still intimidates them. They'd never even *seen* a horse in person before Reese brought them here, after all. The horses of the Quail Ridge Ranch, likewise, had never seen a Florivan. So far, the consensus among the horses seems to be that Merlani is a creature who is unsettling, but not necessarily a threat. The feeling is somewhat mutual.

Tío Esteban chuckles. "Well, we can start you off at a *walk*, then... maybe on one of the calmer geldings, too. Reese does tend to pick out the spooky ones."

"Calmer sounds good."

"We'll make a regular cowpoke out of you yet, Little Ocean—heh! I'd like to see the look on George's face when he gets the pictures from all this."

"I'm... sure he'll be surprised." After all, as far as Dad knows, Merlani's plan was to spend the break on campus getting ahead on their assignments—not hiding out on a ranch on the far end of the territory from the Academy.

"Well, naturally! I went and named my squadron for these horses, you know, even though I kept having to explain to the young space-bred types like your dad what a Mustang even *was*—and here *you* are helping me in the barn. There's poetry in that, I'd say." Tío Esteban grins up at them.

Merlani nods, then falls silent for a while as they look up at the sky to the one or two fluffy little poofs of cloud starting to cross overhead. "Dad's never really told us much about his Fleet days, actually."

"Really?" The old man sounds surprised. "I always knew him as the talkative storyteller sort."

"Yeah." Merlani shrugs. "Äiti told me once it's more because of what happened to Nida than anything the two of them went through during the War, but it's hard to know for sure."

"Well, it *was* a long time ago... and some of us do better talking about our old days than others." Tío Esteban nods slowly. "That fool father of yours was a good pilot, though—didn't get to officially keep him long, of course, but definitely one of the better kids who lied about their age and wound up flying for me."

"Oh?" Merlani unwraps their tail from the fence and shifts position so they can focus more on him while still watching Reese and the horse with one eye.

"Yep." Tío Esteban chuckles softly. "Would have gone ahead and promoted him to my wing Sergeant anyway, you know, if he hadn't gotten drafted for Nav when he did."

"*Drafted*?" Merlani raises all three eyebrows. "What do you mean?"

"Oh, he's never told you *that* story either?" Tío Esteban looks up at them and grins. "It's a nice one, I think."

"I don't *think* he has..."

"Well, then, Little Ocean. Here's a bit of family history for you to pass on to those littermates of yours sometime." The old man readjusts his hat again and then leans both arms on the fence and looks up at Merlani. "So, we pilots were half responsible for keeping our darters flying; other half belonged to the squadron mechanics and techies, see? Well, *Gymnasio* was docked at Horizon Prime out at Kapteyn and I was helping our Chief Petty Officer re-educate George in the finer points of putting a darter back together after he'd gone and broke it off crashing into a T'irsh-fel drone during a training exercise—sort of by way of encouraging him *not* to break the thing again."

Merlani nods. They may not have heard the majority of Dad's stories, but Uncle Rudy has told them more than a few from his perspective as a former darter maintenance chief.

"Say, does your dad still have that habit of singing old sailing tunes while he's concentrating?"

"A bit, yeah. Never notices he's doing it, either, unless someone starts singing along. Why?"

"Heh! Nice to hear he hasn't changed—used to do that while he was flying, too."

"Really?" Merlani giggles. "I take it the rest of the squadron didn't like hearing him over their radios?"

"You'd be right about that. My wing leads got to the point of drawing straws every time we went out to see whose team had to fly with the kid and keep a handle on that. Got to the point where I kept him in my wing so they'd *stop* fussing at me."

Merlani is now very much looking forward to passing that bit of information on to their siblings—especially considering that Mir picked up that little singing habit too.

"So, anyway." The old man gestures vaguely out over the fence with one hand. "Picture, if you will, me and CPO Sidney holding up one of the wing struts of this busted-up darter while George is on his back underneath applying his refresher course in micro welding to reattach the thing. And he's got some old shanty or other stuck in his head, so poor Sid and I are having to listen to *that* the whole time. Then, just as we're finishing up and getting ready to move on to the next piece of the darter bits we need to put back together, this Florivan kid appears out of *nowhere* next to me—younger than you are, for sure. If I remember right, they'd not even been formally released from their apprenticeship yet. Doesn't even make an introduction, just looks around and asks me where the 'human with the warm voice' is."

Merlani is *certain* now that they've never heard this story before. "And that was Nida?"

Tío Esteban nods. "Yeah. So Sid and I point under the darter, and the kid thanks us and crawls under there and just point-blank tells George they want him for their Navigator. *He* practically comes out of his skin and bangs his head on the underside of the darter because he didn't notice them before that—knocks himself clean out for a minute, too—and then we all have a good laugh at his expense carrying him up to sick bay to get stitches put in where he'd cut his forehead open and make sure he didn't get a concussion when he hit the floor."

"Wait... *that's* how Dad got the scar? Because Nida *startled* him?"

Tío Esteban grins. "That is indeed!"

Merlani has to take several minutes to get all of the giggles out of their system. When they can finally catch their breath again, they shake their head and look back down to the old pilot. "My sibs and I have been trying for *forever* to get him to tell us the story and he's never done anything more than spin out tall tales instead."

"That's George for you." Tío Esteban chuckles again. "Anyway, we spend the rest of the week working on that darter with a very persistent little Florivan spectator... who, granted, was more helpful than your dad was, but who every day without fail would ask if he was ready to be their Navigator yet before they left. As it turned out, Breezy didn't like any of the official Nav prospects their mentor had been introducing to them and *did* like George's voice, and hearing him from the corridor was all they needed to decide *he* was the human they wanted. Next thing I know we've got a fully functional darter... but I no longer have a full-time pilot to *fly* it because he's finally said yes to that parent of yours."

Merlani smiles, although halfway sadly. "I never knew they'd done that... but it makes a lot of sense."

"Probably makes more sense to you than it does to me. All I know is that after that, it wasn't long before I had one of my Mustangs up running Nav for Gymnasio on nights when her primary team was off-duty and the best adjunct I could ever have asked for down in her Drive Bay. The whole squadron teased your dad for *ages* that he'd picked a real funny-looking darter to replace all the ones he'd crashed." Tío Esteban looks up to Merlani and raises a conspiratorial eyebrow. "Granted, we *also* teased him that Breezy was the better pilot out of the two of them, but that's just a *fact*."

Merlani is about to say something about how they've heard a few stories about that last detail before, but the conversation is interrupted by Reese and her horse coming to a halt in front of where they're sitting on the fence.

"Well? Think you're ready to have a go again yet? Angel here's ready to take a break from showing off." Reese flashes a cheerful smile at them, then reaches down to pat the spotted grey animal on the side of its neck.

Merlani looks down to the horse, who is giving them the same look most of the horses have been since they arrived on the ranch: the one that says the animal is not yet decided on whether they're a danger to the herd or not. The horse makes a soft nickering sound of discontent and flicks her ears at Merlani.

Merlani does their best not to make any sudden movements. "Um... as long as you have a horse around here that's *not* going to try to throw me off and trample me this time, sure."

"I know just the one." Tío Esteban chuckles and heads off in the direction of the pasture connected to the stables. "Come on, Little Ocean, I think we can convince Mercury to give you a chance."

Reluctantly, Merlani comes down from their perch and follows him.

★

As it turns out, Mercury is one of the oldest horses on the ranch: a bay and white painted gelding who is both hard to fluster and easily bribed. He doesn't take long to make the connection between letting Merlani come near him and the manifestation of an apple or a handful of sugar cubes. With a day or two, he seems content to allow them to put a saddle on his back and then climb into it—although with a clear understanding that Merlani *will* continue providing treats in exchange for riding privileges.

Mercury is the sort of horse that converts a person into liking being around horses. As soon as he's decided that Merlani is a creature that's worth his interest, he seems to always be waiting at the pasture or corral fence right when they're walking by. The other horses still give them a cautious look and shy away, but not Mercury. He knows that at least one of the hands under Merlani's borrowed poncho will be holding a sugar cube if he comes over to greet them.

And so it is that by the end of the week, Reese has Merlani confident enough working with this one horse to take them out on trail rides down through the canyon and along banks of the small river running through it. On this particular afternoon, she's taken them out to a little cave on the canyon wall at the far end where she used to go with her cousins to camp out and watch the stars. It's a beautiful place, complete with a tall cluster of cottonwood trees right by the river. There's even a rope swing tied to the largest tree for those adventurous enough to want to launch themselves into the water.

The two of them have made plans to come back out later in the week with the collection of young folks and children from her extended family to have one of those camp outs, since it's not quite too cold yet to enjoy a night outdoors. Merlani has the distinct impression that it will be better than the planetary-survival-training trip they had to endure with the Nav/Quan cohort last year—if only because they're actually *comfortable* around Reese and her relatives.

The fall air is crisp, but the sunshine of the clear day is warm and the blanket-like garment draped over Merlani's shoulders is surprisingly good for keeping the wind out. They're growing to like the poncho—it suits them, somehow, and the thick fabric is *warm* without restricting their movement. Although they're accustomed to their cadet uniform, they definitely want to add one of these brilliant outer garments to their wardrobe before they go back to the cold of space. They've been issued a set of black leather chaps and boots as well for riding trails like this, which, while intended for keeping the taller bits of brush from scratching their legs even through the thick cloth of their equally borrowed jeans, are also good for holding in warmth. Thankfully for Merlani, between the various members of Reese's family there were enough appropriately-sized garments for them to borrow while they're here—which is particularly nice, since they'd arrived with nothing more than the clothes they'd worn when they retreated from their flat.

Reese, of course, seems perfectly at home on horseback and looks every bit the mythic cowgirl figure from the paintings hanging in the old ranch house museum: grey felt hat with a red and black beaded hatband, hair swept back into a pair of braids down her back, long brown-fringed duster, dark jeans, and tall brown boots with constellations worked into the decorative stitching. She's promised Merlani that before the next time she brings them here, she'll help them acquire some proper long-sleeved western shirts like the bright red one she has on.

"So," Reese asks, nudging her grey horse ever so slightly to turn down onto the trail that leads back up to the house and barns, "enjoying yourself?"

"Too much, probably." Merlani reaches down with one of their lower hands to give Mercury a friendly pat on his neck. "I've half a mind to just see if your great-aunt would take me on as a ranch hand and give up on the Academy altogether."

Reese chuckles and shakes her head at them. "You'd miss the stars too much, Cinny—and you know it."

"I know, I know... but it *would* be simpler." Merlani sighs, reaching up to readjust their hat. It's now officially theirs because of the holes Reese's young cousin Jacob insisted on making for their ears to fit through so it could do a hat's proper job and keep the sun out of their eyes. Jacob has also made the joke more than once now that they look like they could be an Old Western outlaw in their full outfit.

He has no idea how close he is to the truth.

"Simpler, maybe. But you couldn't hide out here forever. Besides..." Reese reaches over to nudge their shoulder. "Even if Tía Anita let you stay, I'd be back to claim you for my ship's jumper once I make Captain, remember?"

"I remember." Merlani cracks a small smile. "Wouldn't have it any other way, Captain Reese."

It's just as well they have to go back to Houston when she does at the end of the break. Mercury is a nice horse, but he's no substitute for Reese's company. Merlani is well aware they only have the rest of the school year to enjoy that. Come spring, Reese will be graduating and leaving for her first posting on a Defense Fleet starship somewhere. They may not see their best friend again for *years* after that happens.

"Want to try racing to the bridge?" Reese's broad grin prevents Merlani from thinking too hard about the future. In the here and now, she's the same delightfully cheeky human she always is.

Merlani hesitates. "I just got comfortable with *walking* without falling off..."

"Come on, Cinny! It'll be fun!"

Somehow, before they know it, Merlani is holding onto the saddle horn for dear life with their lower hands and trying to remember how to direct Mercury through the reins with the upper two while he's trotting along behind Reese's horse. She's practically flying up the trail already, all excited laughter and shouting for them to catch up.

The speed of the two horses increases each time Merlani and Mercury get close to closing the gap between them. This is a *game*, after all. Reese must be trying to see how fast she can get them to go without falling off or giving up.

Merlani, for their part, is just glad their horse friend seems to know what he's doing.

Riding at a gallop along the river is *terrifying* and incredibly thrilling all at once. The wind rushes by their ears with a roar just from the speed, blocking out all sounds but the rhythmic beats of the horse's hooves against the ground. Merlani has never experienced anything like it, even in their wanderings in the Strange. Soon, they're catching their friend's enthusiasm and laughing right along with her. They can see why Reese likes riding the way she does, now. There's no room for anything in their mind but holding on and moving with the powerful animal whose back they're perched upon.

By the time the two of them reach the small stone bridge that spans the river, Merlani has forgotten entirely that *they're* supposed to be the one in control of the horse and not the other way around.

Reese pulls up on her reins easily and halts her grey-spotted horse in moments.

It takes Merlani at least a dozen meters of riverbank and a shout from Reese to remember how to get Mercury to stop. When he does, the abrupt change in momentum is enough to make them lose their balance and fall out of the saddle and into a clump of rough greenery right on the edge of the water. The impact is enough to knock the wind out of them, but at least they know from years of drills in judo practice how to fall safely.

"*Stars*, horse," Merlani says to the old paint gelding when he nuzzles their face a few moments later in search of the treats he doubtless can smell in their pockets. "I asked you to *stop*, not to throw me in the river."

Reese trots her horse up and dismounts, offering Merlani a hand to get to their feet. "You're not hurt, are you?"

"No, just my pride—I'll be sore tomorrow, though, for sure." Merlani takes the hand and dusts themself off once they've gotten back upright. They know they were lucky not to be injured or worse.

"Maybe we'll hold off racing again until you can handle a canter better." Reese picks their hat up off the ground by the greenery and gently sets it back on over their ears.

"Might be a good idea."

Mercury nudges Merlani's chest expectantly with his head, nearly knocking them over again.

"Oh, no, mister," Merlani says to the horse, reaching up to pat him on the neck. They look into his eyes pointedly, keeping their tone firm and businesslike. "We have an agreement, remember? You get your sugar *after* we get back to the barn, not before."

Reese chuckles and climbs back up on her grey spotted mare. "You don't get to tease me about talking to my plants anymore, Cinny. At least I don't negotiate with them."

"Plants are a different matter altogether," Merlani tells her, leading their horse friend over to a nearby large rock so they can stand on it to reach the stirrup and pull themself up onto his back. Otherwise, they're short enough that they'd have to jump to get into the saddle—and they have established that horses *don't* appreciate that sort of behavior. "Mercury is *intelligent* and has opinions about his fee for putting up with me."

"He's going to be an absolute pest about letting anyone else ride him at this rate, you know?" Reese giggles. "He didn't even try to wander off while you were on the ground."

Merlani succeeds in getting themself securely into the saddle and directs Mercury back over to where Reese and her mare are waiting. "Pity I can't train Mercury to be a Navigator." They give the horse another affectionate pat on his shoulder. "He's far easier to work with than anyone the Commanders have given me."

"Maybe you should try offering your next Nav cadet sugar cubes?"

"Oh, is *that* what I'm doing wrong?"

"Hey, bringing you sweets worked for me!" Reese grins at them pointedly.

"You hear that, Mercury?" Merlani says, leaning down towards the horse's ear, "She finally admits she thinks I'm a strange four-armed horse."

Mercury twitches his ear in response and snorts at just the right moment to sound like he's laughing at them.

Merlani and Reese have a good long laugh of their own over the whole idea of that on their way back up the trail towards the ranch house.

It's nearly sunset now. Just as they're getting within sight of the pasture fence, they spot another rider galloping down the trail towards them.

"Reese!" calls the rider, "There you are! Abuela sent me to get you!"

"What is it, Jacob?" Reese halts her horse when the boy gets close enough to turn his black horse around and fall in alongside them.

"Flitter landed up on the pad with someone asking after you. She's been talking to Abuela and Tío Esteban for a couple hours now—I think there's trouble."

"Oh?" Reese raises both eyebrows at the boy. He's only eleven, after all—hardly the most trustworthy of messengers.

"She's a *Ranger*, Reese."

Reese looks over to Merlani.

Merlani meets her eyes and sighs lightly. "She'll be here for me, then."

"You don't know that for sure, Cinny."

"Why else?" Merlani shakes their head and nudges Mercury back into a trot to head up the path to the ranch house—even though what they really want to do is go flying on his back in the other direction, all the way to that cave in the canyon side where their problems don't seem to exist.

"For *you*?" Jacob spurs his horse forward to ride right alongside Merlani. "Are you really an outlaw or something now, like in the books?"

"I..." Merlani hesitates, then sighs sadly. "Well, yes, Jacob, sort of. Reese was helping me run away from something I did for a while—I never thought the Rangers would send someone after me."

"What'd you do, Ocean?" asks the boy, eyes wider than Merlani has ever seen a human's go before. "Did you *kill* a guy or something?"

"Jacob!" Reese admonishes, catching up to the two of them and guiding her mare so she's on Merlani's other side. "How could you even *ask* something like that?"

The memory of the sound of Cadet Lewis's arm snapping and how they left him lying on the floor under the fog flits through Merlani's mind. "I... I hope not, Jacob," they say softly before they fall silent for the rest of the ride back, "I sincerely hope not."

Merlani isn't sure what to expect when they leave Reese and Jacob to see to the horses and walk up to the more modern two-story rock-and-planking house which serves as the ranch headquarters. All they know is that there's no sense in delaying the inevitable—especially if they've brought trouble to Reese's family.

They hadn't considered at all that the Ranger would be waiting for them on the porch swing with her white hat down over most of her face and her boots propped up on the railing, apparently having long since finished with her talk with the ranch's elders.

The Ranger doesn't bother to remove her hat or look up when Merlani walks up the stairs. "Ocean Merlani Barker-Hämäläinen."

Merlani winces at the disappointed-sounding pronouncement in the all-to-familiar voice. "...Hi."

She gestures vaguely at the spot on the swing beside her. "*Sit*. We have talking to do, yes?"

"Yes, ma'am." Merlani sits down awkwardly, holding the tufted end of their tail between their lower hands to keep it still.

"Kitten," says the Ranger from under her hat, switching effortlessly from smoothly-accented standard to Finnish, "do you have *any* idea how much trouble you put me through to figure out where you'd disappeared to?"

"I... didn't really think about anyone trying to find me," Merlani admits, answering in the same language and staring down at their hands. "I *was* going to go back at the end of the break—"

"—And what, turn yourself in?"

"...Something like that, yes." Merlani sighs sadly. "I never meant to actually hurt him..."

"Well, now, the problem we have here is that you *did* hurt the boy, yes? I've heard what happened from the witnesses. What I want to know from you is *why*."

"...Cadet Lewis isn't hurt *badly*, is he?"

The Ranger holds up her pinkish-pale fingers and taps each one in turn as she counts off the injuries. "Shattered right arm, dislocated shoulder and minor wrist fracture on the left one, a pretty severe concussion that had him out cold for several days... Oh! And one minor skull fracture, too. He's lucky his neck didn't snap outright when he hit the floor."

Merlani falls silent. The broken arm they'd assumed, but the rest... it's painful just to think about it. They feel like they might as well be swallowed up by the ground right here and now.

"So tell me, Merlakka, child of my heart," says the Ranger, lifting her hat back to the top of her head above her pair of ash-blonde braided buns and leaning over to look directly into Merlani's lower pair of eyes with her own concerned icy blue ones. "What happened?"

"Äiti... I..."

Merlani falls apart, fighting back tears, telling their mother *everything*: Cadet Lewis, how bad a fit he was as a training partner, all his annoying little nicknames and *assumptions* about how they should act towards him, the stupid party, the stupid truth-or-drink game they'd let themself get drawn into, how he'd tried to stop them from leaving, what they think they said when they left him lying there on the floor.

All of it.

"...And since I couldn't face any of them... Reese brought me here."

Their Ranger mother has been watching them closely the whole time they've been talking. She hasn't said anything to interrupt the confused stream of words at all before this. "She's a good friend, your Reese."

"She is, Äiti."

"So it was the Lewis boy trying to use your private name without permission that did it in the end? Or him calling you by your nida's nicknames?"

"...More that he didn't want me to leave... talking like he had a *claim* on me... but... I just... he had his hand on me and..."

"A lot of things added up all at once, yes?"

"...Yes." Merlani has no more words to offer; only shame.

Äiti shakes her head and sets an arm around their shoulders. Merlani leans gratefully into her familiar warmth.

"Ah, Merlakka... sweet kitten, what am I *ever* going to do with you?" She clucks her tongue and then sighs lightly. "I know better than anyone how easy it is to react in haste like that—and I know that you're not *really* this violent person. Well-trained with arts that have their origins in violence, for sure, but not setting out to *harm* anyone, yes?"

Merlani nods, still unable to say anything. They have most of their face buried against the side of their mother's pale grey vest instead.

"You're fortunate we'd just arrived in orbit so I could offer to your instructors to find you. They're worried, you know? Poor Cerulean was about ready to turn over every rock on the continent looking for you *themself* when I spoke to them."

"...Because I hurt someone, or because I left?"

"Both. *Particularly* because you left your pocket-com in your bedroom and no one knew where to look for you or how to contact you."

"...Oh. So *that's* where it's been." Merlani sighs sadly. The ranch doesn't have the best reception, thanks to its geography, and Reese had stashed her own pocket-com in a drawer up in her childhood bedroom when they first arrived so she could relax. They had barely thought about their own little communication device since they first got here, themself. "I'm going to be the first Florivan who gets expelled from an Academy, aren't I?"

"Maybe... maybe not. That's up to your Commanders. *I* just volunteered to track you down because I was in town looking for you anyway, and now I've found you."

"...And now you're going to take me back?"

Their mother nods. "First thing in the morning, kitten. Tonight we're bunking here, and you *aren't* going to run off again now that I've found you, yes?"

"Yes, Äiti." Merlani gets quiet again for a minute or two, and then finally asks the question they've been dreading. "...Does Dad know?"

"Yes, but I was in on the call when Cerulean told him. We'll have a nice *long* chat with him over the relays once we get back to Houston. I left River there to help your Commanders try to sort things out with the Academy Administration."

"...Who's more disappointed in me?"

"Mm... probably River, but you know how they felt about us getting you into judo in the first place. That's why I came alone, yes?"

"...Thanks, Äiti." Merlani is grateful that it's her sitting here for sure. Out of all the people who helped to raise them, this woman they've always known as their äiti—'mother,' in her ancestral language—is the one they've always felt understood them the best.

It's at this point in the conversation that Reese reappears, having finally finished grooming the horses and putting them into the stable for the night. She walks up the porch steps and stops when she sees the two of them on the swing.

"Forgive my impertinence, ma'am," says Reese, leaning against the nearest supporting post of the porch, "but this has to be the oddest-looking arrest in the galaxy."

Äiti chuckles and nudges Merlani lightly. "This is your Reese, I take it, Merlakka?"

"She isn't *mine*, but yes." Merlani looks up from where they've had their eyes hidden against her vest.

"She's sparky, yes? I like it—reminds me of your dad." She offers Reese a handshake, still keeping her other arm wrapped around their shoulders as she shifts seamlessly back to standard to introduce herself. "Ranger Captain Taimri Hämäläinen; nice to meet you, Miss Vasquez. Thanks for keeping an eye on my little outlaw here."

Reese accepts the handshake and raises a perplexed eyebrow in Merlani's direction.

Merlani finally finds their smile again. "My *mother*, Reese. I told you about her."

"Ah! That's why the name's familiar!" Reese nods and then asks, "So, how much trouble are they really in, ma'am?"

Äiti looks at her closely for a moment before answering. "Enough trouble that I need to take them back with me in the morning. Not enough for *you* to need to spirit them off into the night a second time."

"Good to know. What time are we leaving?"

"Teresa," Merlani starts to say, "you don't have to—"

"—I'm going to, though." Reese tilts her head and looks back to their mother. "If it's okay with the Ranger, that is? I'm not letting my best friend get put on trial or whatever without me there to back them up."

Äiti chuckles and gives her a small nod. "All right, then. I'm planning on just after breakfast. Sleep in and I'm liable to leave you behind, yes?"

"Noted. Thank you." Reese gestures towards the door. "Are you two going to come in for dinner?"

Merlani nods. "Go ahead, we'll join you in a bit." For the moment, they're not quite ready to leave the swing. It's been a long time since they've seen their äiti, and if she's not going to be angry with them about what they've done, then they don't want to leave the reassuring warmth of her just yet.

Äiti makes a little wave towards the house with her free hand. "Yes, go on, I need to interrogate my little outlaw a bit longer before I send them in to wash up."

"Okay, then. See you in a bit." Reese gives them a nod and then goes into the house.

Once she's gone, Merlani looks back up to their äiti. "You're not *actually* interrogating me again, right?" they ask, shifting back contentedly into the language she'd taught them and their littermates as kittens.

"You know I am, Merlakka!" Äiti smiles broadly at them. "I haven't seen my favorite kitten in *ages*—of course I'm going to have all sorts of questions for them about the things in their life I've been missing. I was going to track you down for your break from classes anyway, yes?"

Merlani smiles and hugs her with all four arms now. Their äiti has always been one of their favorite humans— their first real memory, even, is of waking up warm and safe snuggled in the inner pocket of her vest and being fascinated by the shiny silver Ranger's badge she wears.

If Äiti still loves them after what they've done, then there's hope for things to work out after all.

★

A WEEK OF SITTING AND LISTENING TO PEOPLE talking about what they've done and having to tell their side of things over and over again culminates in Merlani sitting on the dusky orange couch in their Uncle Julian's office for more than an hour as they wait to be told what's going to happen to them.

It's the first time since they returned to the Academy that they've been actually alone, too—although only because they *forced* Reese to go back to her apartment and sleep. She's been on the edge of one of her infamous caffeine-and-sugar-and-lack-of-sleep crashes all morning, after all. Merlani knows her well enough by now to recognize when she's hit the point of no return on one of those.

Even so, sitting here on the couch staring at the bright red fish swimming in the tank behind their uncle's desk, they dearly wish their best friend *was* here, even in that half-sleeping dragon state of hers. They'd be willing to risk Reese's fight-the-thing-that-woke-her reflex, too, if it meant not sitting alone and cold like this while they wait for their parents and instructors to finish this final discussion with the Academy Administration.

Merlani has no idea what to expect now. Outside of all the meetings, their mother and Aunt Penny are the only authority figures who've spoken to them at all in *days*—everyone else has been too busy dealing with the situation, even Uncle Julian and Entile Wyndi. Their parent's littermate, too, only talked to them long enough to hug them and say they were in trouble for disappearing before they'd had to go back into their meetings with the Administration and Cadet Lewis' family.

Merlani knows they probably *deserve* to be avoided. What they've done goes against both the nature and culture of their species. Right now, they'll be surprised if any Florivan outside their family ever talks to them again.

The door slides open. Uncle Julian walks in and nods when he sees them. He's alone.

Merlani has no idea whether that's a good sign or not.

"Glad to see you're still here, Little Ocean."

"I promised my mother I wouldn't disappear again, sir." Merlani's tail swishes in embarrassment.

"Good. And your Miss Vasquez is...?" He glances around the room as if expecting Reese to jump out from behind his desk or something.

"I sent her home because she needs to sleep, sir."

"Ah. It *has* been a long week, hasn't it?" Uncle Julian pauses to pull the chair over from in front of his desk to face Merlani instead.

Merlani doesn't know what else to do than just sit there on the couch straightening the fluff on the end of their tail and wait for him to speak again.

"So, Little Ocean. I don't think I have to tell you that this is something of an unprecedented situation?"

"...No, sir, that's been made quite clear."

"I'm sure. And you're aware that we have to make at least *some* gesture towards a punishment so that this doesn't all come out badly when people hear of it?"

"I'm aware that I deserve to face the consequences for what I've done, sir."

Uncle Julian raises an eyebrow momentarily, and then nods. "Well, we've finally come to an agreement with the Administration."

Merlani sits up a little straighter, holding all four hands tightly interlaced now so he won't be able to see them fidget.

Their uncle steeples his own fingers together and gestures lightly at them with the paired index fingers as he talks. "The short version goes like this: We're *not* going to expel you or transfer you to one of the other Academies— no matter how much Assistant Chancellor Lewis has been demanding we do that—although there are some *conditions* we've had to put on that to get the rest of the Administration to agree to let us keep you. You'll also be sending Cadet Lewis a formal apology letter by the end of this week—*and* writing a statement explaining yourself for us to have on hand for the rest of the department and anyone else who needs it."

"...Yes, sir." Merlani nods slowly, relieved to some extent but wondering if *anything* they could possibly write would actually improve matters. "And the conditions?"

"Well, we all know that you won't be making your compact with either of the Maltby twins even if you go through rotations with them, and I wasn't able to argue to my way into bringing in any of my Nav cadet alternates to work with you instead like we'd talked about. The Administration isn't willing to 'risk' having another 'incident' and losing more of their 'highly qualified candidates' because of you." Uncle Julian pointedly makes air quotation gestures as he says this and rolls his eyes.

"What does that mean, then, sir?" Merlani asks, doing their best to keep their tail from twitching nervously.

"Short version: I won't have any new Nav cadets coming in before we run trials at the end of next term. To that end, you're to be *suspended* from Nav/Quan outright... with the understanding that you will *remain* suspended only until I manage to find a training partner who will be willing to 'take a chance on you' for a full school year. You'll be allowed to continue the rest of your course of studies for your secondary in the meantime."

"That's... generous, sir." Merlani can't help their ears drooping to hear this, even if it's better news than they ever expected.

"I'm not done, Little Ocean." Uncle Julian pauses for a moment, likely to make sure they're listening. Merlani swivels their ears to focus entirely on his voice. "As far as your units over in Sec/Tac... Penny made a strong case for allowing you to remain there on a probationary status—she seems to think you require remedial lessons in controlling yourself and your abilities, and I trust her judgment. She's taken responsibility for keeping you out of trouble. Until you're reinstated in our program, you report to *her*. And when you *are* reinstated, it'll be subject to her approval as well. As far as the Administration is concerned, you're *her* personal project now."

"...Yes, sir."

"As for whether you'll be allowed to continue participating with her team... that's up to Penny, although she's assured the Administration she won't be letting you do anything of the sort until you've earned her trust that you won't do something like this again. In any case, you *won't* be allowed to compete alongside them until you've been reinstated. Do you understand all of that, Little Ocean?"

"Yes, sir." Merlani hadn't thought they'd be allowed to continue with any of their martial arts classes at all. It's a complete surprise, somehow, that Aunt Penny has been willing to take a chance on them.

"Additionally: Since you seem to have acquired a knack for disappearing and going out of contact, you'll be required to keep Penny informed of your whereabouts at all times, particularly if you have occasion to leave the city. That's more for *your* protection than anything else, mind you—and the peace of mind of all of us who are responsible for you."

Merlani nods. Mentally, they note that it could be far worse than this—Äiti had said something or other as a joke recently regarding fitting them with a set of tracking bracelets. At least, they *hope* that was a joke.

"As far as your housing situation... we spoke to your housemates during the hearings. As much as Cadet Condrey and the Maltby twins have made it clear they'd prefer to have *you* back if they had a choice in the matter, Assistant Chancellor Lewis insisted that you be removed from Academy Accommodation altogether because of this incident. Unfortunately, we couldn't find a way around that."

"I'm... not surprised you couldn't." Merlani's impression of Cadet Lewis' mother during the hearings was that she was a rather intense woman who was just as protective of her offspring as their own family is of them—but with a vindictive streak a light-year wide.

"Don't worry, Little Ocean, we're not going to leave you homeless." Uncle Julian smiles reassuringly. "You have the choice between whether you're going to move back in with us or take Penny's spare room. She lives closer to campus than we do, so that might be a better option for you to keep a bit of your independence and routine. Either way, your family has room for you."

Merlani hesitates. "If Aunt Penny's going to be my guardian, it might be easier to stay with her—if she's really okay with that?"

"She is." He rubs at his beard thoughtfully with one hand. "Might keep her from following through with that threat to show the Assistant Chancellor what it looks like when a trained martial artist actually *wants* to hurt someone, too."

"...She didn't *really* threaten Cadet Lewis' mother, did she?"

"No, luckily she said that quietly enough that Wyndi was the only person who heard it." He chuckles. "Anyway. From what I understand, Penny's excited about the prospect of having you stay with her for a while... and that's about the long and short of it. Any questions?"

"...No, sir, not really." Merlani holds back a sigh. "This is all... very kind, really. Far kinder than I probably deserve."

Uncle Julian's eyes soften. "Do you want a hug, kiddo? I'm done with the official stuff—and I've been meaning to give you one ever since your mother brought you back."

Merlani silently nods.

He stands, plops over onto the couch beside them, and opens his arms. Merlani had forgotten just how warm and comforting their uncle's hugs can be. They cling to him for a long time, just trying to let that warmth re-center them so they can face whatever comes next.

"Now, kitten." Uncle Julian wipes an errant tear from Merlani's third eye and lightly pats them on the head. "Listen to me, this is all going to blow over eventually."

"...You think so?"

"It always does." He smiles at them. "Look, it may be unprecedented for me to have to have a conversation like this with a *Florivan*, but really, Little Ocean? You wouldn't *believe* the number of times I've had to discipline my human cadets for getting into fights—especially during the party season around spring finals. For that matter, well..." their uncle pauses and chuckles lightly to himself, stroking his beard thoughtfully again. "...Let's just say that

Penny's giving you the same sort of chance she and the girls gave *me* a long time ago and leave it at that."

"Sir?" Merlani tilts their head slightly to one side. They've heard a lot of Aunt Penny's stories about what her squadron got up to during the War, but they have no idea what their uncle is talking about this time.

Uncle Julian grins. "Remind me once you're reinstated and I'll tell you the story."

"Yes, sir."

"So. Think you can live with those consequences, Little Ocean?"

"...Yes, sir. I think so."

"Good." Uncle Julian gestures toward the door. "You're free to go now, whenever you're ready. Your mother has custody of you for the rest of her stay with us, but she and Penny are both waiting for you outside."

Merlani reluctantly extracts themself from the hug and stands. They take a hesitant step towards the door before turning back to the kind, warm man on the couch. "Uncle Julian... may I ask why—"

"—Why *I'm* the one debriefing you instead of either of them or Wyndi?"

"...Yes. That."

"Pretty simple, really." Uncle Julian stands too, moving the chair he'd started out sitting in back to its usual place by his desk. "Until you walk through that door, you're still under Nav/Quan's jurisdiction... and Wyndi and River are in a meeting over the relays right now with a few of the Elders explaining the decisions we've made."

Merlani's tail and ears droop again at that. They knew Dad was involved in the discussions, and they assumed that Elder Celadon was being consulted as well, but they never expected that anyone *else* would be brought in—not that that's much of a surprise, in hindsight. The entire scattered membership of the Florivan Council of Elders is probably going to be informed about their mistakes before all of this is over.

"Oh."

"Don't worry, Little Ocean." Uncle Julian comes over and gives them an encouraging pat on the shoulder. "No one's going to disown you over this."

"I hope not." Merlani isn't entirely sure they believe him.

"Now, go on before your mother and Penny come in looking for you." Uncle Julian makes a little shooing motion towards the door. "I have paperwork to fill out."

"Yes, sir."

And with that, Merlani steps through the door, unsure at all what their future could hold.

Part 3: The Meddling of Navigators in the Course of Fate

A MONTH OR SO BEFORE THE END OF THEIR SECOND year as a student at the Sol Central Space Service Academy, Merlani finds themself not on Earth, but in the VIP section of arena-side seating at the newly-constructed *Spirit* Memorial Athletics Center at the domed city of Elysium Mons on Mars.

The *Spirit* Center is massive, with a translucent dome of its own for a ceiling over the main arena and facilities for seemingly every variety of competitive sport humans have come up with. Today, the main arena is set up to host the first day of the *Spirit* Center's inaugural event: the Quinquennial Intra-System Martial Arts Competition and Exhibition. The team Aunt Penny leads at the Academy has earned the honor of an invitation to participate, and even though Merlani isn't allowed to compete with their teammates, they're still thrilled to have gotten to come along.

"Comfy, kiddo?" Aunt Penny asks, hopping over the low railing separating their reserved area from the walkway at the base of the grandstands to take her seat beside Merlani.

"I am." Merlani's tail swishes happily. "Is everyone set for their first events?"

"I'd think so." She makes a vague gesture out at the group of young humans preparing to perform for the audience. They're all primary school aged from what Merlani can tell, and wearing rusty red tops edged in gold and black trousers. "Tàijíquán preliminaries for our division start once the Martian Children's Tai Chi Association is done with their group presentation." Aunt Penny coos softly. "They're just *adorable*, aren't they?"

"They're a cute collection of human kittens," Merlani agrees. "Which ones are Lavine's little sibs?"

"Ah, the two on the end there." Aunt Penny gestures to a pair of girls near the edge of the group, one about a head taller than the other. "And their mum's the one leading the cuties."

Merlani nods. "I can see the resemblance. Is that who the extra seats here are reserved for?" They wave their tail towards the two empty chairs on the other side of them.

"Oh, no, Claudia's going to be sitting with her students." Aunt Penny laughs. "*Our* guests are just running a touch late, that's all."

"Do I get to know who they are?" Merlani asks, raising their third eyebrow, "Or are you trying to be sneaky again?"

"Who, me? *Sneaky*?" Aunt Penny grins at them. "When am *I* ever the sneaky one in the family?"

Merlani rolls all three eyes at their aunt. "I never said you were *good* at being sneaky, Aunt Penny."

"Cheeky kitten," Aunt Penny teases back. "Maybe I'm just so good that you only *think* I'm bad at being sneaky."

"Or," says a familiarly gruff man's voice from behind the two of them, clearly holding back a laugh, "maybe it's just that the *rest* of our odd collection of family is better at being sneaky than you are, Penny."

"Uncle Rudy!" Merlani bounces up from their seat to give the old Navigator a hug over the railing. "What are *you* doing here?"

"Heya, kiddo." Their uncle affectionately ruffles their hair with one of his exceptionally warm ruddy-pale hands, tossing his long, graying golden-brown braid back over his shoulder with the other before he properly lifts them up and hugs them back. "Miss us?"

Merlani nods. "Always." They look over their uncle's shoulder and wave to the equally welcome sight of his counterpart standing behind him. "Hello, Elder Celadon."

"Hello, Little Ocean!" Ai-Nida Celadon waves back, stifling a giggle. They're dressed up in their formal Elder's robes, all in layers of translucent amber silks with a matching beaded headdress covering the complex silver braided hair buns behind their pale blue-green ears. They look up at Merlani affectionately through the shaded lens over their third eye; the lower pair are hidden under a fully opaque band of black lensing that perches over their nose and is secured to a thin silver harness that circles their head and crosses over the top of it behind their ears and under their headdress. As usual, they're leaning on their ornately-carved wooden cane with their lower two hands. "Do I get a hug too, once my Navigator's done with you?"

"Of course!" Merlani taps their uncle on the shoulder. "You can put me down now."

Uncle Rudy laughs, making a point of setting them on the aisle side of the railing. "Fine, fine, here you go, Dons, it's your turn for hugs."

"Thank you, Elias." His counterpart wraps all four of their arms around Merlani. "It's good to see you, Merlani-kitten," they whisper, quietly enough that no one else around them could hear the breach in 'formal public space' etiquette.

"It's good to see you too, Ai-Nida Celadon," Merlani whispers back.

"I hate to break up the adorable family reunion," says Aunt Penny, "but the performance is about to start. Come sit down, will you? It's a bit early in the week for me to get in trouble for disrupting things."

Ai-Nida Celadon laughs, letting go of Merlani but taking one of their hands. "Okay, Penny, I *promise* we'll be good and not embarrass you. Little Ocean, dear, help me find my seat?"

"Yes, Elder Celadon." Merlani guides them through the small gate in the railing that their uncle is holding open. "There's three steps down here," they say, "and then it's all level to the chairs after that."

"Thank you, kitten." With Merlani's assistance, Ai-Nida Celadon carefully makes their way down the steps and over to the seat beside Aunt Penny. They're not entirely blind in their third eye, but outside of the familiar setting of *Starbright's* corridors and in a crowded and brightly-lit place like the arena, they tend to rely on Uncle Rudy or one of their other family members to help them get around without incident.

Merlani takes the seat beside their household's Elder with their uncle on their other side. As usual, he casually drapes his arm around Merlani's chair and lets them scoot in close to soak up a bit of his warmth. Uncle Rudy's always good at telling when the various Florivans in his life are getting chilly—it's not *too* cold in the arena for Merlani just yet, but they appreciate the gesture all the same.

"So, Penny," Ai-Nida Celadon asks, flicking up the shielding lens over their third eye briefly and squinting out at the arena before putting it back down, "what are we watching?"

"Adorable little martians showing off their Tai Chi sequences," Aunt Penny replies, similarly draping her arm around Ai-Nida Celadon's chair. "And then my kiddos Lavine and Martins will be performing in a bit in the singles and doubles routines—oh, and as part of the taijishan and taijijian competitions tomorrow!"

"I can hear it in your voice how proud you are of them, Penny." Ai-Nida Celadon gives her arm a gentle pat.

"Oh, I *am*—and I'll tell you all about them once there's a break." She giggles softly and holds a finger up to her lips as the performance accompanying music begins to fill the air of the arena. "This isn't a hoverpolo match, after all... the judges get a bit testy with people cheering and interrupting."

"Noted," Ai-Nida Celadon whispers with an amused flick of their ears.

Merlani makes themself comfortable sitting snuggled up under their uncle's arm. The only thing that could *possibly* be better than being here to watch their teammates perform is to be sitting here with members of their family whom they haven't seen in ages.

On the last day of the competition, during the break before the final round of championship matches and exhibition performances, Merlani receives yet another surprise from their aunt—this time under the pretense of going with her to give her "encouragement speech" of the evening to their teammates who will be competing.

"All right!" says Aunt Penny once she's decided that the team's three seniors look suitably encouraged, "go on out there and do your best, kiddos." She claps her hands together and heads for the door. When Merlani moves to follow her, she laughs and turns them around, nudging them back towards Reese, Kouassi, and da Silva. "Oh, no, Little Ocean, you're going the wrong way. Vasquez has your things for you—she'll fill you in, since da Silva here has to scamper on out and be ready for the capoeira finals."

"Ma'am?" Merlani asks, but to no avail. Their aunt has already disappeared from the changing room altogether, as has da Silva. They turn back to Reese, more confused than curious.

Reese laughs. "You didn't *really* think we'd bring you all the way here and not find a loophole so we could show you off to everyone, did you?" She pulls a neatly-folded bundle of soft white cloth and a familiar black cloth belt out of her locker and holds it out to Merlani. "Here, go ahead and get changed. You're going to be my sparring partner for my technique exhibition match."

Merlani takes their judogi and belt, tilting their head curiously at their best friend now. "But I thought you and Kouassi were each other's partners for that."

"We can be, if you're not up for it," says Kouassi, tugging on the red slipper-socks he always wears when he's not out on the mat to keep his feet warm. He pauses to grin at Merlani. "I was looking forward to having you be *my* sparring partner too, though, Barker."

Merlani looks at both of their friends, not certain what to think about this.

Reese flashes them an encouraging grin as well. "Well, we've been training against you all this time… and if you're the one we're sparring with, we *really* get to show off."

Kouassi nods. "The Colonel already okayed it with the judges so you can be a 'demonstration assistant' instead of a competitor—just don't go holding back on us too much."

Merlani stifles a laugh. Their tail swishes with unexpected joy. "I wouldn't dream of it, Kouassi."

As they slip into one of the changing alcoves and pull the privacy curtain, Merlani can't help giggling with the nervous excitement that's now washing over them. They certainly weren't expecting to be allowed to participate at all today—especially not with their friends in the finals, of all things—but this is an experience they know they'll never forget.

Once all of the day's events are over and the closing awards ceremony is done, Merlani makes their way back over to the VIP seats where their family is waiting. They'd sat with their teammates for the finals and all of the ceremonies, since they were officially a participating member of the team rather than a spectator. Now, the thrill of it all is still putting a bounce in their step and a happy swish in their tail as they scamper across the arena.

Aunt Penny, of course, is off taking photos with her newly-named champions, but Uncle Rudy and Ai-Nida Celadon are there waiting for them. Their uncle, true to form, pulls Merlani up into a bear hug when they get there.

"Congratulations, kid." Uncle Rudy gives them a gentle squeeze before setting them down and ruffling their ears affectionately. "You put on a good show out there."

"Thanks, Uncle Rudy." Merlani beams, then makes an appropriate little bow of gratitude to him since they're still dressed in their judogi. He returns it with a warm chuckle.

"You did us proud, Little Ocean," says Ai-Nida Celadon, similarly enveloping them in a warm four-armed hug. "I'm glad you were allowed to participate in the end."

"Thank you, Elder Celadon." Merlani's tail continues waving happily. "I'm glad I had the opportunity."

"We took plenty of pictures to send to the rest of the family," Uncle Rudy tells them. "I'll bet that father of yours will be bloody *thrilled* when he sees them."

Merlani hesitates. "Are you sending them to Entile River too?"

"Already did!" Their uncle grins. "All of the family Rangers demanded photos when we told them we'd be here to see you and your friends competing."

"Ah." Merlani feels themself blushing slightly.

"Don't worry, kitten." Ai-Nida Celadon gives them a reassuring pat on the head. "Your performance was wonderful and no one is going to be upset that I'm still encouraging you to participate in things you enjoy." They laugh brightly. "And if they are, they all know that's something to take up with *me*, not you."

Uncle Rudy gives his counterpart a knowing nudge on the shoulder. "As if *anyone* bothers arguing with your decisions anymore, Dons."

"My reputation *does* have its perks, yes." Ai-Nida Celadon grins at him before turning back to Merlani. "Your Navigator performed admirably as well," they say. "I look forward to having an opportunity to congratulate her personally."

"What? Oh! No, I—" Merlani startles when they realize who their household's Elder is talking about. "Reese isn't my—she's a tactical pilot and all that, Elder Celadon, not a Navigator."

"Hmm. I suppose I was mistaken, then." Ai-Nida Celadon lifts the lens from in front of their third eye to look at Merlani more closely. "I could have *sworn* Jade said you'd made your compact with her."

"Why do people keep thinking that?" Merlani puts both upper hands over their face to hide their embarrassment now. "Even Entile Jade now? Reese is my *best friend*, that's all."

"Well, kid," says Uncle Rudy, chuckling, "you'd hardly be the *first* in the family to—"

Said best friend chooses this moment to manifest out of the crowd and interrupt before he can finish whatever teasing statement he was about to make. Merlani couldn't be more grateful for her good timing.

"—Cinny! There you are!" Reese is still wearing her blue competition judogi and her newly-awarded champion's ribbons. She looks brightly at Merlani's uncle and his counterpart and offers them a crisp salute. "Hello again, sirs! Did you enjoy the show?"

"We did, Miss Teresa!" Ai-Nida Celadon flips their upper shielding lens back down, smiling broadly at Reese. "You performed admirably. Congratulations."

Uncle Rudy nods in agreement. "If you fly bloody *half* as well as you spar, Vasquez, the Fleet's going to snap you up in a heartbeat."

"Thank you, sirs. That means a lot, coming from you." Reese is all beaming grins and leftover adrenaline.

She still doesn't seem to have quite gotten over her awed awkwardness around the heads of Merlani's family. They told her whose household they belonged to ages ago, of course—but knowing that one's best friend is related to and apprenticed under people one has written papers about and actually meeting those people are very different things for a human. Merlani themself has never thought of the two of them as "war heroes" or "Fleet legends," even if they are. In their eyes, the pair are simply their Nida's grumpy line-adopted brother and the Elder who's the closest thing to a grandparent they and their littermates have ever known.

After a few moments, Reese shakes her head a little and turns back to Merlani. "The Colonel sent me to find you, since you weren't in the changing rooms."

Merlani tries their best to hold in a small eye-roll. "I'm hardly going to run off on an unfamiliar planet, Reese, she knows that..."

"Not without *me*, at least!" Reese laughs. "But no, she wanted me to let you know she's releasing you to me and Toby for the night to celebrate with the rest of the team—Lavine's family is taking us all to that legendary all-night breakfast place that they kept talking about on the journey here, since this is their hometown and all."

Lavine and Aunt Penny have had a running argument of sorts ever since the team left Earth over which of the local points of interest the team should visit in their free time. It's been a source of great amusement for as long as anyone on the team can remember, of course, how much stronger both of their martian accents become when those arguments take off—almost to the point where no one but Merlani and Martins can understand a word of what they're saying. It's not an infrequent occurrence, too, since Aunt Penny is from one of the other domed cities that has a sports rivalry of sorts with Lavine's hometown. Despite all of the playful arguments, though, on the journey here the two of them had agreed on precisely one thing: Carter's Waffles and Karaoke. Apparently *that* of all things is something no martian can imagine a visit to their planet being complete without experiencing.

"She's not celebrating with us, then?" Merlani twitches their ears curiously.

"Apparently she has a prior engagement with old friends she owes a round of 'sunblock-flavored mock-tails' or something?" Reese shrugs. "That's what she told me, anyway."

Uncle Rudy laughs outright, shaking his head.

"That would be us, Miss Teresa," Ai-Nida Celadon says, giving the man a bit of a knowing nudge and silencing his laughter.

"Sir?" Merlani will never cease to be amused by the wide-eyed look Reese gets when someone manages to actually startle her.

"Penny's never appreciated the wonders of a well-made piña colada even *with* the rum," the old Navigator supplies, stifling another chuckle, "but we all have our traditions to uphold."

"That we do." Ai-Nida Celadon now nudges Merlani towards Reese with two hands. "Go on, kittens, have fun! We'll keep Penny out of trouble tonight—just make sure you're all at the City Transportation Hub on time tomorrow. *Starbright's* sending a shuttle to collect all of us directly."

"*Starbright* is picking us up?" Merlani's tail swishes with excitement again. "Why didn't you tell me earlier?"

"You know us, Little Ocean." Ai-Nida Celadon grins at them. "We like our sneaky little secrets—now shoo, your friends are probably looking for the two of you."

"Yes, Elder Celadon." Merlani makes their deepest, most formal bow, then takes Reese by the hand and hops back over the railing to head toward the changing rooms.

As the two of them are scampering away, Merlani hears their uncle laughing again.

"So, by 'keeping Penny out of trouble'... you mean I'll keep *both* of you from getting into trouble or accidentally starting any bloody bar brawls tonight?"

"That's your job, Navigator, isn't it?"

More laughter. "That it is, Dons, that it is."

★

THE STARSHIP LSS *STARBRIGHT'S* MAIN DINING area is, as usual, practically deserted during the ship's designated night period. Most of her crew and passengers are either asleep or on duty elsewhere on the ship. From the end of dinner service to the beginning of breakfast for the first daytime watch, very few people have any reason to be in the mess.

On the night *Starbright* leaves Mars' orbit bound for Earth, only three people are in the room at all. One of them is an Academy cadet in loose athletic clothing, with one red and one ivory departmental stripe around each cuff of the uniform jacket that's draped over her shoulders.

One of the ship's senior officers has just finished eating his regular midnight shift-break sandwich and gone to top off the cooling coffee in his mostly-empty cup when he happens to look over and see the cadet. The tall, ruddy-pale man's long graying golden-brown braid swishes behind him as he changes directions to approach her.

"Well, now, kid! I thought all of you young folks would have turned in by now."

The dark-haired cadet looks up from the empty mug she's been staring into for the last twenty minutes and at the officer who's just walked over to her table. She doesn't say anything, just blinks a couple of times and rubs at her eyes briefly.

"Can't sleep, then?" The officer takes a sip from his coffee and sits down opposite her with his back to the wall.

"No, sir."

"Strange disrupting you? Or something else?"

"...Mostly other things," the cadet admits with a vague gesture of one hand, "but the freaky Quantum Space Transit dreams didn't help."

"Ah. Sounds familiar. Used to give me weird nightmares too, back in the day—still does, on occasion." The officer takes another sip. "You planning to stay up for the whole second jump cycle, I take it?"

"I suppose so. Worked well enough on the way out..."

"All right, then." He gestures at the cadet's empty mug. "How do you take your coffee, kid?"

"Sir?" The cadet looks down, then back at the officer. "Oh. Black, double-strong, three or four spoons of sugar. Why?"

"Of *course* you'd be another bloody hummingbird." The officer chuckles and stands, picking up her mug when he does. "Come on, then. If you're going to be awake, you might as well make yourself *useful*."

"Sir?"

"I'm conscripting you as my assistant. First stop: refilling coffee cups to take up to Nav with us."

"Yes, sir!" The cadet brightens and hops up from her chair to follow him.

Once coffee has been acquired, the officer leads the cadet up to a little cubbyhole of a compartment just off the ship's command bridge. He gestures to a small round swivel stool next to the mobile chair in the center of all of the holoscreen displays and control panel counters.

"Welcome to the Nav closet, kid. That's your spot. Your main job is going to be paying attention to everything that happens in here and fetching coffee when I tell you. If that sounds too boring, you might as well leave now."

"No, sir," says the cadet, brightening. "It doesn't sound boring at all—I've *always* wanted to see how this works."

"Good. Let's see if you can keep up." The officer tosses a headset to her that matches the one he's already pulled on himself. "Here, put this on."

"Yes, sir." The cadet rearranges her hair so it won't be in the way and then dons the headset. It's composed of a simple padded headband that goes across from one ear to the other, with a single headphone over the left ear and a small microphone bar on the right.

The officer reaches over and flips the cadet's microphone bar up for her before pressing a button on the side that starts up a bit of a white noise hum in her ear.

"So! This is synced up with mine. You won't be needing it, but that third little button on the side switches it between receive-only and active; second one cycles through the channels, and the microphone only switches on when it's flipped down. You're keeping it how I have it set now unless I tell you otherwise, got it?"

"Yes, sir."

"Good. Now…" The officer turns the chair towards the display closest to her perch and pulls up a checklist. "Dons'll call in when everything's ready to start back up again down in the Drive Bay, but before anything happens, *I* have to go through *this*."

"What is it, sir?" The cadet tilts her head curiously at the display.

"It's a long bloody *mess* of system checks and safety protocols, and I *swear* it gets longer every time we move to a new ship." The officer pulls out a stylus and hands it to her. "You read them off, and then tap the check when I confirm it. Got it?"

"Yes, sir."

"Good. Let's get this show on the road."

Twenty minutes later, the cadet is finally reaching the end of the checklist.

"The last ones are… ship-wide Nav override confirmation and Nav/Quan com checks?"

"Right. Those we wait a moment on, Dons should be calling up any—"

As if they'd heard him say this, a wind-chime-toned Florivan voice surrounded by electronic interference crackles into the space where the white noise hum has been in the Cadet's headset. "*—Final Drive Bay checks confirmed! You ready up there with some stars for me, Elias?*"

The officer chuckles. "Ready as always, Dons. Half a sec, I'll get that static cleared out." He reaches over without even looking and does something with the interface on the console beside him that almost immediately removes the interference and returns the subtle hum on the headset. "Try it now, that should have done it."

"*I think it did,*" says the voice over the headset, now clear. "*Check on Primary Nav/Quan com link?*"

"Confirmed," says the officer. "How's our Secondary com link?"

"*Secondary's coming through clear,*" a second, younger Florivan voice replies. The cadet smiles when she hears them.

"Confirmed, Cinny." The officer checks the backup com links the same way and then nods to the cadet. "All com checks confirmed. Stand by, you two, we'll be ready to go in a bit."

The cadet taps the check box next to that item on the list.

The officer whirls his chair over to one of the other display monitors and flips a few switches on the console below it before tapping on one of the buttons on the side of his headset.

"Bridge, this is Nav/Quan calling in. All our systems show green, we're ready to engage Nav overrides on your mark and begin our second Quantum Space Transit cycle."

"*We hear you, Lt. Commander Rudolph.*" The no-nonsense feminine voice on the main intercom now is human; it belongs to Starbright's first officer. "*Safety protocols have confirmed, all sections report in clear for continuing Quantum Space transit. Engage Nav overrides and get us underway."*

"Yes ma'am." The officer reaches over and flips a few more switches. "Nav overrides are in place. Ready to begin jump cycle in ten."

"You have the ship, Nav."

The officer gestures to the cadet to complete her checklist and then goes back to his com link to the two Quantum Space Drive Engineers. "All right, we're ready to go in for the first jump. Engage Drive when you're ready, Dons."

"Engaging Drive and jumping to Strange in ten... nine... eight..."

When the older Florivan's voice reaches the end of the countdown, an almost imperceptible static charge seems to float over the whole ship for a few moments as the com link falls dead silent. The officer flips up the microphone on his headset and then turns to the cadet, gesturing for her to hand him his coffee cup.

She does so, tilting her head to one side curiously. If she has a question in mind, she doesn't ask it.

"And now," says the officer, taking a long sip from his coffee, "we wait."

"Sir?"

"First rule of Nav, kid: Never interrupt at the start or end of jumps. We just wait for them to call up that they're ready for landmarks."

"How long does that take?"

"Oh... depends on the jump, really. Inside a star system always takes longer, seems like—should be something like fifteen, maybe twenty minutes on average—but I've seen

Dons and Jade pull the whole bloody process off in two a few times, back in the day."

The cadet takes a sip from her own coffee. "Was that when you served on Admiral Marvin's flagship, sir?"

The officer nods solemnly. "That was a long time ago, kid."

"I've studied most of the battles, sir."

"Oh, have you, now?" The officer gestures with his coffee cup and raises an eyebrow. "Some unit on war history and tactics or something?"

The cadet is the one to nod this time. "I'm aiming for Fleet Captain someday, sir. Your counterpart's exploits—and yours, too, sir—are sort of required reading for deep-space combat theory. I have a paper due on the final battle of the Luyten-Procyon corridor when we get back to Earth, actually... I wasn't expecting to meet any of the people who *developed* the tactics I'm studying, you know?"

The officer halfway chuckles at that.

The cadet seems to be trying to will herself not to blush.

"That explains why you've been so awkward since Cinny introduced us, at least."

"...I suppose it does, sir."

"Well, no need to keep that up—Dons and I are only mortal, same as you. If what we did made any bloody difference in the end, that's one thing... but don't go putting us up on pedestals for having done any of it."

"Yes, sir." The cadet seems more at ease now, if also a bit deflated.

"Besides," the officer says with a wry smile, "Penny's probably told you all sorts of stories about us that those bloody textbooks leave out, hasn't she?"

The cadet hesitates and takes another sip of her coffee. "She might have? The Colonel talks a lot about her Fleet days, but she doesn't always use names."

"I'd be the hotheaded mechanic who kept her and the rest of the Musketeers flying no matter how many times they brought me back piles of parts instead of darters, if that jogs your memory."

The cadet manages not to choke on her drink. "Really, sir?" Her eyes widen.

"Really." The officer laughs for a moment, then grows quieter as he absently twists the worn gold band on his left ring finger with his thumb. "Lucky for me, most of the history texts you kids study pick up my name *after* Dons and I inherited each other, so I get to keep a bit of my bloody *privacy* from folks who aren't connected to the family." He takes a long sip from the coffee he's holding in the other hand before setting it back down. "So," he asks, turning his eyes back to the displays surrounding them where all of his various sets of star charts and readouts are now popping up, "Fleet command track, then?"

The cadet nods, regaining her composure a bit. "Yes, sir—it's what I've been aiming for since I got my letters. I'd thought about trying for Nav certification once I got to the Academy, too, but I didn't meet the minimums to even do trials."

"Oh? Why not?"

"My Tech and Engineering aptitude scores were 'unsatisfactory' according to the Academy criteria. The

Administration doesn't take anything lower than T/E 9 for the Astral Navigation program, and…" The cadet takes on a slightly embarrassed posture, hesitating for a moment before she shrugs and continues, "well, according to the Academy Registrars, 8.8 doesn't hit close enough."

An amused look crosses the officer's face. He doesn't laugh this time, but he certainly looks like he wants to—although not necessarily at the cadet. "Well. That's Academy Administration for you. Bloody bean-counters… how are you with star charts, though?"

"I can read them, sir, if that's what you mean."

"Good. That's better than me when I started, believe it or not." The officer gestures to each of the screens surrounding them in turn. "Now, pay attention: System chart is on screen one, recorded flight paths of all the other nearby vessels with relay transponders is screen two, our planned course from the Bridge is screen three, and twenty-light-year star position index chart is screen four. If you can keep all that in your head, you'll be able to follow along."

The cadet focuses her eyes on the charts. "It's a lot of information, sir."

"It is." The officer reaches over and pops up another smaller holoscreen out of the armrest of his chair. "*We* condense it down to landmarks; the jumpers do the rest." With a second small silver stylus he produces out of one of his pockets, the officer sets about tapping on one point after another on the various maps and charts spread out on the screens around him.

The cadet is silent, watching him and sipping slowly from her coffee. It's a while before she speaks up again. "May I ask a... well, probably a stupid question, sir?"

"Go ahead." The officer doesn't look away from his work.

"Why can't a computer compile all of this for you?"

The officer chuckles briefly. "One *could*, but not in a way that would suit Dons—or any other jumper, for that matter. They won't work with computers running the show. It's just not in their nature... and they can't hear artificial voices over the earpiece to begin with."

"Really? Why not?"

"Kid, I've been working with Dons for..." The officer pauses and then shakes his head. "Well, a *long* time now— known them a few years longer than that—and they have *yet* to give me a satisfactory answer to that one, so don't expect me to tell you everything." He chuckles. "Second rule of Nav, kid: in this business, you learn things when your jumper needs you to know them and not a bloody *second* earlier."

Before the cadet can respond, the headset speakers come to life once again. The older Florivan's voice comes across clearly, although with a distinct faraway sort of effect in their tone. "*We're ready for your landmarks, Elias—all's calm and quiet in the mists tonight.*"

The officer flips down his microphone. "Glad to hear it, Dons." He looks down to the list on his small screen. "Your Primal's Sol, and local origin point is 2A by 15 and 8."

"*Got it. And our directions?*"

"Max Forward's 5B by 134 and 8. Back's 29 by E and 0..." The officer goes on to read off hexadecimal coordinate points for the rest of the cardinal markers: Left, Right, Up, Down.

The cadet does her best to follow along and try to spot the points on the various maps. The local origin point matches the coordinates for the location in Normal space where the ship was sitting prior to the jump into Quantum Space. The rest, though, to anyone but a Navigator or their counterpart, would seem a painfully *arbitrary* mix of coordinates for planets and other ships—the Down point, for example, is far closer to being on a line towards the relative location of Venus, while Up seems to be referencing one of the ships on the proximity list.

The veiled dimension of Quantum Space might be the best shortcut around long-distance journeys between planets and star systems, but it's a shortcut that more than lives up to its Florivan name: Strange. The normal laws of physics and time don't completely apply there, enough so that humans can't safely withstand any kind of direct exposure to its miasmas for more than a few minutes. Madness, blindness, hallucinations, even death are among the known side effects of long-duration contact. That danger is the source of more than half of the items on the Navigator's checklist, all of which deal with ensuring that the ship's safety seals and viewport shutters are functioning properly to prevent miasma leaks while the team skips the vessel across space like a smooth stone on the surface of a lake.

Meanwhile, a ship's Florivan Quantum Space Drive Engineer spends their duty shifts down in the Drive Bay fully immersed in the Strange and somehow maneuvering the ship through it. Their species gave humanity the Drive and introduced them to the shortcut, after all—but *they* still have to be the ones running it.

"*All right, Elias, I've got your field of play sorted. What are you calling our destination point?*"

"2B by 17 and 8, if you think you two can handle pulling full-skips for the rest of the night. I have points to keep going with halves marked out if that's more up to the kid's speed."

"*I'm not that badly out of practice, Uncle Rudy!*" says the younger Florivan over the earpiece, only half protesting.

"*Full-skips will be fine, thank you,*" the older Florivan declares. "*I'll let you know when we're ready to come up for air.*"

"Roger on that, Dons." The silence returns to the headset speakers. The officer flips up his microphone and gestures for the cadet to hand him back his coffee.

"And now we wait again?"

"Got it in one, kid." He takes a long slow sip. "This part's where I have time to go through if I need to and make sure all of my charts are correct and there's no issues with any of the relays or transponders—should take around half an hour for them to get us to the jump-out point, give or take."

The cadet drinks some more of her own coffee. "And after that, we wait for them to jump us back to Normal space?"

"You catch on quick. Yes. Then we take ten minutes or so to let the ship even out and confirm the Bridge doesn't want any major course changes before we make the next jump."

"And then you just keep doing jumps until morning?"

"Yep." The officer is looking over his system chart now, still taking sips from his cup every now and then.

"I never realized Nav was so..."

"So what?"

"...*Calm*, sir, I guess?"

The officer chuckles. "Calm is good. Means nothing's going pear-shaped tonight. Exciting nights come in two flavors, kid: annoying and *dangerous*. Sometimes both. If you're smart, you learn to head that off before it happens."

"Ah."

"Nav isn't quite the glamorous thing people make it out to be, is it?"

"...Maybe not, sir." The cadet stifles a laugh. "At least, not if someone was the impatient sort. The rest of it is still neat."

"Neat's one word for it, I suppose." The officer smirks and hands his empty cup over to her.

"This is the part where I go refill the coffee?"

"It is indeed. Keep your headset on, I'll call for you if something interesting happens while you're gone."

The cadet finishes her own cup and stands. "Splash of milk, no sugar, right?"

"You're observant!" The old Navigator grins. "Good. There might be hope for you yet."

18

"GOOD MORNING!" MERLANI SLIDES INTO ONE of the free seats at the table in the middle of *Starbright's* mess where the rest of their teammates are already eating lunch. The only person they don't see is Reese, but they assume she's just stepped out of the room for some reason or another.

"It's *ship's noon*," Kouassi declares, only half-teasing. "What are you on about?"

"*Breakfast*, as far as I'm concerned." Merlani sets about sprinkling the raisins and cinnamon-sugar blend they'd picked up in the robo-automat service line out of the little white cup and onto the top of their oatmeal. "I was in the Drive Bay all night. 'Morning' is when the day starts, you know... regardless of what the ship's official time is."

Kouassi laughs. "Fair enough, Barker, fair enough."

"So you've been signed over to the Nav/Quan folks for the trip back to Earth, then?" Katz raises an eyebrow.

"Yes, thankfully." Merlani stirs the fruit and sweet-spice mixture into their bowl of tasty grain sludge. "It was just *unnatural* being a passenger while we were with *Tetrabrachium* for the flight out and having to sit out of all the jumps."

"You being rewarded for good behavior or something, then?" asks da Silva, gesturing at Merlani vaguely with his fork. "It's about time, if that's the case. I still say you shouldn't have had the book thrown at you—I mean, sooner or later *someone* was going to deck that guy. I would have been more than happy to do it myself, you know."

"Please don't remind me..." Merlani sighs, then twitches the mixed feelings out of their ears. "Anyway, as far as my getting a reprieve from my sentence? Eh... sort of?" They shrug. "I lived on this ship for nearly six years while I was Elder Celadon's apprentice—they were determined to have me back in the Drive Bay with them for this trip whether I'm technically *supposed* to be there or not."

"They're allowed to do that?" Kouassi raises an eyebrow. "I'd have thought your 'warden' would be required to object."

"Elder Celadon's been friends with the Colonel since before my Uncle Rudy became their Navigator." After a small bite of their oatmeal and a sip of tea, Merlani smirks and adds, "and they're an *Elder*... and the Fleet's Elder, at that. There aren't many people who are good at saying no to *them* in the first place."

"Sounds like we're not going to see you in the mornings at all, then," Martins comments, spearing one of the tomatoes remaining in her salad.

"Well, it's just Elder Celadon who's made an exception to my restrictions. I'll be free some on the days Cyan and Lt. Marshal are running jumps."

"Good," says da Silva, grinning. "Then you'll be around for practice?"

"I should be," Merlani tells him, "as long as I don't get called in for any other apprentice-type duties and Lt. Felix doesn't need me."

"Which one's Lt. Felix?" Lavine asks, looking up from the chips they've been stacking carefully into a tower on the side of their plate.

Merlani takes another bite of the oatmeal before answering. "He's *Starbright's* head geologist—and the mestre who got me into capoeira. I wouldn't be surprised if he shows up at practice sometime to meet all of you. He came down to watch a few of the rodas with us on one of the days of the competition, actually, but I haven't seen him yet since we've been aboard."

"Now, *there's* something for all of us to look forward to, da Silva," Kouassi teases, nudging his friend playfully, "seeing you go up against a geologist who's *not* on the Colonel's leash."

"Speaking of my leash!" says Aunt Penny, appearing seemingly out of nowhere at the head of the table. "I'm glad to see all of you bright-eyed and bushy-tailed today—especially you, Little Ocean. Rudy gave me a *stellar* report on how your first night back in your natural habitat went."

"I'm glad I met with his approval, ma'am." Merlani nods, a little bit embarrassed that she's saying this in front of the rest of the team—although they couldn't necessarily put a finger on why it's embarrassing.

"Now... we seem to be missing Vasquez?" Aunt Penny looks over to Lavine and Martins.

"We left her asleep in our cabin this morning," Martins says, brushing some of her ginger waves back out of her face. "She came in around ship's dawn and had one of her smaller sleep-crash moments—"

"—And neither of *us* was interested in waking her up and having to dodge punches before breakfast, ma'am," Lavine continues. They're close friends with Martins, as Merlani has learned, and have been for so long that the two of them often finish each other's sentences with this sort of eerie accuracy.

"Ah... that's right! I need to talk to her when she does wake up my plan to shift her over to a nocturnal schedule for this trip so we don't have to drag her down to the infirmary again." Aunt Penny reaches for her pocket com and taps out a message that Merlani assumes is to Reese. "As long as the poor girl's actually *sleeping*, though, we might as well let her."

Merlani is concerned for their friend too, considering that she'd had such a hard time on the journey out from Earth. The effects of Strange transit on sleeping humans are somewhat hit or miss: some don't to have any problems with it; others are subjected to nightmares and other unsettling disturbances to their sleep. Reese, unfortunately, is one of the ones whose dreams are severely affected. Coupled with her tendency towards running on as little sleep as possible to begin with, that had made the team's journey to Mars one of *dangerous* levels of insomnia for her.

Merlani had initially spent most of those sleepless nights keeping Reese company, since Florivans don't require the same amount of rest humans do. Once Aunt Penny figured out just how bad a state she was heading into and helped her sort out a solution with the ship's surgeon, Merlani had taken on the task of guarding their best friend's dreams from the influence of the Strange. The sedatives had dealt with Reese's insomnia, thankfully, but not with the disturbances that had caused it.

Still, Merlani is glad to hear that she seems to be doing at least a little better with this return trip. They'd been worried for Reese last night, but there wasn't much they could do when they had to be in the Strange themself instead of with her.

"Although…" Aunt Penny puts her pocket-com away and turns most of her attention to her soup. "Little Ocean, I'd like you to check on the sleeping dragon for us once you're done here—see if she'll be up to joining us for afternoon practice, if you can manage to wake her."

"Yes, ma'am."

"Anyone want to run odds on whether she wakes up punchy?" da Silva jokes, grinning broadly at the rest of the team.

"Now *really*, da Silva," says Aunt Penny, "haven't I taught you better than that?"

"Yes, ma'am. Sorry, ma'am."

Aunt Penny smirks at him through her tinted lenses and slurps her soup. "Rule twenty-eight: Never run odds on a sure thing—or on people who will come after you if they find out about the bet."

Da Silva laughs so hard at this he almost chokes on his drink.

The rest of the humans are equally amused.

Merlani just shakes their head. It's the small moments like this where they appreciate their little collection of human friends the most.

Once they're done with their breakfast, Merlani slips quietly into the cabin Reese is sharing with Martins and Lavine, taking advantage of the fact that their friends had programmed the door to give them access when they all first arrived on the ship.

Reese seems to still be asleep when they arrive—or rather, the room is dark and quiet aside from the sound of her steady breathing and she's curled up under a blanket in the top of the three bunks built into the left-hands wall. If she's *not* asleep, she's certainly making a good show of it.

Merlani can see well enough in the darkness to not need to turn on the light when they enter and risk disturbing their best friend's rest. Even the dim glow from the stars outside the open viewport is enough for their keen trio of eyes to function. They set the tray they've been carrying down on the table at the far wall and make their way over to check on her.

Merlani climbs up one of the two bunk-access ladders as quietly as they possibly can. Steadying themself at the top of it with three hands and their tail, they peer over into the dark person-sized cubbyhole containing their friend.

Her face is close to them, although obscured partly by both the blanket and some of her hair. They note briefly that she must have really been out of it when she climbed up into her little nest, since she hasn't bothered to take her hair down out of its usual high ponytail.

Merlani gently rests their free hand on her nearest exposed arm. Reese doesn't react to the contact any more than to shift her arm a little further back under the blanket. They keep their hand lightly in place as they close their eyes and let themself drift lightly into the warmth their hand is touching.

Back on the *Tetrabrachium*, Merlani had spent more time than anyone had expected would be needed to drive the Strange out of Reese's dreams, even after the medical staff had helped her—enough that it's easy now for them to find their way along the edges of her sleeping mind with only a small anchor point.

This is one of the traits their species seldom discusses outside of the Nav/Quan community: Florivans may not experience dreaming themselves, but they're sensitive enough to the brainwaves of sleeping humans to be able to slip into them and float alongside the dreamer. It's not a skill many of them fully develop, of course. To go deep enough to affect what the human experiences usually requires either a strong imprint between the two of them or being asleep themself and in close contact.

Merlani, though, was raised almost entirely by humans. They've been doing this since they were a kitten. Even with the difficulties they had in their lessons with their other innate abilities, *this* has always come easily regardless of how well they know the human in question. That skill had been one their Entile Wyndi had helped them hone, too, during their first year on Earth.

Even if they weren't trained for this, of course, Reese is Merlani's best friend. Slipping into her dreams to watch over her and chase away the nightmares is almost effortless, and was even when she'd first accepted their offer to try doing so. After a few moments, Merlani can tell that she's been sleeping peacefully and *deeply*, for once. The edges of her show no traces of disturbed dreams, either, which is a relieving change from the last time they were asked to do this. There's nothing they'll need to intervene with today.

Reese is back to the light drifting stage of slumber now, just on the edge of waking.

Opening their eyes and withdrawing their hand, Merlani decides that she's close enough to being awake anyway that they might as well see if she wants to get up and join the team for practice. "Reese?" They gently nudge her shoulder.

Reese reaches up half-heartedly to bat their hand away. That's better than Merlani was expecting. Waking her too abruptly is a potentially hazardous exercise—not for Reese, but for whoever or whatever is waking her up. The team's jokes about her being a sleeping dragon are founded in *fact*, after all.

Merlani's reflexes are good enough that they don't usually need to worry about that, though. They nudge her again. "Teresa... come on, it's just me."

Reese makes a kitten-like sound of sleepy displeasure at being woken up and then cracks open one of her eyes to stare at Merlani.

"Aunt Penny wants to know if you're coming to afternoon practice."

"It's not..." Reese yawns halfway through her response. "...*That* late in the day already, is it?"

"Something like thirteen-thirty or so." Merlani twitches their ears at her cheerfully. "I brought breakfast!"

"I thought I smelled waffle..."

"Pancake, actually—there's also fruit!"

"Mm."

"Oh, and *coffee*."

"You win, Cinny, I'm up." Reese stretches and reluctantly starts extracting herself from the blankets. From the look of it, she never fully changed out of her workout clothes when she went to sleep.

Merlani hops down from the bunk ladder and turns the room lights on to a comfortably dim setting. They make themself comfortable sitting on the padded bench under the viewport so they can watch the stars while they wait for their best friend.

Once Reese has come down and sorted herself out in the little adjoining washroom, she joins them, bringing the tray Merlani had left on the table for her. She takes a long savoring sip from the coffee first. "Mm. I'll say this for *Starbright*... whoever the quartermaster is, they certainly know how to acquire good coffee."

"Used to be Lt. Colverson—but I think they must have gotten someone new. Uncle Rudy and Marsh used to complain all the time about this ship having the *worst* coffee of any they've ever served on... not that it ever stopped the two of them from drinking the stuff, of course."

"Ah." Reese takes another sip, smiling contentedly. "Well, *I* think it's good, at any rate."

"I'll take your word for it. I can't tell any difference from the smell."

Reese shakes her head. "You don't know what you're missing, Cinny."

"I'm just glad that it's a *nice-smelling* poison that all of the humans I like best drink."

Reese chuckles and then takes a pointedly exaggerated slurping sip before turning her attention to the pancakes they'd brought for her. After a few bites she looks back up to Merlani. "So, did last night go okay for you? Being back in the saddle and all?"

"It went well!" Merlani smiles at her and then glances back out to the stars for a moment with their two lower eyes. "Kind of rough at first, since it's been *months* since I've even been in sims, much less out in the Strange... but it was good to get to work with Elder Celadon again—and Uncle Rudy, too! I'd almost forgotten how *nice* it is to work with a Navigator who actually knows what he's doing."

"I'm glad they let you help out, then. It'll be nice not having to see you all antsy again like you were on the flight out."

Merlani rolls their third eye teasingly. "*You're* one to talk about antsy-ness, Teresa."

"True..." Reese yawns again, briefly. "Some Captain *I'm* going to be, if I can't figure out how to sleep through Quantum Space Transit."

"I'm sure you'll find a way to make it work..." Merlani runs the tuft of their tail through their lower set of fingers, absently straightening out the soft silver fluff. "I'm just sorry *you* have to be the one out of the team that's sensitive to it."

"Well, at least I'm used to keeping odd hours." Reese smirks at them. "And I can see why you got into the habit of it too."

"What can I say? We don't need as much sleep and Nav/Quan is nocturnal on most ships. I'd never had to try to keep to a daytime-focused schedule before I got to the Academy, you know." Merlani pauses, remembering why they came in to wake her in the first place. "Oh! Aunt Penny also said she wants to talk to you—something about setting you up on the night shift so you don't have any problems with this trip."

"That could work." Reese nods and continues nibbling away at her breakfast. "I did pretty much half of that last night anyway."

"The nice thing about it, of course, is that then I won't be the only one eating breakfast at ship's noon—so the team can try teasing *both* of us instead of just me."

Reese laughs. "I take it they gave you a hard time this morning?"

"Not as bad as usual—they still don't come near to what my littermates can be like."

"Good. That means I can go easy on them at practice for once."

Merlani chuckles. "Since when do *you* go easy on anyone during practice?"

"Mm. Point taken." Reese grins. "Wouldn't want them to go *soft* by the time we get back to Earth."

"Naturally."

JUST AFTER THE COORDINATES HAVE BEEN CALLED down for the first jump into Quantum Space on the second day of LSS *Starbright's* voyage to Earth, the ship's Primary Astral Navigator is still standing in the doorway of the Nav closet waiting to continue his discussion with her Secondary Astral Navigator about a certain arrangement he's just made for the department.

The younger man runs a freckled olive-tan hand through his closely cropped brown hair to readjust his headset now that he won't need to talk through it for a while. Microphone secured, he turns his attention back to his superior.

"Well?" the old Navigator asks.

"I don't recall being classed as a *child-minder*, sir."

"She's just going to observe and fetch coffee, Marsh."

"I can get my *own* coffee, sir."

"Yes… if you want to call that stuff you drink *coffee*…" The old Navigator chuckles softly. "But since I've got the kid on loan from Penny until we drop the lot of them off at Earth, you might as well get some use out of her too."

The younger Navigator raises an eyebrow. "Just how big of a favor did you owe the Colonel, sir?"

"Well…" The old Navigator shrugs. "Let me put it this way, Marsh: Penny and I go far enough back that we've lost *count* of who owes what. If any bloody favors were called in, I'm not entirely sure I could tell you whose they were."

"Ah."

"Besides," says the old Navigator, taking on a teasing glint in his eyes, "the kid has the same taste for coffee-flavored syrup that you do, so you should get along just fine!"

"Now, don't go dragging my coffee into this, sir," the younger Navigator replies in jovial protest.

"Fine, fine. If you don't want to have some reasonably good company up here for once, I'm not going to order you to let her stay."

"You mean better company than *you* were when I started out, sir?"

The older Navigator laughs. "More like better than you were when *you* first darkened my door. At least this one doesn't think she bloody well knows everything."

The younger Navigator rolls his eyes. "She's not even studying for Nav, sir—what are you up to?"

"Just giving the girl something to do since she's on nights anyway." The older Navigator shrugs innocently. "That's all."

"Sir, please." The younger Navigator stifles a laugh. "When you try to use Celadon's cryptic tone you just come off as devious."

"What can I say, Marsh? I learned my scheming from the best—but I'm not scheming anything." The older Navigator thoughtfully sets a hand on his clean-shaven chin for a moment. "Well, not *yet*, at least. Accuse me again in a week or so, will you?"

"Sure, sir..."

At this point, the cadet in question appears in the doorway of the Nav closet, carrying three tall insulated cups on a tray with a small plate covered over with a napkin. She hands one cup to the older Navigator first, smiling, and then offers another to the younger one. "Double-strong black coffee on ice, two shots of cinnamon syrup and a dash of vanilla? Oh, and I brought some ginger cookies too, sir. Lt. Cyan mentioned you like them."

The younger Navigator accepts the cup with a suspicious look at his superior, and then takes a cautious sip through the metal straw sticking up out of the center of the lid. "Huh..." he takes a cookie from the plate and gestures to the stool beside him with it before taking a bite. "All right, then. Have a seat, cadet."

The cadet happily takes her place on the small stool and accepts the backup headset the younger Navigator passes to her.

"I had a *feeling* you'd see my way of thinking, Marsh." The older Navigator grins at his subordinate and then turns to the Cadet. "Lieutenant Marshal here is in charge tonight. Try to behave for him, kid, will you?"

"Of course, sir."

"Good." The old Navigator takes a cookie from the plate and then leaves the two of them, a small glint of a growing conspiracy flashing in the corner of his eye.

A few hours into the final jump cycle of the night, the younger Navigator finally strikes up an actual conversation with the young woman sitting on the stool beside him during the long period of waiting after giving his counterpart their latest set of landmark coordinates. "So, cadet. You getting anything out of all this?"

"Yes, sir. It's interesting seeing how this actually works—even in the tactical sims I've been in for class, we never really do much more than com down to ask for a course change and eta, you know?"

"Ah. Heard something similar from one of my old housemates back at KCA who was doing Command track—always cracked me up when he complained about the 'inefficiency' of only running jumps during the ship's night on standard protocols." The young Navigator chuckles, shaking his head ruefully. "Even *Cy* couldn't ever manage to talk sense into him."

"It's a safety thing, though, isn't it, Lieutenant?" The cadet takes a sip from her coffee and looks at him curiously.

"Indeed. The bigger the ship, less time it can take in Quantum Space without risking miasma leaks... and the harder it is for the Drive to jump us along in the first place.

And, surprisingly, accidents are less likely to happen with the crew if most of the ship is asleep."

"Even though it gives some of them nightmares?"

"Yeah. Most are on watch rotations, though, so it evens out for them eventually. It's just us odd folk that take nights as standard—and you, at the moment."

After a moment of silence, the cadet tilts her head at him and asks a question of her own. "So, Lieutenant, if you don't mind me asking... how'd *you* end up in Nav?"

The young Navigator chuckles. "Oh, I don't mind. It's in my blood, really."

"Really, sir?"

"My mum's the Navigator for our sister-ship, *Stargazer*, and my dad's partnered with Cy's parent on ESS *Diaphus*. Cy and their littermates and I grew up together—and Cy's a stubborn enough sort that they wouldn't *let* anyone else have a chance at being their counterpart."

"Stubborn?"

"Kept up with me over the relays the whole time they were gone for their apprenticeship and everything." The young Navigator smiles fondly. "I wanted to follow the parental footsteps anyway, though, so having my best friend all set on making their compact with me made things pretty simple there. Met back up with them when they signed for Kapteyn's Academy, and here we are."

"That's neat, really, sir. Reminds me of my family's legacies, a bit."

"Fleet, right?"

"Yeah, and the ranch... but I'm heading for the stars *first*, you know?"

"I get that, cadet." The young Navigator nods. "So you've always been aiming for pilot, then?"

"Pretty much." The cadet shrugs. "I looked into trying out for your line when I applied to the Academy, actually—but my classifications aren't high enough in the right places, you know?"

"Yeah, I know—not that any Navigator worth their salt would let a little thing like *that* stop them."

"Sir?"

"It's like this." The young Navigator gestures vaguely towards the charts on his displays. "If there's a jumper who *wants* you—"

"*—All right, Sean,*" calls a distinctive wind-chime toned Florivan voice over the headset, interrupting him. "*I've got us to the marker. Ready to confirm those jump-out coordinates?*"

The Lieutenant flips down his microphone bar and nods to the cadet. "Ready, Cy." He looks back to his list on the small holoscreen at his right hand. "Your point's 34 by 3 and 2E. Standing by for jump-out."

"*Coordinate confirmed. Jumping back to Normal in thirty seconds.*"

The young Navigator switches over to the ship's intercom while his counterpart begins their countdown. "All hands, stand by for return to Normal space."

By the time the countdown ends, he's fully forgotten whatever it was he meant to say to the cadet—and so has she.

Several days before *Starbright* is expected to make port at Earth's Luna Orbital Space Station, Merlani is enjoying a quiet evening with Ai-Nida Celadon and Uncle Rudy. The two of them are off-duty tonight; as on most ships with more than one Nav/Quan team, they alternate which team is running the night's Quantum Space Transit cycles. Instead, they're sitting in their quarters playing cards with Merlani.

"So, kid," asks Uncle Rudy, gathering up all of the cards from the table and passing them over so Ai-Nida Celadon can shuffle them and deal out the next hand, "you looking forward to getting back to your classes?"

Merlani shrugs, absently stacking and re-stacking the small pile of colored stones they've won so far this evening.

"I've already turned in all of my final projects for the term... and I haven't decided which summer units to sign up for yet."

"Fair enough." He shoots them a teasing smirk. "You could always take the summer off from studying, you know. Nothing in the rules saying you *have* to stay in Houston up to your ears in homework..."

"I *like* the homework, Uncle Rudy." Merlani rolls their eyes and swishes their tail playfully at him. "Besides, I'd have to clear it with Aunt Penny if I was going to go anywhere else."

Ai-Nida Celadon laughs brightly as they begin to distribute cards around the table. "Now, really, kitten. If I know Penny, she'd be *delighted* to have an excuse to take a few months off from the Academy herself and go on a planetside adventure with you and Teresa."

Merlani sighs. "Maybe... but Reese will probably be heading off to whatever ship the Fleet assigns her to after she graduates. I don't think she'll have much time for adventures before she leaves."

"You never know, Merlani." Ai-Nida Celadon gives them a reassuring pat on the hand. "Your friends all seem to be the sort who would be up for some adventuring."

"Maybe." Merlani shrugs lightly. "I *had* been planning a caving trip of some sort with Condrey and the Maltbys before... well, everything happened... and at least Katz and Lavine and Martins aren't graduating..." Their tail betrays a disappointment they don't want to acknowledge with its sedated swishing. "It wouldn't be as much fun without Reese around, though."

"You know, kid," Uncle Rudy starts to say, "you *could* ask—" He's interrupted by an urgent call alert sounding over the cabin's computer system. "—Oh, now what?" He leans his chair back onto its two rear legs and reaches up on the wall to activate the intercom connection. "I'm listening. What's going on?"

"*Marshal here, sir,*" says the voice over the intercom. "*Sorry to interrupt your night off—We've just come back into the Normal and are waiting for the ship to equalize before we jump again; Cy says they need you and Celadon down in the Drive Bay.*"

"Nothing serious, I hope?" Uncle Rudy gets up and pulls his uniform jacket back on.

"*No, they didn't say what it was, just that they need the two of you to come take care of it.*" Something in Lt. Marshal's voice sounds almost like he's attempting to hold back a laugh. Merlani isn't sure why.

Ai-Nida Celadon sets down the rest of the cards as they stand and flick their tinted shielding lens back down over their third eye, since they'll need it once they leave the more comfortably dim lighting of their quarters. "You can tell them we'll be down there in a few minutes, Sean."

"*I'll do that. Marshal out.*" The intercom falls silent.

Merlani stands as well now. "Do you want me to come too?"

Uncle Rudy shrugs. "Might as well, kid—if anything, I may need an extra hand or three to fix whatever Cy's gone and broken this time."

"Oh, now, Elias," Ai-Nida Celadon says with just a touch of amusement coloring their voice, "it was hardly poor Cyan's fault the *last* time something broke."

Uncle Rudy shakes his head with rueful amusement of his own, offering his counterpart his arm to hold as they head out. "No, Dons, it wasn't. That was *you* and your bloody vendetta against artigrav systems..."

Merlani stifles a giggle lest the teasing turn their way next.

"Okay, Cy," Uncle Rudy calls as the three of them enter the antechamber separating *Starbright's* Drive Bay from the rest of the ship, "we're here. What do you—"

He doesn't get a chance to finish the sentence. A familiar figure leaps out of the open Drive Bay doorway and pounces him with a high-velocity four-armed hug. "—Hello, Stepdad!"

"Hello yourself!" Uncle Rudy laughs and spins the newly arrived Florivan around in a circle as he hugs them back before setting them down in front of Ai-Nida Celadon. "Seriously, Stepchild, are you *ever* going to get tired of giving me a bloody heart attack every time you show up?"

"Nope! It's too much fun pouncing you." Entile Ilmi smirks at him and then turns and embraces Ai-Nida Celadon. "Hi Nida."

"Hello, Ilmi!" Ai-Nida Celadon hugs their eldest kitten almost as tightly as Uncle Rudy had. "I was wondering when you'd get here."

"Well, I promised 'before you get to Earth', didn't I?"

"You did," says Uncle Rudy, "but you *could* have said how many days out so we'd be expecting you." He makes a rather unsuccessful attempt at a gruff pouting tone.

The grin he's wearing is too broad to allow him to sound sincerely upset.

"Oh, now, where's the fun in being *expected*?" Entile Ilmi waves their tail at him teasingly.

Floating on the Drive Bay side of the doorway, Cyan giggles at the sight. "See, Rudy? I didn't break anything tonight! Now you can all go back to whatever it is you do when you're off-duty. Marsh and I can handle things." With that, they wave to Merlani, set Entile Ilmi's other travel-bag out into the antechamber, and close the door. The door seal system begins its usual set of clicks and whirs as each of the redundant locking and airtight sealing mechanisms engages.

"Well... expected or not, it's good to see you got here without any icicles hanging off your ears this time," Uncle Rudy teases, picking up Entile Ilmi's patch-covered duffel bag from where Cyan had set it and slinging its carrying strap over his shoulder.

Entile Ilmi readjusts the backpack they're wearing and flicks their ears in amusement. "Oh, it wasn't *that* big of a jump this time. *Aransas* gave me a lift from Europa on their way to Waco to pick up the new crop of junior Rangers." They turn and offer Merlani a hug now. "Ah! Hello, kitten! I didn't know if you'd be coming down to greet me or not."

Merlani happily accepts the hug. "It's good to see you again, Entile Ilmi."

"Likewise, Merlani—I take it your friends are all sleeping?"

"Probably." Merlani shrugs. "Except Reese. She's helping the night crew up on the Bridge."

"Why don't you invite her to come have midnight lunch with us, dear?" asks Ai-Nida Celadon with a knowing smile. "She can help us plan our family meal with all of your teammates for tomorrow."

Merlani nods and pulls out their pocket-com while the four of them are walking back down the corridor towards the lift that will take them up to the ship's crew mess.

"So, Stepchild," asks Uncle Rudy, setting an arm casually around Entile Ilmi's shoulders, "what sort of chaos have you been causing lately, then?"

Entile Ilmi smirks at him. "Oh, I wouldn't call it *chaos*, Rudy! Just an errand here and there for the Council, perhaps a bit of favor trading to sort out some plans down the line, that sort of thing. You know me, I'm the calm, reserved one in the family."

"That's right," Uncle Rudy teases, "you're the one who supposedly *didn't* inherit Dons' troublemaker streak."

"Hmm. Of course they didn't... any more than Little Ocean here didn't inherit one from *their* parent." Ai-Nida Celadon stifles a laugh. "Next you'll be telling me the galaxy spins through the efforts of a rather large hamster running on a wheel..."

Late the next afternoon, Merlani finds themself dressed in their formal amber-embroidered long tunic and trousers, waiting patiently outside the doors to the two cabins their teammates are sharing for the voyage. They re-tie the sheer white-edged amber sash around their waist so that the knot is sitting in a more pleasing position to show off the beaded fringe at the sash ends while they wait.

They can't help wishing their littermate Miradyn was here to tie it for them. Mir is the *best* at tying bows and sashes and things and making them look effortlessly perfect.

Finally, Aunt Penny emerges from her cabin across the hall. She absently readjusts her vermilion-fringed amber shawl as the door closes behind her so it's sitting in the correct place over her shoulders. The shawl is embroidered on the back with a sparkling beadwork version of the same fleur-de-lis and trio of crossed swords she and the other 2nd Darter Squadron pilots all wear on their jackets, also in vermilion. The shimmery fabric of the ivory dress she's wearing sets off the colors of her shawl beautifully, as does the matching hair-ribbons with which she's pulled her two signature white poofy ponytails back.

"Still waiting, kiddo?"

Merlani nods. "They have exactly three minutes to finish getting ready before we're all going to be late, Ma'am."

Aunt Penny laughs. "I thought I told you you're off-duty as my personal assistant until we dock at Luna Orbital?"

Merlani cracks a small smile, swishing their tail softly to match. "Force of habit, Aunt Penny. You trained me to be the team's minder too well."

Aunt Penny comes over and gives Merlani an affectionate pat on the head, since no one else is in the corridor at the moment. "Hmm... maybe I should ask what the rest think about you being their team captain after da Silva and Vasquez graduate..."

Merlani looks up at her in mock horror. "Oh, no, but then I'd be *responsible* for them."

"That *is* the idea, yes." She grins.

"What's the idea, Colonel?" asks da Silva, just now stepping out of the cabin he's sharing with Kouassi and Katz. He's dressed in his crisply-pressed Academy dress uniform, although he's still fussing about a bit with the wide necktie that marks him as a soon-to-graduate senior student.

Kouassi and Katz are close behind him, also in their Academy dress uniforms. Kouassi doesn't seem to have had any trouble getting his tie to lie straight. The ever-present circular cap on the back of Katz' head is edged with the same silver trim as decorates the lapels and sleeve cuffs of all of their jackets.

"Here, kiddo, let me fix that for you—" Aunt Penny laughs as she comes over to sort out da Silva's stubborn necktie. "Oh, the idea is to conscript Ocean here as the next poor soul who has to serve as a team captain for me."

Katz chuckles. "You have my vote, Barker. I've certainly had my fill of keeping Lavine and Martins in line—and we only had the *one* group project together this year."

Merlani rolls all three eyes at him. "And what makes everyone think they or any of the new folks next year are going to listen to *me?*"

The door behind them to their other teammates' cabin opens now, apparently just in time for Lavine and Martins to have caught the last bit of the conversation.

"Oh, I don't know, Barker—" Lavine begins, appearing in their dress uniform with a cheeky grin on one side of Merlani.

Martins manifests on the other side to complete the sentence. "—We listen to you pretty well in practice!" The optional long pleated uniform skirt she's elected to wear instead of the trousers everyone else has on swishes as she moves.

Merlani shakes their head. "Only because you both know my reflexes are better than yours."

Reese appears now too, offering Merlani her arm. "So, *Team Captain Elect*... ready to escort us all to this formal dinner thing before you get volunteered for anything else?"

Merlani looks up to their best friend with an incredulous twitch of their ears. After a moment, they sigh and accept her arm, gesturing with one of their free hands in the direction they need to go to get to the ship's private function room. "Yes—but since when am I elected?"

Aunt Penny laughs. "Well, that sounded like a unanimous enough vote to me."

"Don't worry," says da Silva, now walking on Merlani's other side, "you can always ping one of us if they get unruly so we can growl at them for you."

Merlani shakes their head. "As long as all of you *behave* at this dinner? I guess I'll go along with it."

"All hail the team captain elect!" calls Lavine.

The rest of the team cheers in response. Merlani swishes the embarrassment away with their tail—they're more honored than anything, if they're honest. "All right, settle down, though? There are people *sleeping* in some of these cabins."

"Yes, Barker!" chorus their teammates in cheerful stage whispers.

"We'll be good tonight, Cinny, don't worry." Reese gives their hand that's resting on her arm a brief, reassuring squeeze. "So, what's the special occasion that has Elder Celadon wanting us all over for dinner, anyway?"

"It's a family dinner," Merlani says, smiling up at their friend. "And they and Entile Jade both like all of you."

"If 'appearing out of *nowhere* at the breakfast table and scaring the daylights out of people' is how Jade shows people affection," quips da Silva, "I'd hate to know what happens to someone they *don't* like."

"Yeah," says Martins, shaking her head, "I practically came out of my *skin* this morning when they popped up from the booth next to us."

Merlani giggles. "You should see what they put my Uncle Rudy through every time they come to visit him..."

Starbright's private function room is divided into a neatly decorated lounge area with a wide viewport on the far wall and a dining space with a large wooden table in the middle which can be lengthened or shortened to suit the size of the gathering. A collection of shimmering jellyfish occupy the large fish tank built into the wall beside the dining table. From what Merlani remembers being told when they first came to live on this ship as an apprentice, the tank has only had to be converted for its *official* use in welcoming a traveling Europan ambassadorial observer twice since *Starbright* was commissioned. The rest of the time, the Captain keeps some of his pet jellyfish on display to amuse other visitors or crew members who've reserved the room for the evening.

Aside from the way everyone is dressed, the dinner tonight is less formal than most other occasions this room sees. It's certainly not the sort of prim and proper affair Merlani's teammates were expecting. It's more of a family meal than anything—tasty food and socializing, with more than a few of Aunt Penny and Uncle Rudy's tall tales thrown in for the amusement of all. Da Silva and Kouassi's attempts to tell stories of their Academy exploits to match are fun too, if only because everyone *else* is around to cut in from time to time with corrections on the parts the boys have forgotten.

It's nice to get to spend time with their family and teammates like this. Merlani sits between their best friend and their household's Elder, silent for the most part as they do their best to absorb all of it into their memory. They can't help but feel a bit bittersweet about the evening, since they know this is likely one of the last times they'll ever have all of these people in the same room.

Towards the end of the meal, Ai-Nida Celadon clinks their spoon against their glass of sparkling peach juice to get everyone's attention. "Now, before we take the fresher dome off of that lovely blueberry pie we'll be sharing for dessert... I believe we *do* have a bit of formal family business to deal with first." They stand, smoothing out the sheer layers of amber silks in their lower robes with their lower hands and picking their cane up from its resting place against the wall behind their chair with their long prehensile tail. "If you'd all come over to the lounge area with me?"

Merlani and their friends follow. Once they've all assembled in the lounge area, Uncle Rudy and Aunt Penny each sit on one end of the longer sofa. Uncle Rudy pats the space between them and gestures with his head for Merlani to sit down. They're still amazed that *he's* dressed in his formal family clothes too, complete with a shimmer-embroidered white scarf draped loosely over his shoulders rather than wrapped around his neck to match the loose shirt he's wearing; the rest of his vest and trousers are white-embroidered amber like Merlani and their siblings wear.

Merlani sits, still a bit confused as to what's going on. Ai-Nida Celadon and Entile Ilmi have been even more cryptic about it than usual every time they asked today, to the point where Merlani finally gave up on asking and simply decided to wait and see what happens. That's usually the easier path, though, when the two of them have a conspiracy of some sort going on.

"Ah, stay standing here for a moment, kittens." Ai-Nida Celadon gestures to Merlani's teammates with their cane before they take a seat in the armchair beside the couch. "Okay, Jade, dear, the floor is all yours. I would be all official and stand," they add with a wry laugh, "but my leg has decided you'll have to be content with me *sitting* in witness of this."

"Thank you, Nida." Entile Ilmi retrieves the bag they'd carried in with them and sets it on one of the other armchairs before turning to Merlani's friends. "I would have arranged to do this as a part of the graduation festivities when those happen, but once we get to Luna Orbital I have to hop to a different ship to take care of some business for the Council, so here we are now." After a pause, they fold all four hands together in front of them and take on their most formal Star-Keeper's tone of voice. "I have no kittens of my own; the Strange's plans for me have never included that. I walk the stars alone, but that does not mean I am alone. The family I was born to is small, but the family we have chosen grows regularly."

Merlani catches their friends looking at them with a matched set of utterly confused looks. They smile and give a reassuring flick of their ears. They think they've figured out now what Entile Ilmi is up to, and they're *delighted* by the prospect.

"Elder Celadon," says Entile Ilmi, still in their most formal voice, "I would present these young humans to you, the head of my household. Will you receive them?"

"I receive them gladly, Jade." Ai-Nida Celadon nods, their voice formal but their tail swishing in a way that betrays how thoroughly pleased they are with the whole situation. "Please, proceed." They make a genial gesture with one of their upper hands, leaving the lower two on their lap.

"Thank you, Elder Celadon." Entile Ilmi bows deeply, as called for by the deep formality of the ritual they're enacting. They take a small stack of neatly-folded bundles of amber fabric out of their bag and give them to Ai-Nida Celadon before approaching Merlani's teammates. Kouassi is nearest to them. Entile Ilmi motions to him with one of their upper hands. "Would you mind bending down, Paul?" they whisper, falling into their more casual voice for a moment. "You're too tall for me to reach without being all undignified hopping about."

Ever the dramatic one, Kouassi grins at them and goes down on one knee like a knight in one of the old stories he reads in his free time standing before his monarch. The rest of the team share a look, then follow suit. Martins and Lavine do their best not to giggle.

Next to Merlani, Uncle Rudy has his pocket-com out and is either taking pictures or filming the ritual—knowing him and how much the rest of their family will want to see this, it's probably both.

"That works. Thank you." Entile Ilmi whispers with an amused swish of their tail which makes the bangles on it jingle brightly before they return to their formal ritual tone. "May all of my people who meet you in the future recognize you as the son of my heart and a true friend of our kind in this world." They briefly press their forehead to his.

As they do this—so briefly that even *Merlani* barely feels it happen—Entile Ilmi touches the fringes of the veil between the Normal and the Strange, flickering for less than a second to mark the young man as *theirs*, as *friend*, as *family*. They have to be extremely precise to do something like that without harming the human, but no one other than the most senior Elders of the Council is more skilled than Entile Ilmi.

Entile Ilmi turns back to Ai-Nida Celadon now, resting their hand on Kouassi's shoulder as they speak. "This is Paul Kouassi of the Two Rivers Colony at Alpha Centauri c. I present him to you as the son of my heart, Elder Celadon; will you accept him?"

"I will." Ai-Nida Celadon smiles and motions for Kouassi to come over to them. When he kneels before their chair, they unfold one of the wide scarves from the pile of fabric in their lap and drape it around his shoulders. "Welcome to the family, Paul."

"...I'm *honored*, Elder Celadon. Thank you." Kouassi is the sort of human who adapts to unexpected situations quickly, and it shows; he's hit upon a proper response without too much effort.

Ai-Nida Celadon pats him on the head affectionately and then gestures for him to move to stand behind them. Kouassi does so, and Entile Ilmi turns back to the line of kneeling humans. One by one, they formally adopt each of Merlani's teammates. Once all six of the young humans are standing together behind Ai-Nida's chair, Entile Ilmi turns back to their parent with a genuine smile.

"These human kittens of mine are special, Elder Celadon. I thank you for welcoming them into your household."

"I'm glad to have them, Jade." With that, Ai-Nida Celadon stands and taps their cane on the floor, returning to their usual informal tone of voice. "And now that we're done welcoming all of my new grandchildren to the family... who wants *pie*?"

Merlani and the two humans sitting with them on the couch raise their hands solemnly.

"No family adoption is complete without dessert, is it?" Aunt Penny asks, bouncing to her feet.

"Not in *my* family, it's not." Ai-Nida Celadon laughs and goes with her to set out the dessert plates and retrieve the pie in question from its fresher dome on the sideboard.

Uncle Rudy also stands, going over and giving Entile Ilmi a brief hug. "Good job, Stepchild. You picked some sparky ones."

"Thanks, Rudy—don't go being *too* rough on them now that they're mine, okay?"

"Me? Give *your* children a hard time?" Uncle Rudy laughs. "I'd never dream of it, Jade."

While the two of them go over to help serve the pie, the rest of the team circles around Merlani at the couch.

"So," asks Reese, plopping down beside them, "… did we really just get adopted?"

"Yep!" Merlani grins at her. "Congratulations, you're all my cousins now. Entile Jade *really* likes all of you—and this way, you're family so it's easier for them to ask to borrow you as companions sometimes once you graduate and are all off in the Fleet and things. They've never adopted anyone before that I know of, but it means all of the rest of the Florivans you ever meet will know you're part of Ai-Nida Celadon's household just like Aunt Penny and my parents are."

"Sounds nice," says da Silva, taking the seat on the other side of them. "So, you *are* going to explain all of the etiquette to us, right?"

"There's not much of it, but yes, don't worry, we'll teach you everything you need to know." Merlani nods. They're excited too, to be able to call this group of wonderful people who've come into their life *family.*

"Come on, kittens," calls Entile Ilmi from the table with a genuine laugh, "there's *pie* over here."

With no small amount of stifled giggling, the team does as they're told and reassembles at the table to accept the rather generous slices of pie that have been cut for them.

Once they're all back in their chairs enjoying their dessert, Entile Ilmi stands again and pulls two old-fashioned paper envelopes out of the folds of their tunic. "Before I forget: Paul, Tobias? These are for you—consider them your graduation presents from me and Nida." Entile Ilmi gives one of the envelopes to each of them, then sits back down and looks to Reese. "Teresa, I'm still working on your gift, but I'll be sure to talk to you about it before we get to Earth."

Reese nods with an appreciative smile before savoring another bite of pie.

"Go on, kittens," says Ai-Nida Celadon with a knowing smile, "open them."

Kouassi and da Silva open the envelopes and read the contents simultaneously, then both turn their resulting wide-eyed incredulous stares to Entile Ilmi.

"This is... *wow*." Kouassi, for once, is at a loss for words. "I haven't even signed my papers for joining the Fleet, though..."

"Neither have I," says da Silva. "They don't let us do that until after we officially graduate. But still... thank you, Jade."

"Yes," echoes Kouassi, "thank you."

"Well, I *did* make sure to ask Penny what sort of career path the two of you were looking at first." Entile Ilmi's tail makes a pleased, jingling swish. "And you'll still have to go through with the interview and make it *happen* for yourselves... but I think you'll both be perfect for the positions. Your records and letters of recommendation have already been sorted out; all you have to do is respond to the messages that will be waiting for you when we get to Earth and arrange a time for your interviews."

"Do we get to know what you're talking about?" Martins asks, gesturing curiously with her fork, "Or is it supposed to be a secret?"

Da Silva looks to Entile Ilmi, who nods and gives him a little 'go on' sort of a gesture. He holds up the piece of paper that was in his envelope. "I'll be interviewing for one of the open positions on Europa's Argadnel Outpost security staff—normally they don't take fresh graduates at all unless they're from there originally." His eyes are still disbelievingly wide.

"Wow, Toby!" Reese grins. "That's your dream post, isn't it? You've been talking my ear off about Argadnel since we were what... fourteen?"

Da Silva blushes softly. "Yeah." He looks over to Entile Ilmi again. "So, is it polite for me to ask if I can hug you? I feel like I should for something like this."

Entile Ilmi nods with another happy swish of their tail. "You're my heart's-children, all of you. Hugs are most welcome."

One rather enthusiastic hug later, da Silva has returned to his chair. He nudges Kouassi, who's sitting beside him. "Okay, your turn. What's in your envelope?"

Kouassi smiles softly, still at a loss for words. He hands the paper to da Silva and wordlessly gets up and gives Entile Ilmi a hug as well.

"I wouldn't have recommended you if I didn't think you were the right man for the job, dear," Entile Ilmi tells him, "and I'm *certain* Yuliana will agree with me."

If da Silva's eyes had been wide when he read what was on his own paper, they're practically bulging out altogether now. "'Admiral Setiawan invites you to interview for the post of her administrative assistant'—*wow*, Kouassi. I can't think of anything that's more *you* than that." He looks between Entile Ilmi and Ai-Nida Celadon, shaking his head. "You two give gifts that are *impossible* for us to ever dream of matching, you know that?"

"Now, Tobias," says Ai-Nida Celadon, stifling a laugh, "there's no need to match anything. We both just have friends who consult us when they're looking for good people to fill out their staff, that's all... and we like seeing the bright young humans we meet have the opportunity to reach for their dreams."

"Thank you," da Silva says again. "We'll do our best to make the most of the opportunity."

"We will," Kouassi agrees.

"Don't worry," Entile Ilmi tells them. "I'm already proud of all of you! It's not every parent who gets to say their human kittens are *system champions*, after all." They flash a smirk. "I'm still disappointed I couldn't be there in person to cheer for you... but the broadcasts were fun to watch."

Uncle Rudy laughs. "So, how many favors did you win from whatever ship you were watching from betting on these kids of yours?"

Entile Ilmi stifles a laugh themself. "Enough that I think *Curiosity's* crew have all learned their lesson about betting against me."

"You would think everyone would know better than to bet against you in the first place by now," Aunt Penny quips. "You're just as bad as Celadon here is for making it seem like you can predict the future."

Ai-Nida Celadon shakes their head. "Now, now, Penny, I've told you that's just an *illusion*... the world would be a very different place if either of us could know what the future holds."

"Point taken." Aunt Penny nods, a light somber note coloring her voice for a moment. She raises her glass of sparkling juice. "A toast, then, to the newest members of your household."

Merlani raises theirs as well. "Here, here. Welcome to the family, cousins—I couldn't have asked for a better present *myself* than all of you."

As the glasses clink around the table, Merlani can't help smiling. They can't wait to tell their littermates about all of this.

TWO DAYS BEFORE THEIR ARRIVAL AT EARTH AND not long after finishing their night's work in the Drive Bay, Merlani is floating alone in *Starbright*'s lower observation dome. The full expanse of the galaxy around them extends all around, crisp pure darkness spangled with faraway lights of stars and nebulae and closer, brighter points of the system's own sun and planets. There isn't another view like it anywhere.

This is Merlani's favorite spot on the whole ship. When *Starbright* was their home, they would spend hours here whenever they needed some time to themself, just floating and soaking up the starlight.

It's colder than the rest of the ship, unfortunately, because the whole dome is made of translucent poly-glass and reinforcing bars and the heating only fully kicks on if someone's actively occupying the place. Back when Merlani first came to this ship as a provisional apprentice with their littermates, the three of them would often bring a blanket up and float all cuddled together while they practiced listening to the stars. They miss those days.

Now, though, Merlani is alone and wrapped in their Academy uniform jacket, doing their best to ignore the temperature—and wishing they'd taken the time to stop by their family's quarters and pick up their poncho so they'd be a bit warmer. It's worth being a bit chilled to get their thoughts realigned, tonight—and they *do* have a lot of thoughts to sort through before they're deposited back on Earth's soil.

"Hey, Cinny! Elder Celadon said you might be down here. Mind if I join you?"

Merlani looks to the access ladder that leads back up to the ship's lowest deck. Their best friend has already dropped herself into the dome, of course, legs first.

"Good morning, Reese. I'd have thought you'd be off to sleep by now?"

"Oh, no," Reese replies, stifling a small yawn, "not quite tired yet. Besides, I could say the same to you."

"I'm fine, really... I just needed to soak in some stars for a while." Merlani gestures vaguely towards the dome with their tail. "Clear my head, you know?"

"Makes sense to me. It's been a long night." Reese floats by them with something of an acrobatic tumble, still in the middle of getting herself oriented in the microgravity of the dome.

"Yeah."

"I almost can't believe we'll be back planet-side after tomorrow."

"Yeah... me neither." Merlani hesitates. They haven't been able to decide if they're looking forward to being back at the Academy or not. That's part of the line of thinking that brought them down to the dome.

"I'm going to miss all of this, you know? I mean, I know it won't be that long before I'm back in space, but..." Reese trails off, holding onto one of the inner railings towards the apex of the dome and looking out at the stars.

"...Yeah, I know what you mean." Merlani's tail swishes sadly to match the subtle droop of their ears. Graduation's only a week away for Reese, now. After that, their best friend will be off somewhere as a midshipman-pilot on one of the Defense Fleet's starships.

That was one of the other thoughts Merlani was trying to release to the stars so they can stand a chance of sleeping.

It probably wouldn't be bothering Merlani so much if they'd not been so busy between practice and their jump shifts with Ai-Nida Celadon and their work helping catalogue things for the ship's geosciences department to spend as much time with their best friend on this leg of the trip as they'd thought they'd get to. For her part, Reese has been loaned to the Bridge officers on night duty for some sort of work experience position, so *she's* not really had free time either. Merlani isn't even sure what she's been doing for that. The two of them haven't had much time to talk about it at all.

"But hey," says Reese, still looking out at the stars, "you'll be back in space breaking in your new training partner before long, won't you?"

"...Maybe. Nav trials were this week—I think their last day testing people is tomorrow." Merlani sighs lightly. "Although who knows if they're are actually going to let me near any of the new Nav cadets come fall term or not."

"Commander Potts said he would try to have someone for you, though, didn't he?"

"Yeah... with my luck it'll be another ill-fated mismatch like the last one." Merlani shakes their head. They don't have the energy to let themself think about what happened with the last one.

Reese looks back to them, giving them her most reassuring expression. "I'm sure there's going to be someone who can work with you this time, Cinny. Besides, if all the incoming Nav cadets are like that Lawton guy—"

"—Lewis—"

"—Yeah. Him." Reese lets out a soft chuckle that turns into another yawn. "If all of their incoming cadets are like *him*, your Commanders have way more to worry about than whether or not to keep on punishing you just to satisfy the Administration's weird vendettas."

"Hmm. I guess." Merlani recrosses all four of their arms and sighs again. "I just... after finally getting to be back in the Strange, I'm... well, *not* looking forward to being grounded again, to say the least."

"I'd be surprised if you were." Reese turns her head towards them. The motion makes her ponytail swish and float above her like a living liquid in the microgravity of the dome.

Merlani shakes their head lightly, looking past her towards the stars. "I'm almost starting to think there *isn't* someone out there who's meant to be my Navigator, you know? It feels like I'm just going to spend the rest of my life planet-bound and stuck in the Academy waiting for the Commanders to figure out what to do with me." They wouldn't dream of admitting that to anyone else, of course, but Reese is different. She's named them her best friend, after all. She knows why they feel this way.

"Ocean Merlani Barker Hämäläinen," Reese says, taking on a firm, knowing look in her eyes. "*Trust me*. I'm *certain* there's a Navigator out there for you."

Merlani sighs, although part of them wants to giggle at the fact that she's remembered their full name *and* pronounced it correctly. "...If you say so, Teresa."

"I know so." Reese smiles and offers them a hand. "Cold?"

"A little." Merlani accepts her hand gratefully.

Reese pulls them over into a loose half-hug with her free arm draped over their shoulders so they can share her warmth and look out at the stars together. Reese is a particularly warm human, too—at least as far as Merlani's experience goes.

It's something they're going to dearly miss when she leaves them after graduation.

"So," Reese asks, nodding up to the stars. "What's that big bright one?"

"Sirius," Merlani replies. They gesture with their tail towards another star they can feel clearly. "And the one there is Tabit."

The two of them spend a long time like this, marking and naming the stars, until finally Merlani realizes that Reese is going to fall asleep on them if they don't get her down to her bunk soon.

She might be their best friend, but that hardly means they enjoy having to try to *carry* her.

★

Another night in the Nav closet, and *Starbright*'s lead Astral Navigator has come in during the midnight break. He's now sitting on a second swiveling stool beside the mobile chair the younger Navigator is occupying, grinning at the young woman who's just returned from her usual trip down to the crew mess to acquire refreshments.

"Ah, I'm sorry, sir," the cadet says, handing the younger Navigator his coffee and setting her own down beside the stool she usually perches upon. She sets a plate of almond pastries on the small bit of open space among all of the controls and then leans the tray she'd carried everything on beside the door. "If I'd known you were going to be here, I'd have gotten something for *you* too—"

"—Don't worry, kid, I brought my own." The older Navigator laughs, picking up a lidded cup from beside his chair and gesturing with it. "So! Ready to show off what you've learned?"

"Sir?" The cadet takes her seat on the stool beside him, looking between the two officers with curious confusion.

"It's your last shift as our assistant," says the older Navigator. He pauses to take a sip from his coffee, then gestures to her with it again. "We want to see if you were paying attention."

"I don't understand, sir."

This is the first time since the cadet has been assisting the two of them that the older Navigator has come back for the second half of the younger one's shift. She's clearly not sure what to do with such a break in the routine.

The younger Navigator stands up and gestures to the now-empty Nav command chair. "Have a seat," he says. "Jade and Cy are waiting for you—we ran through all of the checklists while you were out, so you're good to go."

"Sir?"

The older officer reaches over and nudges her lightly to encourage her to stand up. "Really, kid, I *know* you're quicker on the uptake than this. Get in the bloody chair. You're running the jump this time."

"...Yes, sir." The cadet sits hesitantly, still looking at the two officers.

The younger Navigator reaches over and flips the microphone bar of the cadet's headset down for her and taps one of the buttons on the side. "There you go. All set! Now say hello and let's get this thing started—and make sure you use their names so they can anchor onto your voice."

She smiles nervously and nods to both of them before taking a breath and turning her eyes to the various charts set up on the screens around her.

"Hello, Lieutenant Cyan, Jade? This is Cadet Vasquez. Can you hear me?"

"*Cyan here, Miss V.*" says the voice of the younger Navigator's counterpart. "*Reading you loud and clear!*"

"*You're clear and bright to me too, kitten,*" a second Florivan voice says. "*We're ready to make the jump on your mark.*"

"All right, then." The cadet closes her eyes and seems to stifle her nerves with a single deep breath. She's all cheerful confidence when she opens her eyes again. "Jump us in on ten, please."

"*Ten it is, Miss V.! Nine... eight... seven...*"

In a few moments, the countdown is over and the cadet flips up her microphone and looks to the two observing officers.

"Good," says the older Navigator, taking a sip from his coffee. "Bonus points because they could both hear you on the first try without *us* having to chime in. Now, let's see you get some landmarks together for your jumpers. Go with a half-distance for your jump-out point."

"Yes, sir." The cadet pops out the smaller holoscreen on the chair arm and swivels herself around to the various displays to set about choosing a collection of coordinate markers for the two Quantum Space Drive engineers to work from. It takes her a while, but when she's done, she offers the list to the older Navigator in its tablet screen form.

"Is this okay, sir?"

The older Navigator looks over the list and then raises an eyebrow and shows it to the younger Navigator, who nods.

"You're taking MSS *Legacy*'s position for your max Down?" the younger officer asks.

"Um... yes, sir." A note of nervousness returns to the cadet's voice. "Was that wrong?"

The younger officer studies her closely. "What's your reasoning?"

The cadet gestures up at the third display screen. "*Legacy*'s path intersects ours somewhere between now and

Earth. I don't know *why*, sir, but I know you always put the closest intersecting ships as Up or Down."

The two Navigators share a look. The older one nods, taking another casual sip of his coffee. The younger one passes the list back to the cadet.

"If you look at the flight paths," the younger Navigator says, gesturing at the charts, "*Legacy* won't intersect us until we hit our fourth jump, assuming we keep going at halves. But you can leave it in; they shouldn't have any problems working with an advance warning. Don't forget to tell them that Down is a moving reference when you give them the points, though."

"Yes, sir." The cadet nods, making a note on her list.

After a few more moments of silence, the headsets crackle to life again.

"*Jump to Strange completed, Miss V.! You have markers for us yet?*"

"Yes, Lieutenant Cyan, the Navigators just confirmed them for me. Origin point is 5F and 6 by 6..." Soon, the cadet has given them all of the points and flipped up her microphone bar for the long wait while the ship is being carried to the jump-out point.

The younger Navigator passes the cadet the coffee cup she'd left by the stool on which he's now sitting. "You can *relax*, you know," he says with a smile. "You're doing just fine."

The cadet takes a sip, then tilts her head to one side as she looks between the two men. "May I ask a question, sirs?"

"Go ahead, kid," says the older officer.

"Why in the *stars* are you letting me do this?"

The older Navigator chuckles. "What, you *haven't* been wanting to see if you could?"

"Well..." The cadet blushes momentarily. "Yes, of course—but still, I'm not in Nav—"

"—Yet, kid. Not *yet*. But I'm inclined to think you could be, if you wanted to."

The cadet goes silent and takes another slow sip of her coffee.

"Besides," the younger Navigator chimes in, "we're right here with you if you need us."

"If this does work out the way I think it will..." the older Navigator trails off for a moment before chuckling. "Well, the family has a *lot* of favors out in the galaxy waiting to be called in, and this might just warrant pulling one or two of those."

"Sir?"

"Don't worry about it." The older Navigator grins at her, tossing his long graying braid back over his shoulder. "Just do the work, kid, we'll all have a chat at the end of the cycle and see what Jade and Cyan think of your performance."

"Yes, sir." The cadet nods, smiling softly.

"You're lucky, you know?" The younger Navigator tells her after a moment. "Most people who do *official* Nav trials have never even sat in on a simulated jump cycle before. They just get picked up for their aptitudes on the chance they'll be able to have something made of them if the trials go well and the instructors choose them."

"Well, Marsh," says his superior, giving him a nudge, "They can't *all* be bloody prodigies like you or troublemakers like Sarge who start off carrying their counterparts around in their *pockets*."

The younger Navigator laughs. "Point taken, sir."

"It's a bloody *odd* system, though, anymore," the older Navigator muses. "Back in the day, we had folks who got *certified* for astral navigation and all... but there weren't any of these Academy Nav/Quan programs trying to make it so the *only* choices presented were the ones that fit some arcane classification matrix."

"Really, sir?" asks the cadet.

"You're studying Fleet history, kid, you should know this by now." The older officer gestures vaguely with his coffee mug. "Even during the War, no matter *how* many high-classed, certified prospects were ever trained for them to choose from, at least a third of the time the Florivan volunteers would set their sights on just about *anyone* else who'd made a good impression on them instead. Lot of darter pilots wound up in Nav that way..." He trails off, giving the cadet a knowing look. "And I believe you're aware of how bloody *resistant* Florivans can be to working with someone they don't click with?"

The cadet nods. "I certainly am, sir."

"Well, then." The older Navigator smirks and takes a drink. "There you go."

"What's the saying? Ah, right," says the younger Navigator, "the only thing harder than getting into an Academy Nav program in the first place is actually *graduating* from one. You could be a T/E12 and pass trials like *lightning*... but if none of the jumpers click with you?" He laughs, shaking his head lightly. "Well, you'd better have a backup career plan to go with that shiny little certification mark in your file when you wash out. Knew more than a few folks like that back at KCA, myself."

"I'm sure you did, Marsh." The older Navigator turns back to the cadet. "But that's nothing for *you* to worry about, kid. We know you're already graduation-bound and all—this is just our way of thanking you for all the work you've put in helping us."

"...Of course, sir." The cadet seems about to say something else, but the voices over the headset interrupt her.

"Teresa, we've reached the marker. I hope Lt. Marshal and my 'stepfather' aren't distracting you too much for you to confirm the point for us?"

The older Navigator chuckles and silently shakes his head.

"They're being perfect gentlemen, actually, Jade," the cadet replies, stifling a giggle. "Your point is 5F by 10 and D."

"Confirmed, Miss V.!" says the younger Navigator's counterpart. *"Standing by to jump back to Normal space on your mark!"*

The cadet looks over to the two officers.

The younger Navigator nods to her and flips down his microphone bar to give the announcement over the ship's intercom.

"You're clear to jump now, Lieutenant Cyan," says the cadet once he's done. "Thank you."

"All right, Miss V.! Jumping in ten... nine... eight..."

Once the jump is complete and the charts are going through the auto-update cycle with the relay data centered on the ship's new location, the older Navigator stands from his stool and stretches. "Good job, kid," he says, patting the cadet on the shoulder briefly.

"Thank you, sir."

"Well, Marsh, I believe that leaves it to *me* to do the coffee runs for the rest of the night. Help her set up another half-distance, and then after that I think we can have her running full-skips until you and I need to take over for our final jump into orbital proximity." The older Navigator picks up the tray from its place beside the door and sets about collecting the now-empty coffee cups.

"Will do, sir." The younger Navigator nods.

"I thought it was just for that jump, sir?" the cadet asks hesitantly, although she doesn't move to get up from the chair.

The older Navigator turns back to her with a cheeky grin. "You *really* want to stop now, kid?"

"...No, sir, not really." The cadet grins back.

"Didn't think so." The older Navigator flips down his microphone bar. "Say, Jade? Cy? Either of you mind if we have the kid keep running the show for a while?"

"*We'd be delighted, Rudy!*" says the younger Navigator's counterpart.

"*Agreed,*" says the other Florivan in the Drive Bay. A soft jingling sound accompanies their voice over the intercom. "*I see what you and Nida were talking about now.*"

"Well," says the older Navigator, flipping the bar back up. "There you go, kid. Enjoy yourself, try not to break the bloody ship while I'm off getting nectar for you hummingbird types."

"Thank you, sir." The cadet's whole face is lit up with excitement now.

A small pinging sound from the readouts informs them that the updates have completed.

The younger Navigator nods to the cadet and flips his own microphone back into position to tap into the ship's intercom.

"All hands, prepare for the jump to Quantum Space; Nav safety overrides and protocols remain in effect. Jumping in five minutes…"

★

22

"WELCOME BACK, CADET OCEAN," says Entile Wyndi, who seems to be making a *point* of being formal. "I'm sorry we haven't gotten to chat before now, but I'm glad to see you again."

Merlani sits down somewhat awkwardly into the chair in front of their entile's desk. They weren't expecting to be called back into this office before the beginning of the fall term—much less on the day before the Academy's graduation ceremonies.

"Thank you, Commander." Merlani doesn't even know why they're here. Aunt Penny didn't tell them anything when she brought them down to the Nav/Quan wing and left them at their entile's office door. Apparently she had other business to attend to, but she didn't tell them what *that* was either.

"Elder Celadon gave me a good report on your performance during the return journey from Mars. Granted, they weren't *supposed* to allow you to assist them…" Entile Wyndi twitches one of their ears, but is smiling softly all the same. "However, I *do* trust their judgment—and the day they and Rudy stop conspiring and rearranging other people's plans is the day we should *all* start worrying about the state of the galaxy."

"Yes, Commander." Merlani isn't entirely sure they completely understand, but they know the heads of their household well enough that they're sure that their entile is right.

"Anyway, I'm sure you're wondering why you've been brought back here sooner than we expected?"

"…Yes, Commander, I was."

"Well, for a start, I met with Colonel Albright yesterday. She's given me a recommendation for your potential reinstatement starting in the fall term. That's why you're here, and why this conversation is going on the record for the Academy Administration's files on your situation."

Merlani breathes a small sigh of relief.

"She hadn't told you?" Entile Wyndi raises an eyebrow.

"No, Commander, she hadn't."

"Ah. That's Penny for you, I suppose. She's always liked arranging to surprise people almost as much as Jade does." Entile Wyndi shakes their head again and then turns their eyes back to Merlani. "Do you remember the contingency for your reinstatement, Cadet Ocean?"

"Yes, I do." Merlani holds back another sigh. "It's only if you have someone *willing* to work with me, since I... don't exactly have a good reputation anymore."

"Indeed. Particularly since Cadet Lewis has now left us."

"He washed out, Commander? Because of what I... because of what happened?" Merlani had never thought that Cadet Lewis was cut out for Nav, but somehow they'd thought that his mother would have been successful in her attempt to force their instructors to give him a second year to try partnering with something else. One of the most annoying things *about* the boy had been how much he talked about what a great Navigator he was going to be someday.

"Only partly." Entile Wyndi gives them an enigmatic shrug and wave of their tail. "There were some other... personal issues of his that came to light after your incident. His ultimate reasons for dropping out of the program and transferring to another Academy and course of study had far more to do with *that* than with you."

"Commander?"

"Nothing for you to concern yourself with, Cadet Ocean, don't worry. Now, where was I? Ah. Yes." Entile Wyndi steeples all four sets of fingers together and rests their elbows on the desk. "We conducted trials for our new additions to the program while you were on your way back from Mars. I have six new Florivan cadets joining us next term, so we've taken a total of seven new Nav recruits for next year—and Commander Potts and I believe one of them might be a suitable training partner for you."

"Really?" Merlani almost can't believe it.

"Yes. Transfer student, actually—not the most sought-after qualifications by the Administration's standards, but she comes highly recommended by both her former instructors and the Nav/Quan teams who asked us to make an exception and consider her. Their results from running her through field trials were *quite* impressive, too."

"That's... good, then." Merlani can't tell whether the feeling at the back of their ribs is excitement or wariness at the prospect of dealing with another new human who they'll most likely fail to imprint on again.

Entile Wyndi's eyes seem to be watching them very closely. "You're not sure about this, are you?"

"...Not really," Merlani admits.

"You do have a choice in the matter, Ocean. Either you come back to the program next term and stay partnered with this cadet we've chosen for a full year... or you can continue with your current status until we run trials again."

"A full year?" Merlani asks. "Outside the partner rotations?"

"It's the same arrangement I gave the *last* cadet who struggled with keeping a training partner as much as you seem to. You remind me of them enough that I think the longer partner assignment will be good for you." There's a fleeting look of sadness that crosses their entile's eyes, but it's not there long enough for Merlani to recognize what its source might have been.

"And..." Merlani hesitates, catching the end of their tail in one of their lower hands to stop its nervous swishing. "Well... If we *don't* get along?"

"If she doesn't work out, then at the end of the year *she'll* be graduating with her Nav certification and *you'll* go back to the standard track with my other Florivan cadets until you find a partner who does suit you. Rotations and all."

"I see. And she's..." Merlani hesitates, running the tuft of their tail through their lower fingers. "You've told her what happened?"

"She's aware, and she's assured me it isn't something that bothers her at all. She's already consented to the conditions involved in this arrangement."

"Oh."

"Would you like to talk to her before you make your decision, Cadet Ocean? I believe she *should* be finishing up her own little discussion with my counterpart by now." Entile Wyndi gives them a knowing look and a bit of a smile.

"...Yes, if that's possible."

Their entile stands and gestures for them to do the same. "Okay, then, Cadet Ocean, come with me."

Merlani spends the whole walk down the hall to Uncle Julian's office wondering what sort of an impression of them has already been made on this new Nav cadet—especially if she's been told about what happened to their *last* training partner. What they can't figure out is *why* anyone who managed to pass Nav trials in the first place would say yes to an arrangement like this. After all, from the sound of it, she's essentially *guaranteed* to wash out at the end of the year.

When they reach the door, Entile Wyndi taps on the intercom button beside it. "Sarge? I have Cadet Ocean with me; are you ready to see them?"

"Yeah, we figured you'd be coming by soon. Bring them on in."

Upon entering, Merlani is completely shocked by the sight of the back of the person sitting in the chair opposite their uncle at the desk.

For a moment, they think this must be some elaborate joke at their expense, or that it's just their imagination and an uncanny resemblance. That only lasts until the cadet turns around and smiles at them, giving a little wave with one distinctly constellation-tattooed hand.

"Cadet Ocean!" Uncle Julian grins broadly and gestures towards the young human sitting in front of him. "Welcome back! I believe our new recruit needs no introduction?"

Merlani is at an utter loss for words.

There are a lot of things they could have expected, and a lot of things they had been afraid of. The thought had *never* crossed their mind the cadet waiting for them—bright blue Nav/Quan stripes already added onto the cuffs of her uniform jacket above the red and ivory ones that had always been there—would be none other than Teresa Vasquez.

"Well?" asks Entile Wyndi after a few more moments of silence pass, nudging Merlani a little further into the room so the door can finish closing without catching their tail. "Do you think you can work with this one, Little Ocean?"

"I..." Merlani still can't get the words out. There are too many feelings fighting with each other inside them.

Reese seems to pick up that they're struggling. She stands and comes over to them. She has that same bright grin on now that she did when she first sat down at Merlani's table in the cadet mess. "I *would* have told you sooner, Cinny—but the Commanders asked me to wait until everything got cleared through the Administration."

"...I shouldn't let you do this for me," Merlani whispers at last, looking down with all three eyes.

"Why not?"

"You're supposed to be graduating and joining the Defense Fleet—You *told* me you'd already accepted a position, Reese."

"I did!" Reese chuckles softly. "This one."

"...Why?"

"Why not? If it doesn't work out, I'll have an advantage going into the Fleet with Nav certification on my record... but you're my best friend, and I'd *like* to think this could work." Reese pauses and then holds back another laugh. "One way or the other, you're going to be my jumper someday, remember?"

"I did promise that, didn't I?" Merlani finally looks up and smiles back at her. The elation at having their favorite human in the galaxy at their side wins out over all of the other feelings crowding their mind.

Reese offers a hand to them. "What do you say, Cinny? Give me a chance?"

Merlani takes her hand in both of their upper ones. They can't find any words yet to answer her. On an impulse, they pull her into a hug instead.

Reese laughs, wrapping her warm pair of alien arms around them.

The hug feels *right* in a way Merlani couldn't hope to describe. They'd never allowed themself to imagine this being an option, but they know now that there's *no one* else they'd rather work with.

"Well, then!" they hear Uncle Julian say, "I do believe we can put that down as a 'yes'."

"I do believe you're right, Sarge." Entile Wyndi smiles and sets one hand each on Reese and Merlani's shoulders. "Welcome to Nav/Quan, cousin Teresa—and welcome home, Ocean. We've missed having you."

For the first time since they came to Earth, Merlani is certain that they're in *exactly* the place they're supposed to be.

★ **The End** ★

Appendix

Timeline of *Strange Space Adventures*

The following timeline lists all of the published *Strange Space™ Adventures* and Short Stories in roughly chronological order. Where stories feature major time skips, they have been placed based on the earliest events of that story.

Short Stories marked with *[1] can be found in *Tales of the Navigators: Volume 1.*

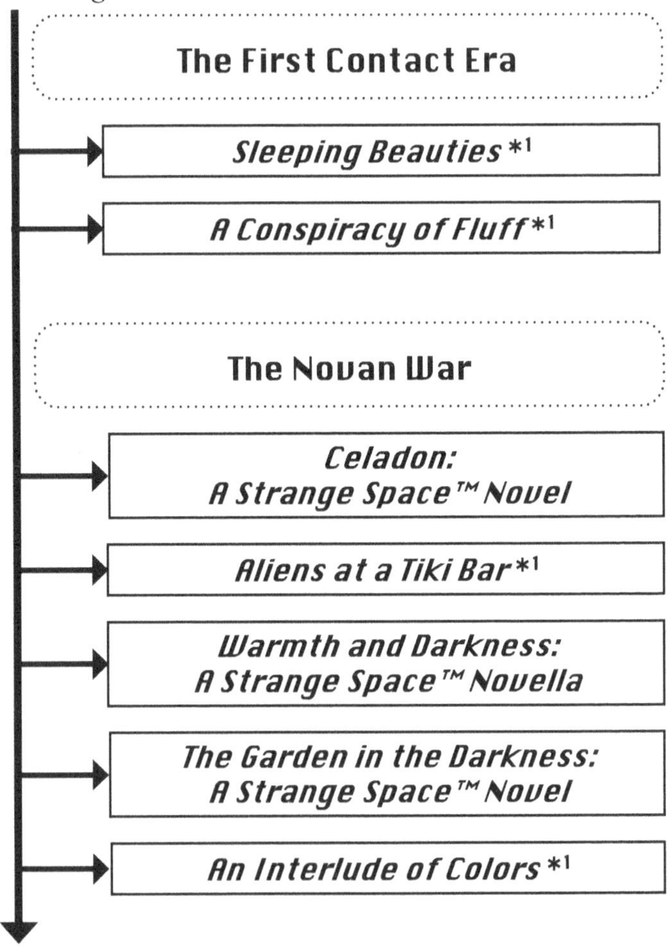

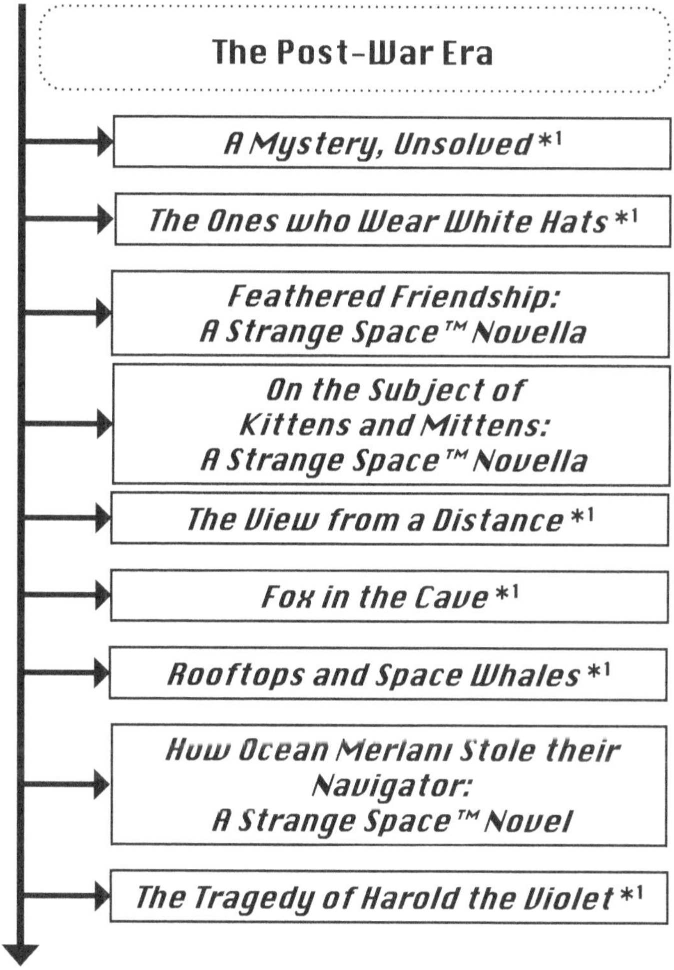

The Post-War Era

A Mystery, Unsolved [1]

The Ones who Wear White Hats [1]

Feathered Friendship:
A Strange Space™ Novella

On the Subject of
Kittens and Mittens:
A Strange Space™ Novella

The View from a Distance [1]

Fox in the Cave [1]

Rooftops and Space Whales [1]

How Ocean Merlani Stole their
Navigator:
A Strange Space™ Novel

The Tragedy of Harold the Violet [1]

ON CHARACTER IDENTITIES AND PRONOUNS

How Ocean Merlani Stole their Navigator takes place in a far future setting in which human society has long since reached the stage of accepting and celebrating all varieties of diversity. This is a sort of world that I, personally, would like to live in. I don't claim it to be a *perfect* setting, but I do take an optimistic view of our potential as a species.

Several of the human characters presented in this story would, in today's terms, likely identify with one or more communities under the LGBTQIA+ umbrella. While the narrative of this story did not call for the characters to specifically state which labels they would use, and I like to imagine that a lot of who they are can be inferred through their interactions, as a member of the LGBTQIA+ community *myself*, I'm aware of the importance of clear representation. Seeing characters like ourselves in stories where they are valued for who they are and able to live without being marginalized for their nature is, in my opinion, *powerful*, and a big part of my philosophy as a writer.

Please note that at the same time, it is impossible to represent an entire community in the form of one character. My characters are simply themselves, and while they draw on my own experiences and those of people I know, they are not meant to be "perfect" renditions of one thing or another. Just like every human, their various identities are *aspects* of them, rather than the entirety of their personality.

That all being said, the following characters who feature in this story would like to "come out" to you and share this aspect of their lives:

Teresa Vasquez would describe herself as bisexual and aromantic.

Tobias da Silva would describe himself as a transgender man who is attracted to women.

Beck Lavine would describe themself as nonbinary and/or agender.

Robin Maltby would describe themself as genderless. (If asked how they identify, Robin usually responds with a noncommittal shrug and then changes the subject to something they find more interesting.)

Elias Rudolph would describe himself as homosexual/ homoromantic. (In his words: "a man who happens to be attracted to other men." Rudy has never been all that interested in labels of any sort.)

(Note: Please keep in mind that this is not an exhaustive list of the LGBTQIA+ characters who appear in this story, any more than it is a full description of each of the characters in question. These are simply the ones who feature most prominently and asked me to clarify their identities.)

On behalf of all of my characters, humans and Florivans alike, I'd like to thank you, dear reader, for being accepting of them and respecting their preferred sets of pronouns. I hope that we all will one day live in a world like the one these characters inhabit, in which a person can openly be themself without fear. I do believe it's possible for us to get there, too; every small step we make in the right direction matters.

—Katie Silverwings

On Florivan Names

Florivan names consist of two parts: the 'public' name and the 'personal' name. The 'personal' or 'kitten-name' is given to a Florivan when they first open their eyes, while the 'public' name is chosen for them when they are old enough to be presented to the Council of Elders. Some kittens receive one or the other half of their name in honor of one of their ancestors or entiles, such as Ocean Merlani, whose personal name was given in memory of their parent, Ocean Marbree.

Personal names come from the ancestral Florivan language, and are largely untranslatable. All of the kittens in a litter will usually be given names with the same or similar initial sounds.

Public names are always words from human languages which connect somehow to the individual's coloring. Kittens, therefore, receive their public names once they have shed enough of their fur to show a large patch of a recognizable color. Elders will often carry a theme through the public names of their kittens such as different stones, plants, or a specific language of origin.

Florivans are most often addressed by their public names. Only Elders, family members, or the closest of friends will address or talk about a Florivan by their personal name, and then only in private. (Private, in this case, also extends to situations where only other Florivans or close friends of the family are present.)

Florivans also commonly take on nicknames which are used by their families, friends, and colleagues. Who can use a certain nickname for them depends on the situation and origin of the nickname. Ocean Merlani, for example, is called "Cinny" by their family and certain close friends, although usually only in private. Elder Celadon Toreval is called "Dons" in public, but only by their Navigator.

Florivan Elders are addressed formally with their title, although most of them will grant close friends and colleagues permission to address them by their public name alone outside of formal situations. The Eldest of the Council is a particular exception to this rule, as they are never referred to by name after assuming the role of Eldest, save by their siblings in private. Younger members of an Elder's line will call them 'Nida' ('Parent') or 'Ai-Nida' ('Grandparent') as appropriate in most situations. Apprentices to an Elder typically use their title as a sign of respect regardless of whose line they belong to, although the Elder may ask them to do otherwise in private.

On the Academy Nav/Quan Programs

At the point in time at which *How Ocean Merlani Stole their Navigator* takes place, humanity and the Florivans have been close friends and allies for just over a century and a half. The spacefaring culture of the integrated Human/Florivan society of the Sol Coalition is dependent upon this relationship. Without a Florivan to run the all-important Quantum Space Drive, the ship is limited to solar sails and basic sub-light propulsion methods; without a human Navigator counterpart to direct them and keep them anchored to Normal space, the Florivan 'jumper' cannot run the Drive.

Before the Novan War, only a small percentage of Florivans had taken Navigators and begun to use their technology to jump human ships between the Coalition's inhabited worlds. The majority of them remained un-partnered either by choice or by chance and lived at their people's Sanctuary planet in the Procyon star system, with a far smaller group living at Luyten's Star with the human colony there at North City. With the utter destruction of the Sanctuary's planet at the hands of the Novan Armada towards the end of the War, however, the fragmentary population of Florivans was centered around the North City residents, the Defense Fleet's small group of Volunteers, and those Florivans who were already out in space with Navigator counterparts.

Soon after the end of the War, the surviving members of the Florivan Council of Elders came together to determine the future of their species. With only a meager five thousand or so adults left, and a mere twenty known reproductive individuals, two of whom were no longer able to bear kittens, the Council was hard pressed to ensure the safety of every remaining Florivan.

Of particular concern were the adolescent Florivans who were still in their apprenticeships on various starships and the orphan kittens whom the Defense Fleet had rescued during the disastrous Battle of Procyon. Where before, these young Florivans would likely return to their home planet to live with their parent's household and undergo training in their chosen career if they did not make a compact with a human Navigator and remain in space, now the majority of them were not only orphans, but the sole surviving members of their families. Florivans being a semi-eusocial species, this posed a distinct additional risk to their wellbeing.

In the end, the Elders decided that it would be best to work towards *every* Florivan taking a human counterpart of some kind in order to compensate for their scattering from their kin and to provide an additional layer of protection. They saw it best that the majority of their species would move out into the starship-jumping role, in order to prevent future losses of large portions of their population. They also put into place what would ultimately become the Academy Nav/Quan system in order to ensure that the younger generations of Florivans would be able both to find appropriate counterparts for themselves and to spend a few additional years after being released from their apprenticeship in the company of other Florivans and similarly-aged humans.

As it stands in Ocean Merlani's time, there is an Astral Navigation and Quantum Space Drive Engineering program at the most prominent Space Service Academy in each of the Coalition's inhabited star systems: Sol Central Space Service Academy at Earth, North City Exploration Technology Institute at Luyten's Star, the University of Teegarden-Millefleur at Teegarden's Star, Kapteyn Central Academy at Kapteyn's Star, West Memorial Academy of Sciences at Proxima Centauri, Alpha Centauri-New West Space Service Academy at Alpha Centauri, and Toliman Interstellar Space Service Institute at Beta Centauri. Each of these programs is theoretically under the jurisdiction of the individual Academy's administration, but the curriculum, appointment of instructors, selection of Astral Navigator student candidates, and core workings of the program are overseen by the Florivan Council of Elders. The lead Florivan instructor for each program reports directly to the Council and has the final say on the program's internal matters, although in most cases they share these duties equally with their Navigator, who serves as the lead instructor for the human half of the program.

Upon completion of their apprenticeship on a working starship, an adolescent Florivan will sign to one of the Academies. Usually, they are between the ages of fourteen and sixteen at this time, having begun their apprenticeship at ten or eleven. In most cases, all of the kittens from a litter will sign to the same Academy program. The apprenticeship stage is seen as the adolescent Florivan's time to grow into independence from their parent, and in the same way their Academy training is when they learn to be independent from their littermates. The transition from being constantly together with members of their family to being largely alone on a starship is softened by the introduction of human friend groups and ultimately the relationship formed with the young Florivan's chosen human counterpart.

The Florivan cadets in an Academy Nav/Quan program take a secondary course of study in their preferred career focus in addition to their main program studies. Each of them will remain in the program until they have both made their compact with a human counterpart and completed first two years of advanced paired training with that counterpart and then a two-year posting as an 'Assistant Secondary' Nav/Quan team on a working starship. Upon graduation, the pair will be recommended to a starship with an open Secondary position.

In order to introduce the young Florivans to a variety of potential human counterparts, the programs bring in new Astral Navigator prospects each year. These prospects will rotate through as training partners to the available Florivan students until either they are chosen as a Navigator, run out of Florivan students who can hear their voice over the intercom channels which reach into Quantum Space during a Transit cycle, or reach the end of the school year. The vast majority of Nav cadets wash out of the program at some point in this process, although those of them who do can be granted 'Nav Certified' status if their performance in the program meets certain criteria. (Nav Certified personnel are sought after on most starships, as they can fill in for an ill or incapacitated Navigator if needed. It is not uncommon for one of these trained people to encounter a Florivan later on in their career who will go on to make a Navigator's compact with them.)

The humans selected as Astral Navigator candidates are either recommended by working Nav/Quan officers, offered the opportunity to go through the application process by the Academy's Administration based on their assessment scores and career goals, or apply to the program directly. All potential Nav Cadets go through a series of further assessments, psychological screenings, background checks, and field trials in simulations with the program's Florivan instructors before being admitted to the program. This is partially in order to gauge the human student's aptitude for the Navigator's duties, and more crucially to ensure that humans with ill intentions or inclinations are removed as prospects before they have the chance to come in close contact with the young Florivans in the program's care.

Occasionally, a young Florivan will be set on making their compact with a specific human from outside their Academy's program. These humans are similarly screened and tested by the program's instructors, as well as the Elder of the Florivan's household. In most cases, such a human will be granted admission to the program even if they would not otherwise meet the Academy Administration's criteria.

Aside from the lifelong friendship the young Florivan forms with their human counterpart, the Academy Nav/Quan system also offers them the opportunity to form friendships with the other Navigator prospects and human students from their secondary studies and extracurricular activities. These friendship groups often carry on into the graduated Nav/Quan pair's career and create a network of support both on their eventual starship posting and throughout the Coalition's inhabited worlds. In addition to helping further compensate for the adult Florivan's separation from the tightly-knit extended family groups they naturally live in, this continues to cement the bond between Florivans and humanity as an integrated society and near symbiotic species.

Katie Silverwings is a glassblower, visual artist, and writer, originally from Texas and now a nomadic creative spirit. She holds a BA in English and History from McMurry University in Abilene, Texas, with minors in Art, Arts Administration, and Biblical Greek Translation, as well as a BA (Hons.) in Glass from the University for the Creative Arts in the UK. Silverwings identifies as aromantic, asexual, and genderfae; "she/her", "they/them", and "fae/faer" pronouns are all welcome.

Long fascinated by nature and space, Silverwings' speculative fiction work centers around notions of optimistic futurism, friendship, found family, and adventurous journeys into the known and unknown. Her characters do most of the driving, and she does her best to keep up and negotiate pleasing stories with them.

Silverwings' two cats are commonly found staring over her shoulder while she's writing. The small cloud of dark matter with eyes likes to sit in her lap and interfere with typing, while the calico makes operatic editorial comments from across the room.

www.KatieSilverwings.com

@KatieSilverwings

MORE BOOKS
BY KATIE SILVERWINGS

Celadon

✦ A Strange Space™ Novel ✦

The Novan War has just begun. All that stands between Humanity and utter destruction are the ships of the Sol Coalition Defense Fleet.

The only problem? None of those ships are equipped with the all-important Quantum Space Drive which allows humanity to travel between planets and stars at a reasonable scale of time. The Drive needs Florivan QSD Engineers to run it, and Florivans are pacifists. Their Council of Elders has never allowed service on military vessels.

The Fleet can do little more than sit at the edges of the Coalition's seven member systems and *wait* for the Novans to attack.

Celadon Toreval is the Youngest of the Florivan Council of Elders. If anyone can come to Fleet Admiral Marvin's aid and help her save her people—and theirs—it's them.

Celadon, though, has their own reasons to get involved…

Warmth and Darkness

The Garden in the Darkness

✦ A Strange Space™ Novel ✦

Adventures happen when you least expect them.

In the time of the Novan War, the pilots of the 2nd Darter Squadron "Musketeers" are no strangers to peril. Even the little Florivan kitten who serves as their mascot has a tendency to get into trouble. When two of the Musketeers and their mascot find themselves stranded on a seemingly deserted mining colony, though, they find themselves in a situation none of their previous adventures could have prepared them for.

With no way to contact the rest of the Defense Fleet, they'll have to find their own way to repair their darters and get back to their starship. To make matters worse, enemy forces are lurking in the nearby asteroids.

The Mayview outpost was abandoned at the start of the War, but the Musketeers aren't alone here. Someone is watching them from behind the overgrown vines...

Feathered Friendship

On the Subject of Kittens and Mittens

Ranger Captain Taimri Hämäläinen loved playing in the snow as a child. Now, on a vacation with her family in the snow-covered mountains of a certain planet in the Beta Centauri sytem, she has a chance to share all of her favorite winter games with her own children.

Taimri's three adopted Florivan kittens, of course, have never seen snow before; they live on a space station with her husband, George Barker. That only makes it more fun to dress Sky, Storm, and Ocean up in their warmest clothes and take them out into the frosted wonderland, in Taimri's opinion.

While her Florivan counterpart, River Myrval, stays behind in the cozy comforts of the lodge, Taimri and her kittens are in for a bit of an adventure they hadn't expected...

Tales of the Navigators (Volume 1)

✶ A Strange Space™ Short Story Collection ✶

The world of *Strange Space™* is full of stories of all sizes.

This first collected volume Katie Silverwings' *Strange Space™ Short Stories* includes ten tales from the lives of the enigmatic Florivans and their human Astral Navigator Counterparts:

- *Sleeping Beauties*
- *A Conspiracy of Fluff*
- *Aliens at a Tiki Bar*
- *An Interlude of Colors*
- *A Mystery, Unsolved*
- *The Ones who Wear White Hats*
- *The View From a Distance*
- *Fox in the Cave*
- *Rooftops and Space Whales*
- *The Tragedy of Harold the Violet*

The Strange is calling you...

Available now from Amazon and Barnes & Noble and at
www.KatieSilverwings.com

9 781959 922346